ARCTIC

RED

James Bultema

P.D. Publishing

Early praise for Arctic Red

"Bultema demonstrates his mastery of the techno-thriller genre with a story that could be torn from tomorrow's headlines."
-Midwest Book Review

"Bultema's underwater game of hide-and-seek rivals the most gripping scenes from Tom Clancy's *The Hunt for Red October*..."Immersive and intelligent, *Arctic Red* transforms the planet's coldest landscape into a mirror of humanity's most volatile impulses. It's a book that lingers long after the final sonar ping fades."
-MilitarThrillers.com

Also By James Bultema

<u>Fiction</u>
Sea of Red series:
  Sea of Red
  Attack From Within
  Red Lines

Invaders of the Heartland

<u>Non-Fiction</u>
Guardians of Angels: A History of the Los Angeles Police Department 1869-2019

The Protectors: A Photographic History of Police Departments in the United States

Unsolved Cold-Case Homicides of Law Enforcement Officers

Gangsters and Cops: Prohibition, Corruption, and LAPD's Scandalous Coming of Age

<u>Documentary Film</u>
Behind the Badge: An Insider's History of the Los Angeles Police Department

Website: https://www.jamesbultema.com
P.D. Publishing – Scottsdale, Arizona

This book was edited by Karen Stoff, www.vocostoff.com, and Jennifer Duty, jduty7304@gmail.com

Cover design by Momir Borocki - Proi! book covers

Author photograph by Carole W. Bultema

For the warriors of the Arctic, past and future, who stand
ready—silent, unseen, and unshaken.

<u>**Acronyms & Abbreviations**</u>

This novel contains numerous military terms and abbreviations used by the US and allied armed forces. Where possible, I have written them out in full upon first use in the narrative. In dialogue, however, characters often use the shorter forms, as they would in real life. For the reader's convenience, the following list includes many of the most frequently used acronyms appearing throughout the book. Although not exhaustive, it should serve as a helpful reference.

ACO	Air Control Officer
ACS	Aegis Combat System
Actual	Aircraft call sign refers to the commanding officer. Also called "ONE"
AESA	Active Electronically Scanned Array
AGL	Above Ground Level
AMRAAM	Advanced Medium-Range Air-to-Air Missile
ASROC	Anti-Submarine Rocket
AO	Area of Operations
ASW	Anti-Submarine Warfare
ATGM	Anti-Tank Guided Missile
ATR	Automatic Target Recognition – mines

BDA	Battle damage assessment
C2	Command and Control
CCC	Command Control Center
CENTCOM	United States Central Command
CICO	Combat Information Center Officer
CIWS	Close-in Weapon System
DDS	Dry Dock Shelter - Submarine
EEZ	Exclusive Economic Zone
ELINT	Electronic Intelligence: focused on intercepting and analyzing non-communication electronic signals
EM	Electromagnetic
EMCON	Emissions control, including radio, restricted emissions control, and reducing the signature of aircraft
EO-DAS	Electro-Optical Distributed Aperture System
EO/IR	Electro-Optical/Infrared
FONOP	Freedom of Navigation Operation
GIUK Gap	Strategically important waterway, framed by Greenland, Iceland, United Kingdom
GRU	Main Directorate of the General Staff of the military – military intelligence
HMDS	Helmet-Mounted Display System
HOTAS	Hands on Throttle-And-Stick
IFF	Identification Friend or Foe
IR	Infrared
ISR	Intelligence, Surveillance, and Reconnaissance

LIDAR	Light Detection and Ranging: pulses of laser light to measure distances and create high-resolution maps
Link-16	Secure, jam-resistant military data link network in real time
MADL	Multifunction Advanced Data Link (used by the F-35)
MANPADS	Man-Portable Air-Defense Systems
MFD	Multi-Function Display
MFTA	Multi-Function Towed Array-Sonar
ROE	Rules of Engagement
RWR	Radar Warning Receiver (in aircraft)
SAM	Surface-to-Air-Missile
SAS	Synthetic Aperture Sonar
SBIRS	Space-Based Infrared System
SIGINT	Signals Intelligence
SOCCENT	Special Operations Command Center Component of CENTCOM
SSTD	Surface Ship Torpedo Defense
TACCO	Tactical coordinator
Thermocline layer	A distinct horizontal layer in a body of water where the temperature changes rapidly with depth.
TLAM	Tomahawk Land Attack Missile
TOT	Time on target
TRN	Terrain-Referenced Navigation
VLS	Vertical Launching System
WEPS	Weapons Officer
XO	Executive Officer, 2nd in command

Principal Characters

United States Government

Mark Taylor	President of the United States
Elena Ramirez	Director of National Intelligence
Troy Kincaid	Chairman, Joint Chiefs of Staff
George Mitchell	Secretary of Defense
Roland Stinson	Secretary of the Treasury
Brad Kelly	Secretary of State
Dan Steele	Central Intelligence Agency

United States Military

Blake Stanton	Captain, USS *Idaho*
Brett Jansen	Lt. Commander, XO USS *Hudner*
David Harrington	XO, USS *Idaho*
Dick "Mad Dog" Johnson	Captain, USS *Ford* CAG
Jessie "Swagger" Hampton	Lieutenant Commander, F-35 pilot
Karen Parsons	Lieutenant, Electronic Warfare, P-8
Norm Jackson	Lieutenant, TACCO, P-8
Robert "Han" Johanson	Co-pilot P-8
Ryan Maddox	Lt Commander-A/C commander, P8
Sarah "Danger" Freeman	Lt. Commander, E-2 Pilot
Ronnie "Razor" Harper	Lt. EA-18G Growler
Emily Reyes	CPO, Sonar tech, *USS Idaho*
Logan "Hawk" Carter	Major, B-21 pilot
Megan "Pixie" Alvarez	1st Lt. Mission Systems Ofcr. B-21
Robert "Frosty" Shepherd	Captain, 2nd Brigade, 11th Airborne Div., Bravo Company
Dani Mercer	1st Lt. 2nd Brigade, 11th Airborne Div., Bravo Company

Alex "Seeker" Hayes Lt. Commander, pilot P-8
Adam Dankworth   Corporal, 1st Battalion, 501st
                    Parachute Infantry Regiment

Russia
Admiral Mikhailovich Commander, Northern Fleet
Alexei Morozov   Lt. General, commander of
                    Nagurskoye Military Base
Andrei Petrov   President, Russian Federation
                    Colonial, GRU – Main Intelligence
                    Director
Ivan Gromov   Commander, K-561 *Kazan*
                    submarine
Ivan Kozlov   Captain, *Merkury* Corvette
Natalia Romanova   Deputy Defense Minister
Nikifor Koltsov   Commander, *Volga Star*
Nikolai Dmitrievich Orlov
                    Planted Russian Flag in North Pole
Nikolai Dmitry Orlov Colonel, Son of Orlov listed above.
                    Nagurskoye Military Base
General Smirnoff   GRU
Viktor Melnikov   Civilian captain *NS ROSSIYA*
Viktor Sokolov   Senior CPO, Sonar operator, *Kazan*
Viktor Zhukov   Major, flight leader pilot, Su-35
Igor Romanov   Captain of *Novosibirsk* submarine
Mikhail Barinov   Colonel, CO of Constable Pynt
                    Airport

Denmark
Mads Iversen   Captain, HDMS *Niels Juel*, Frigate
Anders Nyholm   Captain, HDMS *Ejnar Mikkelsen*
Henrik Hansen   Danish Prime Minister

Arctic Operations Map

The North Atlantic Treaty: Article 5

The Parties agree that an armed attack against one or more of them in Europe or North America shall be considered an attack against them all...

Chapter 1

NS Rossiya
August 2, 2007
North Pole

Captain Viktor Melnikov ignored the fact that, although it was the dead of night, the sun shone as he directed his civilian crew, primarily scientists, on a Russian nuclear icebreaker. Melnikov was a seasoned mariner with over thirty years of experience navigating the treacherous ice fields in the Arctic Ocean. Born and raised in Murmansk, he grew up in the shadow of Russia's icebreaker fleet, inspired by his father, who worked as an engineer on an early-generation diesel-powered icebreaker. He'd attended the Admiral Makarov State Maritime Academy in St. Petersburg and had graduated with honors in Arctic navigation. Melnikov was the perfect captain to command this critical mission for his homeland.

Standing on the bridge, he scanned the white expanse surrounding his ship for the precise route. The sea ice stretched infinitely in all directions, broken only by pools of dark water and occasional ridges of ice up to nine meters thick.

"Slow to 5 knots," he ordered, his voice calm but leaving no doubt who was in charge. His first officer repeated the order to the helmsman. *Rossiya's* twin nuclear reactors powered down. The massive icebreaker slowed as its metal hull ground against the Arctic ice, sending an echo across the frozen expanse.

The *Rossiya* was built for this, its reinforced bow able to carve a path through ice over two meters thick. But the last 50 kilometers would be the most challenging. Recent weather forecasts had shown shifting pressure ridges ahead that could move massive ice formations and slow or halt their progress. Melnikov's caution was a personal trait and a necessity in these unpredictable conditions.

"What are you doing, Viktor?" said Colonel Nikolai Dmitrievich Orlov, a veteran of the GRU, Russia's primary military intelligence agency, and the only military agent on board the ship. "Timing is critical to our mission."

Melnikov glanced at the lean, compact man from the notorious military intelligence organization. Orlov was impeccably dressed in civilian clothes and radiating an air of authority. But Melnikov could have cared less. The captain said firmly, "I will not jeopardize my crew for unnecessary risks. Ice conditions here are unpredictable. It's best to go cautiously."

Orlov glared at the captain, waiting just a few seconds past comfortable to reinforce his authority. "Your caution is noted, Captain, but reaching the North Pole is not optional.

The submersibles will descend where I say and when I say, got it?"

"Colonel, this crew answers to me. If you wish to give orders, I suggest you apply for the ship's captaincy."

The two men stared at one another for a long moment, the hum of the icebreaker's engines filling the void. The crew pretended not to be listening. Finally, Orlov nodded, a gesture more of acknowledgment than of agreement. "Very well, Captain. But understand this: The Kremlin sent me to ensure success. If you fail, I promise you, the consequences will not end with a demotion."

Melnikov took the icebreaker through, allowing the trailing RV *Akademik Fedorov* to reach the precise location at the North Pole and launch two submersibles, the Mir-1 and Mir-2, which descended to a depth of 4,200 meters. There, a Russian tricolor flag made of corrosion-resistant titanium was carefully planted, a symbolic act masked as a scientific mission and meant to signal Russia's claim over vast stretches of the Arctic. The claim covered an area estimated to hold up to 13 percent of the world's oil, 30 percent of its natural gas resources, and numerous rare metals.

The event created an international backlash. Countries like Canada, Denmark, Norway, and the United States, the loudest critic, labeled the Russians' actions as provocative. "This isn't the fifteenth century. You can't go around the world and just plant flags and say, 'We're claiming this territory.'"

What Captain Viktor Melnikov didn't comprehend was that he had been party to Russia's first bellicose step in the Arctic. It was just the beginning.

Chapter 2

OAK HARBOR, WASHINGTON
Present Day

The soft crackling of the fire filled the cozy cottage with peace and warmth on yet another rainy day with near-freezing temperatures. Icy pellets tapped on the windows as if asking to come in. That sure as shit wasn't going to happen, thought Lieutenant Commander Jessie "Swagger" Hampton. The fighter jock was kicking back in surroundings he had to admit were growing on him.

Even after a few weeks of being assigned to Naval Air Station Whidbey Island, he was still getting used to his new digs. He loved the wide-open floor plan and the feeling of space. Hell, the bathroom was about the size his entire wardroom had been aboard the USS *Ford,* but damn, he missed the boat for one simple reason: The dinky wardroom came with an ass-kicking Lockheed Martin F-35 Lightning II, locked and loaded and ready to deliver its might for his country.

My, what a sweet thought.

"Hey, Swagger," said Lieutenant Commander Sarah "Danger" Freeman, his wife of less than a year, "You're way too quiet over there by the fireplace."

Sitting on the floor in his sweatpants and wearing a faded squadron T-shirt, Jessie held a mug of hot coffee with both hands. "Sorry, this is just too weird. Being on shore duty is bad for my reflexes. Hell, if I'm not careful, I could lose my advantage out there where the air's thin and the stakes are life and death."

Sarah nodded her head. She was absorbed in her own world, working on a project on the dining room table. It wasn't for some fancy dinner; instead, the Northrop Grumman E2-D Advanced Hawkeye pilot was carefully pressing her new squadron patches onto the Velcro panels of her flight suit, adjusting each one until they sat just right.

"If anyone's worried about losing touch, it shouldn't be you. I've heard you muttering radio calls in your sleep. Hell, the other night you must have been dreaming of throwing your sidestick while chasing an Iranian fighter because you hit me right in the gut with your fist."

Hearing that, Jessie jumped up like a circus performer, without spilling a drop of coffee, and ran over to Sarah, giving her a gentle kiss on the top of her head. "Sorry, dear. How will you ever forgive me?"

"Dinner and wine at my favorite restaurant should be just the cure," she said, straight-faced.

"Not in this weather, Danger. My kiss will have to do," he said as he returned to his resting spot in front of the fire and took a sip from his cup of coffee.

Sarah finished the last patch, neatly folded it, and walked over to him, plopping down to his right, the co-pilot's position, only because there was not enough room on his left side. "At least you're not flying in this weather. Half the time I'm up there, I feel like I'm navigating through soup."

"Soup, huh?" Jessie leaned close to her. "Remind me, how many times did you have to catch a three-wire in seventy-knot crosswinds off Iran?"

"Touché," she said, nudging his leg with her foot. "But my Hawkeye isn't about glamorous landings. It's about keeping you hotshots alive."

"You're right," Jessie said, his tone soft. "You're the one who keeps us from flying into a mess we can't handle. But you are sure as shit not flying much right now, running the squadron while your skipper's on leave."

Sarah rolled her eyes but couldn't hide a smile. "It's been interesting. Lots of paperwork. Lots of babysitting junior officers. There are lots of scheduling hassles in qualifying all the pilots for aerial refueling. I swear, one of them doesn't know the difference between port and starboard."

Jessie chuckled. "Sucks being in charge."

"It's exhausting," she admitted, cuddling closer to him. "But at least I get to come home to this quiet, normal life. Well, as normal as we get."

He brushed a strand of hair from her face. "Yeah, it's nice. Just us, no alarms, no catapults launching us into the void, no one shooting at us. I could get used to it."

Sarah raised her head and looked at him intently. "Could you, though? I'm not sure you know how to sit still for long."

"Fair point," he said, chuckling. "But this—this is good for us. It's a chance to breathe, even if just for a little while."

The two naval pilots were fortunate to live under the same roof, a result of the Joint Spouse Assignment Program. In a way, Iran had played a significant role in that. During the war, two Iranian Shahed-136 drones struck the *Ford*. One of the hundred-pound bombs hit Catapult 1, and the other hit Elevator 3. Both bombs killed numerous sailors, and although the massive carrier could still carry on with combat missions, operations had been severely hampered.

After the war, orders eventually came down for the *Ford* to be repaired at Naval Base Kitsap. Jessie was told he would get shore flight duty in the same area and wouldn't go with his air wing to a different carrier. The powers that be decided he needed career and leadership broadening, and that his tactical experience was ideal for a new program at the Electronic Attack Weapons School, a program designed to better train Boeing EA-18G Growler pilots. Sarah then applied for reassignment and received orders to report to NAS Whidbey Island, where the gods of war had happened to form a squadron of E-2s, the first to fly operationally out of a land-based station, rather than an aircraft carrier. She had heard through the grapevine, which was very accurate in the Navy, that the unit was created because the Russians were engaging in some saber-rattling in the Arctic, and the US wasn't going to allow it.

Neither of the newlyweds knew how long their peace would last, but both agreed to make the most of it while they could. They completely understood that the Navy's needs took precedence over family. And neither was of a mind to let anything keep them from their aircraft. Such was a naval aviator's life.

Chapter 3

MERKURIY
1305 Hours, 21 June
Southwest Baltic Sea

The Steregushchiy-class corvette *Merkuriy* sliced through icy waters not far from Bornholm, a Danish island in the Baltic Sea between Sweden and Poland. The ship's sleek, angular hull almost disappeared against the gray horizon as wind-whipped waves pounded against one of the newest ships in the Russian fleet. Captain Ivan Kozlov stood on the bridge with his hands clasped behind his back, his steel-blue eyes fixed on the radar display. Kozlov didn't waver an inch as the ship rolled in the swells. His eyes were glued to the radar.

The commanding officer of the *Merkuriy* was at one with the sea. The son of a shipyard engineer and a schoolteacher, he was raised with a mix of technical curiosity from his father and academic discipline from his mother. His upbringing stressed patriotism to Russia and, more importantly, loyalty to its maritime legacy. His early career was on various frigates and destroyers, where he gained extensive experience in littoral and open-ocean operations. As a junior officer during a naval exercise, his decisive leadership while commanding the bridge, not to mention his ability to avoid a near collision with a surfaced submarine, had earned him rapid promotions, culminating in his present command.

Just ahead of his warship, the hulking silhouette of the oil tanker *Primorye* loomed in the mist, her tanks full of crude destined for Kaliningrad. Kozlov's mission was twofold. He was to ensure the tanker's safe passage through the contested waters near Denmark, where the presence of NATO warships had become too familiar for the comfort of his leaders in Moscow. He had explicit orders that if NATO ships interfered with his operation in any way, he was to send them a clear message about who ruled the strategically essential Baltic waters. The nature of his orders clearly indicated that the status quo in the waters surrounding his country was no longer acceptable and that Russia would bring about a change.

"Contact, Captain," his radar officer announced. "Surface vessel, bearing two-seven-zero, 20 kilometers. German signature."

Kozlov didn't flinch, as his team had expected the announcement. The Royal Danish Navy's HDMS *Niels Juel*, an Iver Huitfeldt-class frigate, had been shadowing the Russians' movements for days. Now, it was time for him to deal with this meddlesome captain. He expected the Danish CO to mind his business and remain a safe distance away. However, that was thrown out the window when his tactical officer barked: "Airborne contact. Helicopter launch detected from the Danish frigate. It's a Romeo, sir, and heading our direction."

Kozlov was familiar with the Sikorsky MH-60R Seahawk, a helo armed with weapons including torpedoes, Hellfire missiles, and door-mounted machine guns. With its state-of-the-art avionics and modern sensors optimized for anti-surface warfare missions, the Seahawk was an explicit threat to his ship. He questioned what the Danes were up to, but that thought didn't matter; he had to protect his ship and crew.

"Helm, slow to 12 knots. Tactical, ready the EW suite. Let's remind those NATO bastards who rules these seas."

DANISH MH-60R SEAHAWK
1310 Hours, 21 June
Southwest Baltic Sea

Flying low and fast, the Seahawk pilot carefully monitored his instruments while keeping an eye on the choppy waves just below his aircraft. His orders were straightforward: approach the Russian escort, gather intelligence on it and its movements, and remind them that the seas belong to the world, not the Russians. What the helo crew was doing even had a classification—Freedom of Navigation Operations, FONOP.

"Closing on target," the co-pilot said as he scanned his displays.

"We'll make a couple of passes and—"

The electronics in the cockpit flickered once and then went black.

"Systems failure," the pilot shouted. "We've lost radar and comms."

On *Merkuriy*, the tactical officer provided an update shortly after using the ship's electronic warfare capabilities. "Target neutralized, sir. They're flying blind."

"Helm, bring us starboard," Kozlov said calmly. "Close the gap with the tanker. Tactical, arm Paket-E/NK torpedoes. I want them to see we're not defenseless."

The ship turned sharply, throwing the sailors around the ship while carving white slashes in the dark gray sea. Hydraulic systems opened the hatches, exposing the torpedo launchers as they received real-time firing solutions.

Aboard the *Niels Juel*, Captain Mads Iversen didn't like the direction this encounter was taking with the Russians jamming his helicopter's electronics. As that thought passed, his second-in-command blurted out, "Sir, the Russians have just armed their torpedoes. They're painting us with targeting radar."

Iversen grimaced. "XO, order our helicopter back immediately. Do not arm any of our weapons, confirm?"

The XO didn't like it, but it wasn't his call. He relayed the order.

Captain Kozlov watched intently as the helicopter abruptly turned and headed back toward its ship. Not about to give up his advantage, he said, "Helm, return to original course and maintain speed. Tactical, keep the EW suite in active mode."

The Russian corvette resumed its protective formation with the *Primorye*. Behind them, the Danish ship turned away.

A longtime historian of the Russian Navy, Kozlov turned to his XO. A slight smile formed on the captain's lips before he said, "Let them send their reports. NATO likes to provoke, but they need reminding that we're not the same Navy from twenty years ago."

The icy waters of the Baltic seemed to embrace the two ships as the oil tanker and its escort pushed onward. Kozlov was gratified that he had just sent a message to NATO, which would report the near-shooting encounter to the US. His message had been simple but straightforward: Sea lane ownership in waters bordering Russia was no longer negotiable; it belonged to the Motherland.

Chapter 4

CONFERENCE ROOM 1, THE KREMLIN
16 July
Moscow, Russia

The neatly etched sign on the door, "Conference Room 1," gives no hint at what lies inside. In a country where cameras and listening devices are the norm, high-level talks such as the one scheduled for today were held at CR-1. This dedicated, secure room, equipped with anti-surveillance countermeasures, was the go-to room for the president.

Andrei Petrov, president of the Russian Federation, sat at the end of a long mahogany table surrounded by some of the most powerful people in his country. He held up his right arm, barely extending it beyond his body. He didn't have to. Everyone in the room understood that the meeting was about to start and that Petrov was in charge; he was always in charge.

"Comrades," Petrov began, using his most commanding voice, "Our success in Ukraine has shown the world that decisive action backed by our strong will can reshape not only borders but the consciousness." He scanned the room of fifteen leaders, looking for any sign of dissent or disagreement. Luckily for those present, he saw none. "But our ambitions cannot end there. We must now look outward to secure our borders from the West.

"The Arctic represents future resources, strategic control, and dominance over the Northern Hemisphere. After Ukraine, we now have the resources to continue our expansion to what is rightfully ours." There was a chorus of agreement, accompanied by nodding heads.

"Russia has always faced the persistent reality of encirclement by hostile forces, a challenge that cannot be ignored. This is not merely a theoretical concern but a strategic reality we must address decisively to safeguard our sovereignty and national interests.

"Comrades, the decision by Sweden and Finland to join NATO is nothing less than a deliberate provocation and a direct threat to our country's security. This is not an isolated event. It is part of the West's relentless campaign to encircle our nation, weaken our influence, and undermine our sovereignty. Our Scandinavian neighbors have abandoned their neutrality and chosen to align themselves with an alliance that openly seeks to contain and destabilize us. That is not going to happen."

Once again, the people in the room made supportive comments in just the right tone to support and not disrupt their president. The generals were the loudest in agreement.

"Let me be absolutely clear," Petrov said, "NATO expansion will not go unanswered. We will now begin decisive measures to neutralize the threat posed by NATO's alliance with Sweden and Finland. We will reinforce our military capabilities in the northwest, deploy advanced weapons systems to the Baltic region and Alexandra Land, and put pressure on strategically important Greenland. We will ensure the Arctic remains under our tactical control. Kaliningrad will be further fortified, and our forces on the Kola Peninsula will operate at the highest levels of readiness."

Petrov paused to draw more attention to himself and what he was about to say. "I want the final push in our successful efforts to support the pro-independence Greenlandic politicians through transparent financial support and behind-the-scenes bribes. We must continue to push the narrative of how the US and Denmark are militarizing Greenland and dragging it into an unwanted superpower conflict. The key is to continue shifting public opinion toward greater autonomy and a neutral stance, which then leaves the door open for us. With those politicians influencing the 52,000 inhabitants of the island, Greenland will declare its independence. As that shift occurs, with us filling their pockets with cash and winning them over to our side, NATO's Article 5 guarantees become increasingly murky, allowing us the time to establish a strong foothold.

"Additionally, we will use every tool—economic, cyber, and informational—to expose the hypocrisy and aggression of NATO's actions. If Sweden and Finland believe they can act without consequence, they are gravely mistaken. Admiral Mikhailovich, please update us on our Northern Fleet."

Mikhailovich was at the table because of his responsibility as commander of the most powerful and strategically important fleet of the Russian Navy, which was based in the Arctic.

With most of his last fifteen years spent in the Arctic, the well-worn naval veteran was ready. "Comrade President, the Arctic belongs to us. Our investment in icebreakers and military bases along the northern coast gives us an advantage that NATO cannot match. However, we must update our assets and bases with our most modern weapons. And in any direct action, we must be swift and overwhelming in our response."

Pointing with a trembling hand to a map projected on the wall, Mikhailovich said, "The major choke points are the Barents Sea, the Greenland-Iceland-United Kingdom Gap, and the Northwest Passage. They are key to our Arctic strategy. Under all circumstances, we must control these areas and deploy our forces to secure critical Arctic islands, including Franz Josef Land, Svalbard, and potentially even islands in Canadian territory. Then we can establish a de facto zone of control before NATO has time to react." Once again, there were murmurs of agreement around the room.

The Minister of Energy added, "The Arctic contains an estimated 13 percent of the world's undiscovered oil and 30 percent of its natural gas. Climate change is melting the ice and opening access to these resources. If we act decisively, we can secure these reserves before they fall into Western hands. This would not only strengthen our economy but also give us leverage over Europe."

"I agree," said the president. "Leverage is power. General Smirnoff, what do you have to add?"

"Thank you, Comrade President," said General Andrei Smirnoff of the GRU, Russia's military intelligence agency. "Our success depends on two factors, misdirection and deniability. We must ensure the world is too divided to respond effectively, and we can achieve this by leveraging our cyber capabilities to sow discord among NATO allies and target their supply chains and communications networks. At the same time, we will launch information campaigns framing our actions as defensive, as protecting Arctic wildlife and Indigenous peoples, and as combating Western overreach. The narrative must always be that we are responding to their aggression, not instigating it."

Barely letting Smirnoff finish, the one woman in the room, Deputy Defense Minister Natalia Romanova, spoke up. "Comrades, our Arctic bases are well-positioned, but supply lines remain a serious problem. If NATO, along with the US, decides to escalate, they could target these areas with long-range strikes. We must expand our logistic network by building additional airstrips and fortifying key installations and lines of communication."

Romanova's pragmatism earned nods from several senior officials. Still, General Smirnoff, the hawk in the room, interjected, "Which is precisely why we need to act now before the enemy enhances its presence in the region. Their president talks often of this. A pre-emptive strike can neutralize their capabilities long before we have time to upgrade ours."

A silence fell over the room while everyone took a few moments to comprehend what the general was proposing. All eyes went to President Petrov, who unconsciously tapped his right index finger on the massive table. It was the only sound in the room, and those present knew that what he had to say would change the course of history, not only for Russia but for the world. The rhythmic thumping of the president's finger began to sound like a clock ticking. Then it stopped.

"General Smirnoff is correct." The president's words filled the room like thunder rolling across a quiet valley. "We must act swiftly and decisively. But we will not repeat the mistakes of our actions in Ukraine. I take some of the blame for this, but mistakes were made. Our intelligence service underestimated the Ukrainian resistance and the resolve of both the military and civilian populations. We could have done better with our logistics while we underestimated NATO and Western unity." Most in the room agreed, but carefully hid their thoughts.

The president stopped and let his criticisms resonate. He slowly scanned the room, every high-level person at the table feeling guilty when the most powerful man in Russia let his eyes fall on them. When he completed his exam of each person, he continued, "This operation will be a blend of overwhelming military force, strategic deception, and economic exploitation. I want cyber and information operations to destabilize NATO and US communications and to create fractures within leadership."

Turning to Romanova, he said, "Prepare our Arctic forces for deployment. Prioritize control of Greenland and ensure our icebreakers can escort reinforcements through contested waters."

The president addressed the room, "Comrades, the Arctic is not just a prize; it is the future. It will define Russia's position in the world for the next century. The West may claim their principles, but we will claim the land. Now get to it."

As the last person left the room, Petrov gazed at the map of the Arctic still filling the large screen. His expression was determined and resolute. The next chapter of his expansionist playbook was now in motion.

Chapter 5

PENTAGON
17 July
Washington, DC

You would get no argument from Navy brass if you said Captain Blake Stanton's unorthodox style of submarine command made him a maverick in the fleet. He had butted heads with most flag officers at one time or another, earning a reputation as both a brilliant tactician and a persistent pain in the ass. But all would agree on one point: He was a fighter. Despite his hard-headed, take-no-prisoners approach, he was chosen as the first commanding officer of the newest submarine in the US fleet, the USS *Idaho*. To say his appointment was controversial would not do justice to the intense debates that had echoed through the corridors of the Pentagon.

On one side, you had factions who recalled his sinking of two Chinese submarines during the war with China. His instinct for reading the undersea battlespace was unmatched, and despite his reputation for challenging authority, his results were undeniable.

On the opposing side were those who viewed Stanton as a wild card, a maverick who didn't follow strict Navy protocols. He was a loose cannon, and they agreed that there was no way they would put him in command of the *Idaho*.

But not so fast. The Navy High Command also recognized that the Arctic was undergoing significant changes, marked by growing tensions along contested waterways. Most agreed the Navy needed an aggressive commander to compete with the Russians.

The debate ended at the desk of a four-star admiral, the Chief of Naval Operations. As an old submariner, the CNO favored assigning Stanton to *Idaho*. With additional input from another four-star, the Commander of Submarine Forces Atlantic, they agreed that Stanton's appointment would come with the conditions of tight oversight from fleet command and a handpicked XO to balance his aggression.

That person was Lieutenant Commander David "Books" Harrington, as second-in-command of the *Idaho*. He was the opposite of Stanton, a by-the-book officer with a reputation for discipline and unwavering adherence to protocol. He was a career officer who had climbed the ranks through sheer precision and respect for the chain of command. Some battle-tested commanders would call him a talented ass-kisser.

However, if those naysayers looked closely, they would see that Harrington was a decorated officer renowned for his excellence in submarine operations, and his fitness reports consistently praised his ability to maintain cohesive and efficient crews. He was the kind of officer the brass could trust implicitly, and that was precisely why he was assigned as Stanton's XO.

As Stanton took command of *Idaho's* Arctic operations, the crew whispered their theories about why he'd been chosen. The truth was simple, he wasn't picked for being agreeable. He was picked because, in the Arctic, the Navy couldn't afford to lose.

Chapter 6

VOLOGDA STAR
0816 Hours, 17 July
Norwegian Sea

Colonel Nikifor Koltsov contemplated how there were five oceans in the world and that he had sailed them all. And he admitted that the smallest of them all, the Arctic Ocean, offered the most challenges, even to a seasoned sailor like himself. Almost entirely surrounded by the land masses of North America, Europe, and Asia, the Arctic Ocean was unique because it was almost always covered by unforgiving ice. However, that was all changing due to climate warming, and the ocean had been opened up to new shipping routes and previously untapped natural resources.

"Captain?" His XO's voice snapped him out of his reverie. "You had asked me to tell you when we were nearing the Arctic Circle."

"Yes, thank you, XO."

"Aye, sir."

Even though Koltsov had been alone in his thoughts, he and his crew hadn't been alone in the sea. On a parallel course, a second Russian ship with visibly marked military cargo on its deck had also reached the coordinates for the Arctic Circle. And as planned, that ship turned away from the *Vologda Star*, hoping to draw the attention of NATO's spying eyes away from his ship.

"Helm," Koltsov stated, "make a turn to two-four degrees, increase speed to 12 knots."

"Helm, roger, turn to two-four degrees, increase speed to 12 knots."

Koltsov had commanded many warships, but this was his first time at the helm of a cargo vessel. The *Vologda Star*, however, was no ordinary freighter. It was an Arc9/LU9-classified Super type cargo ship, which meant two things: There was no need for an icebreaker, and it could carry a hidden payload. Beneath a deck stacked in numbered containers marked "Steel Beams" were NDB/NPO-Machinostroyeniya 3M22 Tsirkon maneuvering hypersonic cruise missiles capable of reaching Mach 9. Koltsov's orders were clear, but implementation was another matter. He was tasked with delivering the missiles to Alexandra Land, an island in Franz Josef Land, without drawing the attention of NATO or the US Navy.

BOEING P-8A POSEIDON
0818 Hours, 17 July
Greenland, Iceland, United Kingdom Gap patrol

Lieutenant Commander Ryan "Ghost" Maddox banked the P-8 in a sweeping, gentle turn. The noise of the engines was steady against the wind shear that was cutting across the

Arctic Circle and causing his military version of the Boeing 737 commercial aircraft to shake quite fiercely. He sat in the left seat as aircraft commander, responsible for himself and eight other crew members, monitoring the GIUK Gap, a strategically vital waterway framed by Greenland, Iceland, and the United Kingdom. A seasoned pilot with more than twelve years of service to the Navy, Maddox had flown these routes for months, logging hundreds of hours tracking Russian submarines and cargo vessels that moved suspiciously close to contested waters.

"Ghost, target vessels in quadrant three-five-zero," reported Lieutenant Karen Parsons, the electronic warfare officer sitting just behind Maddox. As always, her voice was calm and matter-of-fact. "Positive ID on both."

"Got visual?"

"Got eyes on the westernmost ship, container stacks loaded with military gear, plain as day. The second vessel has nothing obvious, just a standard cargo load on deck, but I ran thermal, and its hull temperatures are higher than usual. Something's cooking below, and I don't mean food."

"Copy," said Maddox, "mark the ship with noticeable military gear on deck as Alpha 1 and the other as Alpha 2."

Maddox exchanged a glance with his co-pilot, Lieutenant Robert "Han" Johanson. He was young but sharp, the kind of officer Maddox trusted to watch his six. "That's our guy," Maddox muttered to the crew. "Keep your sensors tight. We don't want to spook him."

"Ghost, Alpha 1 just altered course," said Parsons. "It's breaking off from the other vessel."

Maddox checked the radar and confirmed Alpha 1 was cutting a wide arc away from Alpha 2. The veteran pilot considered what he had: two cargo ships, one with obvious military cargo and the other appearing to be transporting civilian cargo. Logic told him to concentrate on Alpha 1, but his instincts told him otherwise.

The tactical coordinator, Lieutenant Norm Jackson, said, "Comms traffic just spiked. Alpha 2 is still on course heading east, but Alpha 1 is throwing everything at making itself visible, like running high-frequency bursts and elevating its radar cross section. Alpha 1 is practically screaming, 'I'm going this way, so follow me.'"

"Roger that, TACCO," said Maddox. "Agree that Alpha 1 is way too obvious. They want us to divert our attention away from Alpha 2, so keep your eyes on Alpha 2. That's where the real action is."

"Han," said Maddox, "I have the aircraft."

"Roger that. Ghost, you have the aircraft."

As soon as Jackson turned over the controls, Maddox brought the P-8 into a tight turn but kept their sensors passive, careful not to alert the ships they were tracking. He said, "Tag both vessels. But let's stay locked onto Alpha 2."

"Ghost," said TACCO, the Tactical coordinator, "we've got a thermal disturbance just off Alpha 2's wake that matches the hydrodynamic profile of a small submerged vessel. No buoys are down, but it's trailing close. Classifying as a suspected Russian submarine."

"That's no coincidence," Maddox said. "Give me a heading and prep the sonobuoys. If they're shadowing that ship, they're guarding something important. Stay passive on sensors. Drop a barrier pattern ahead of the sub's course. Tag the new contact as Bravo 1."

Dropping the P-8 to 500 feet to limit parachute drift in the gusting winds, Maddox eased the speed back to 200 knots, low enough for precise buoy placement but cautious not to linger in one place long enough to be an easy target. "Marking position," he called out over comms.

"Perfect," said TACCO. "Hold at 200 knots. Is the buoy bay ready?"

Johanson answered back, "Buoy bay green. Ready to launch."

Roger," said TACCO, "deploy the first set now."

As the buoys dropped from the P-8, a mechanical *clunk* filled the cabin, telling everyone the buoys had just been discharged.

"Buoys away, parachutes deployed, and tracking," said TACCO. After a moment of listening, he said, "Buoys in the water, clean signal. Baseline noise only, nothing active yet."

Chapter 7

K-561 KAZAN Russian SUBMARINE
0829 Hours, 17 July
Arctic Ocean

Pacing the control room of the Yasen-class submarine *Kazan*, Captain 1st Rank Ivan Gromov was concerned about his next move to protect the *Vologda Star* as it carried its extremely valuable cargo of Tsirkon hypersonic cruise missiles. His crew had been operating with the silence and precision he demanded. This was important since the Arctic presented so many unique challenges: surface ice everywhere, ice keels deep underwater, hull stress from operating in freezing temperatures, magnetic anomalies, inconsistent satellite coverage, and the list went on and on.

Whether from nature, warships, or aircraft, staying undetected was the key to staying alive, and playing babysitter for a cargo ship made that more difficult. His orders were explicit: get the cargo ship to Alexandra Land safely without the US or NATO finding out.

If only it were that easy.

"Captain, new contact," reported his sonar operator, Senior Chief Petty Officer Viktor Sokolov. "Multiple buoy drops, bearing two-seven-zero." Seconds later, he added, "Passive. Pattern spread."

Gromov knew from a previous secure message that an American P-8 was patrolling the GIUK Gap. It looked as if they'd arrived.

"Hold course and speed," Gromov ordered, his voice calm but firm. He moved to the sonar console for a closer look. The screen displayed the buoy pattern, a loose net spread over the waters in hopes of discovering him and his next move. A lesser commander might have panicked, but Gromov had spent years mastering the art of submarine warfare. This was just another drill for the veteran submariner.

"Weapons, deploy the Korund-2 decoy," he ordered. "Make it slow-drift starboard." The *Kazan* was outfitted with the trusted MG-74, which enhanced his survivability by simulating his sub's acoustic signature while slowly drifting away from it. The decoy emitted signals that were designed to confuse enemy sonar operators.

"XO, make notifications for silent running," Gromov added. "Take all non-essential systems to minimum power."

"Captain, sonar. Thermocline layer present at 128 meters."

Gromov was pleased to hear that. "Helm, take us below the layer, speed 3 knots."

"Helm, roger, going below thermocline at 3 knots."

Now let them chase a ghost, thought Gromov.

0832 Hours, 17 July

Arctic Ocean

While flying in a pattern over the buoys, Jackson heard from the sonar operator, a young Petty Officer Third Class on her first assignment. "TACCO, I've got transient noise, faint and bearing zero-eight-five."

Jackson came back instantly, "Sonar, lock it down and classify."

"Sir, I mean TACCO, sounds like a Yasen in an S-pattern cavitation signature. It's faint, but it's there."

"Sonar, sounds like or is?"

"TACCO, yes, computer models ID it as a Yasen-class submarine."

Just as Jackson was going to contact the pilot and mission commander, the sonar operator said, "Wait, something's off. Bearing shift now zero-nine-three. With increased screw RPMs."

"Is it speeding up?"

"That's the thing, the pattern feels artificial, too clean. Could be a decoy."

"Copy," said TACCO, "stay on it."

Jackson toggled the intercom to speak to the pilot. "Ghost, TACCO. We've got a possible decoy situation. The Russian sub might've dropped below the thermal layer. I need you to maintain a steady orbit and adjust the heading ten degrees to the left. We're going to need to redeploy buoys to punch through the layer."

As Maddox adjusted his flight pattern, he said, "Copy that, ten left. Holding orbit. How deep are you thinking?"

"Acoustic picture's showing a layer near four-hundred feet, looks like a thermocline. Drop below and stagger the buoys. If she's in the layer, we'll pick her up."

"Understood. How many buoys do you need in the water?"

"More than I like. We'll start with six, spaced tight. I'll call for more if needed."

After dropping the buoys and waiting a short time, the sonar tech reported, "Negative contact on all new buoy drops. I'm not picking up anything below the layer."

Jackson leaned closer to his console, hoping this action would help find the submarine. "Sonar, run a full sweep. Check for anomalies, anything faint or intermittent."

"Already did, sir. It's clean."

Jackson liked that his new sonar operator, Jane Foster, had taken the initiative on her first real test of chasing Russian submarines. She seemed to catch on fast. "Thanks, Foster. Good job."

Toggling the intercom again, Jackson said, "Ghost, TACCO. Nothing coming up on sonar. The decoy was bait, and we took it. That sub captain knows we're up here, and there's no way he's going to make noise unless he's forced to."

"Copy. So what's the play? More drops?"

"Negative. If we spread out too far, we're just burning buoys. He's not running. He's hiding, probably drifting below the thermocline layer, engines cold. We'll give this round to him, but now we know a little more about his tactics and why he's out there. Our time is up on this one."

"Roger that. We're heading home."

Chapter 8

USS THOMAS HUDNER
2358 Hours, 17 July
Kara Sea

It was nearly midnight, and the sun was still out as Lieutenant Commander Brett Jansen, the XO, was standing watch on the Arleigh Burke-class guided-missile destroyer USS *Thomas Hudner*, taking in the vastness of the Kara Sea.

Usually, the officer of the deck would be in his position, but this was no ordinary night, and the XO had taken the watch from the OOD. The *Hudner* was on a Freedom of Navigation operation near Russia's strategically significant Severnaya Zemlya archipelago north of Siberia. This was a disputed territory, with Russia, the US, Canada, Denmark (via Greenland), and Norway all having competing claims. As with all US naval operations near Russia, this FONOP was intended as a reminder of the lawful uses of the sea as recognized by international law. The whole FONOP concept reminded Jansen of playground kids putting their thumbs in their ears, wiggling their fingers like flapping wings, and sticking out their tongues or singing nya-nya-nya, the universal anthem of playground teasing. But one had to be careful, as some kids on the receiving end fight back.

"Beautiful sight, isn't it, sir?" said the helmsman without taking his eyes off the sea.

"Yes, it is. But it can become distracting, and that's why we remind each other to stay vigilant. Right?"

"Yes, sir."

"Bridge, Comms," came a call over the intercom, "distress call coming in from the *Polar Star*, a Norwegian research vessel. They are reporting that they're trapped in an ice drift. Coordinates put them near Severnaya Zemlya."

"Nav, Bridge," said Jansen, "plot a course to the distress call. Find out how many are aboard and if any are injured." Jansen switched to the overall shipboard comm system and announced over 1MC, "Captain to the bridge."

Jansen's commanding officer on the *Hudner* was Commander Don Reynolds, a career surface warfare officer known for his decisive leadership, tactical acumen, and unwavering sense of duty. He was awarded the Navy Cross for his actions during the recent war with Iran.

Within five minutes, Reynolds was standing in front of Jansen. "What do you have, XO?"

After Jansen explained the situation and his course change to intercept the *Polar Star*, Reynolds said, "Pull up a map, and let's see what we've got."

Jansen touched a few buttons on his tablet. A large digital map was projected on the bulkhead. On the blue-tinted screen, the Arctic region was displayed in sharp detail, and the *Polar Star*'s coordinates blinked as a red dot near the ice shelf.

The captain, using the trackpad, zoomed in on the location. "Looks like they're 18 nautical miles off Severnaya Zemlya and right on the ice shelf's edge."

"If they drift much further east," said Jansen, "they'll cross into the Russian EEZ. That whole section is under surveillance."

"Yes, sir. The last thing we need is for the Russians to think we're running ops near their northern stations."

Reynolds pulled up a satellite overlay. Red boundary lines delineated Russian maritime zones, including the Exclusive Economic Zone. The *Polar Star* was drifting closer to the highly secure area of Severnaya Zemlya.

"Jansen, I want you to work with the Seahawk crews to form a rescue plan. Put yourself on a helo, too, so we've got some rank out there in case the Russians come in. As we get more info here, I'll feed it to you."

"Yes, sir."

The captain glanced at Jansen. "There's a high possibility that this could get dicey. The *Polar Star* is expected to breach the EEZ in approximately three hours. You need to get there before that happens."

"Yes, sir. I'll make sure the crews understand the situation and plan their ingress to stay below radar until we're close. The less attention we draw, the better."

As Jansen exited the bridge, both men glanced back at the map and saw the *Polar Star*'s red dot moving closer to Russian territory.

Chapter 9

MERKURIY

0016 Hours, 18 July

Kara Sea

It had been three weeks since the incident with the Danish frigate *Niels Juel,* and Russian command now had Captain Ivan Kozlov patrolling near Severnaya Zemlya in the Kara Sea. He had just received a report of a Norwegian vessel, the *Polar Star,* getting close to the archipelago. The Arctic was no place for missteps. His country had long asserted dominance in these waters, and the *Polar Star*'s location near the maritime boundary was irritating. It was time to shoo them off.

Pacing the bridge because he hated sitting, he stopped mid-step when Comms said, "Captain, radar contact confirmed. H-60 helicopter inbound, likely American. They're on course to the coordinates of the *Polar Star.*"

"Helm, bring us thirty degrees starboard," Kozlov said without hesitation. "Close the gap between us and the Norwegian vessel. Let them see we're coming."

The *Merkuriy* went to full military power, slicing through thin sheets of drifting ice. Within minutes, the shadow of the American helicopter appeared over the horizon and circled the *Polar Star* like a vulture. It was decision time.

0017 Hours, 18 July
Kara Sea

Jansen was accustomed to cold weather, having grown up in western Michigan near the Big Lake, in Grand Haven. But this type of cold was a whole new experience. As he headed to one of the two reconfigured Sikorsky MH-60R Seahawks, the Arctic wind cut through his flight suit and thermal gear as if he had not layered up at all. The spinning rotor stirred up the cold air, making it even worse.

Looking out the pilot-side window, Lieutenant Sally Harris greeted him with a smile. Once Jansen was settled in the helo and wearing a radio headset, she said, "All set, XO. I just received additional mission data. *Polar Star* says to expect clear skies with dropping temps. Ice is creeping in all around them, so we should be able to land on the ice instead of using the hoists."

"Copy that, Lieutenant."

Within moments, everyone was strapped in and ready, including a heavily armed Marine on each helo, who had been added once they'd found out they would be picking up only fifteen people, none of whom were injured. The roar of the engine made Jansen glad he was wearing the radio headset. Looking out the back portside window, he watched the deck of the *Hudner* fade away as the helicopter gained altitude.

The flight was smooth, and they passed over occasional icebergs floating along on calm seas. Eventually, water gave way to ice sheets, and after an hour, the silhouette of the *Polar Star* was spotted, surrounded by ice. As they did a slow flyover, the Americans were greeted with frantic waves from some of the stranded crew who were standing in groups on the ice surrounding their ship.

As the large helicopter came in, its powerful rotors whipped up snow, creating a whiteout. Once it cleared, the aircrewman opened the side door, and despite the rotor noise, Jansen could hear the groans of the ship's hull echoing through the air. The research vessel was slowly being squeezed to death by the encroaching ice, and the eerie sound made Jansen very uncomfortable. He couldn't imagine how the ship's crew had endured it while they'd waited.

With the Marine waiting just outside the helo's door, Jansen walked carefully but quickly over to the captain, who was one of the few in uniform. As he approached, the captain called out, "We thought you would never make it."

Jansen shook his hand firmly. "We got here as fast as we could. Let's get your crew aboard the helicopters and back to solid ground."

As the *Polar Star*'s crew split up and the helicopters' aircrewmen began ushering them toward the choppers, a sharp voice crackled through Jansen's headset. "XO, Tommy 11. We have radar contact. Russian vessel closing in fast from the east. ETA fifteen minutes."

Jansen turned to the civilian ship's captain. "We have a problem." The captain looked at him like, *now what?* and Jansen continued, "We have a Russian ship hauling ass to intercept us. Let's get your crew moving faster and get out of here. We have fewer than fifteen minutes."

Jansen then yelled, "Everyone needs to expedite. We have a Russian warship inbound."

The atmosphere went from relatively calm to near panic in seconds. Everyone quickened their pace as much as they could, despite their heavy Arctic clothing.

On the emergency guard channel, Jansen heard someone speaking with heavily-accented English. "This is Captain Ivan Kozlov of the Russian Navy. You are in Russian territorial waters. The vessel you are attempting to remove is in violation of maritime law and will remain. Stand down immediately."

Jansen didn't hesitate to answer. "Captain Kozlov, this is Lieutenant Commander Brett Jansen of the USS *Thomas Hudner*. The *Polar Star* is a Norwegian vessel engaged in lawful research. We are conducting a humanitarian rescue mission. I suggest you allow us to proceed."

"Negative, Commander. Any action you take is a violation of international law and an encroachment on Russian territory. You have ten minutes to leave."

On the *Merkuriy*, Kozlov knew that the Americans would test his limits. He studied the *Polar Star* with his binoculars. It was trapped fast by ice, its crew scrambling toward the helicopters. Ten minutes passed. The rotors of the MH-60Rs churned the cold air yet stayed on the ground, defying his command. A few more people were struggling to board.

"Weapons," Kozlov said, "I want you to light up the helicopters with targeting radar and be ready to fire on my command."

"Weapons, roger, sir."

Back on the ice, standing just outside of the lead helo's door next to the Marine, Jansen toggled his headset. "XO to Tommy 11, get ready. I want out of here as soon as the last person enters, and that will be me. You copy?"

Harris answered, "Tommy 11, roger. I read your mind, XO. We're fired up and ready to go as soon as you're aboard."

"XO, Tommy 12," said the other pilot, "the Russians have lit us up with their targeting radar."

Jansen didn't like the way this was going. Even though he didn't really believe the Russians would fire on them and start a war over a rescue mission, he would feel better if he could get some support.

He toggled his radio. *"Hudner,* XO. We've got a Russian ship locking on our helicopters with targeting radar. Request immediate air cover and interception."

"Roger that, XO, but there are no assets in the area. You're on your own."

As the last of the civilian crew were pulled aboard, the *Merkuriy* could easily be seen close-in. Jansen saw the Marine and aircrewman from the other helo get in and shut the side door. He motioned for his escort and aircrewman to get in his helo's cabin and quickly followed them. The Seahawks' engine was revving higher than Jansen could have ever imagined.

As the last one in, he pulled the door shut and yelled, "Go, go, go."

Within seconds, the two helicopters were airborne, immediately turning away from the Russian warship but staying close to the ice and sea, making them challenging targets.

On the Russian ship, *Merkuriy*'s XO excitedly said, "Captain, they're taking off. Should we fire?"

Kozlov hesitated before replying, "No. Weapons, stand down. Turn off targeting radar."

Today wasn't the day to fire, but he sensed that day was getting closer.

Chapter 10

ELECTRONIC ATTACK WEAPONS SCHOOL
0730 Hours, 18 July
NAS Whidbey Island, WA

Division ran deep. Jessie "Swagger" Hampton had thought that kind of tribalism had faded with time, until he stepped into the large classroom at Naval Air Station Whidbey Island. The rift was plain. On one side, the F-35 pilots sat upright, eyes locked on the screen, jotting down notes with precision. On the other, the Growler crews lounged back in their seats, their posture casual, as if this was just another round of tired doctrine they'd heard a hundred times before. Commander Richard Lawson, the instructor, directed his operations brief to the Growler pilots. "Your primary mission is jamming enemy radar so the F-35s can sneak through. Think of it like holding the flashlight for your dad while he works on the family car."

"Yeah," said Lieutenant Ronnie "Razor" Harper, "except we're the ones keeping the wolves at bay while the stealth guys tiptoe around, hoping not to get frostbite." He directed a smart-ass grin to the F-35 guys. "Oh, and stay out of my light, like my daddy always said."

Jessie couldn't help himself. "We'd love to stay and fight, but someone's gotta be invisible. You can't just blast

Wagner's 'Ride of the Valkyries' and show up on every radar from here to Moscow."

"Because stealth is real helpful when you run out of missiles. Don't worry, buddy, we'll jam their radar and carry enough firepower to clean up your mess. Like we always do."

"Mess?" Jessie said. "We're the ones dropping precision bombs while you guys are playing with knobs."

Lawson jumped in, "Guys, please act like the professionals you're supposed to be. Save this shit for the chow line."

"Precision bombs are cute," Harper said. "But when that Russian Flanker looks at you funny, guess who you'll be calling for backup?"

Jessie smiled. "I'll call you, Razor, right after I've splashed him from fifty miles out. Then you can jam his ejection seat."

"Attention," shouted Lawson. Everyone jumped to their feet and stood at rigid attention, wondering which captain or admiral had just entered the room. "Any more of this grade-school shit and class is over, flights are cancelled, and you smart-asses will be spending the rest of the day with the principal. Got it?"

The room echoed with a single "Yes, sir."

"Now take your seats and shut the fuck up."

Harper and Jessie locked eyes and smiled, each thinking they had won the little bullshit session.

Lawson reviewed several areas where the conditions in the Arctic impacted each aircraft. Jessie paid particular attention to the effects on an F-35, including those on hydraulics, sensors, and avionics. Due to the subzero temperatures, he could expect reduced battery performance and decreased engine efficiency as the fuel thickened. Thrown into the mix was magnetic interference with traditional nav systems because of proximity to the magnetic pole. The best practice was to use GPS and inertial navigation systems. Lawson also reminded everyone that the Arctic had limited infrastructure, with fewer airstrips, fuel depots, and maintenance facilities. And lastly, he said that radar-absorbing materials could be affected, so pilots needed to balance the effects of external loadouts on stealth performance for any Arctic missions.

Good to know, thought Jessie.

Chapter 11

THE HAMPTON-FREEMAN RESIDENCE
1733 Hours, 18 July
Oak Harbor, Washington

When Jessie pulled into his driveway, his wife pulled in beside him. Good timing, he thought.

Sarah stepped out of her car and peeled off her flight jacket, a small smile tugging at the corners of her lips. Jessie knew that look. It was the one she wore when she had news and wasn't sure how he would take it.

"Long day, sweetheart?" Jessie asked as they walked toward the front door. He carried his duffel bag over one shoulder and had his flight suit zipped halfway down.

Sarah loved it when he wore his uniform like that, but had never told him. She didn't know why, but probably because, knowing him, he would do something to spoil her fun.

"You could say that," Sarah replied, "but I finally got all my pilots AR-qualified." She glanced at him. "How about you? You look like you've been hearding Growler drivers all day."

Jessie smirked. "They put up a fight. You know how they are, cocky as hell."

"And you're not?"

"There's a guy, calls himself Razor, who thinks he's God's gift to flying. Shit, I could fly circles around him, and he wouldn't even know I was there."

"I sense some competition."

"Not yet, but we'll finally be flying an exercise against a Russian attack of some sort. I think my skill with the F-35 will top anything he can do with his Growler."

They both stepped into the house as Jessie closed the door and locked it. He dropped his duffel bag, pulled Sarah into a loving hug, then spun her around twice. Her foot nearly knocked over the floor lamp, but they didn't care as they locked into a long, passionate kiss.

"Whoa, cowboy," Sarah said when she pulled away, "I want to discuss something with you first."

"It can't wait?"

"Not if you want a good time," Sarah said, smiling.

Jessie knew that look. "All right, out with it. What's on your mind?"

She hesitated for a second, then exhaled before saying, "My squadron's been selected for temporary duty at Pituffik Space Base. It should be for just a few months, but it's going down fast."

Jessie stared at her in disbelief because he thought they had finally settled down together. "Greenland?"

"Yup. They want to test E-2s in Arctic conditions, and apparently, the brass thinks it's a perfect opportunity to also give the Russians something else to think about."

Jessie leaned back against the wall, crossing his arms. He wasn't surprised. Sarah's new unit was cutting-edge, constantly pushing boundaries. But Greenland meant long, cold flights and being apart.

Get it together, he told himself. "When do you leave?"

"Next week," she said, watching him closely. She didn't like this any more than he did, but deep down, she was excited about this new opportunity.

He nodded slowly. "Well, I guess I'll have the house to myself for a while." Smiling, he added, "Maybe I'll get some peace and quiet."

Sarah fluttered her eyes. "Oh, please. You'll be calling me after three days asking when I'm coming back."

"Probably," Jessie admitted. He stepped closer, wrapping his arms around her waist. "You do know I'll worry a little, right? Arctic operations, I'm learning, can get tricky."

Sarah rested her forehead against his. "I know, but it's a short deployment. And if it helps, I heard there might be some F-35s tagging along for air cover."

Jessie looked happier. "Now that's more like it. Maybe I'll put in for a ride-along."

"You would just get in my way," she teased.

Chapter 12

THE WHITE HOUSE
0800 Hours, 19 July
Washington, DC

As he headed for the Situation Room for yet another meeting with his National Security Council, President Mark Taylor reflected on his nearly eight years in office. During his first term, there was a war or conflict or whatever with China after they used military force in an attempt to seize Taiwan. Thankfully, that didn't happen, and they'd been minding their p's and q's ever since.

Then Iran got brave. The fact that terrorists had blown up Independence Hall still haunted him. The resulting war with Iran had been deadly for both sides, but on a positive note, Iran now had a democratically based government that continued to attempt to win over all their people.

The president suddenly slowed his walk. His lead Secret Service agent, who always followed him closely, was caught off guard, and he almost ran into the leader of the free world. "Sorry, sir. My bad."

"No problem, Jerry. I have a lot on my mind."

As he was about to enter the Situation Room, Taylor hoped today's National Security meeting about Russia's provocative moves in the Arctic would not lead to the third conflict in his two terms as president.

When he entered the room, all stood. Present were the National Security Advisor, the Secretary of Defense, the Secretary of State, the Chairman of the Joint Chiefs of Staff, the Director of National Intelligence, and other senior advisors.

"Be seated, please," said Taylor.

Once everyone got settled, he said, "Good afternoon, and thank you for attending this vital policy meeting. I think we can all agree that the Arctic is becoming one of the most contested regions in the world. What was once a remote and frozen frontier is now a strategic hot spot. Climate change is accelerating the ice melt, opening new shipping lanes and exposing vast reserves of oil, gas, and rare earth minerals. These developments are transforming the Arctic into an arena of great power competition, one with significant implications for our national security, the global economy, and the environment."

The president took a moment to scan the room, making eye contact with some of the country's brightest minds. "Russia has been aggressively expanding its presence in the Arctic. They've militarized the region with new bases and advanced weapon systems, and conducted frequent military exercises, even at times with China. This isn't just posturing. It's a deliberate strategy to dominate the Arctic and control critical shipping lanes, such as the Northern Sea Route. If left unchecked, Russia's actions could not only threaten our interests but also destabilize the rules-based international order we've worked so hard to maintain."

Taylor adjusted his chair to be a bit closer to the large table. "Ladies and gentlemen, before we discuss the broader security posture, I want to begin with what now must be our top priority: Greenland. What we're seeing unfold with Russia isn't just a territorial provocation. It's a calculated move aimed at the heart of our Arctic defense architecture. Greenland isn't just a frozen land mass on a map. It anchors our missile early warning system at Pituffik, controls access to the Arctic sea lanes, and flanks the GIUK Gap, the naval choke point through which Russia projects power into the North Atlantic."

As the president continued, his voice sounded more urgent, capturing the undivided attention of everyone in the room. "If we lose control or credibility in Greenland, we compromise the northern shield of the continental United States. We risk losing strategic oversight over both the Atlantic and polar approaches. And let's be clear, Russia isn't interested in snow and ice. They're after leverage: military positioning, mineral dominance, and freedom of maneuver in an increasingly accessible Arctic. We cannot afford to fall behind. Our military, diplomatic, and economic policies in the Arctic and Greenland must be aligned to ensure we're prepared for the challenges ahead. That's why we're here today to assess the threats, identify our strategic priorities, and decide on the actions necessary to safeguard our national interests and those of our allies.

"I would like each of you to share your assessments and recommendations, and I expect an honest and clear discussion. The Arctic may seem distant, but what happens there will have far-reaching consequences for us and the rest of the world. I believe the Arctic is insufficiently prioritized amid our competing global interests. The future battlefield is melting and demands our attention. Please, let's get started. Elena?"

As she always was, Director of National Intelligence Elena Ramirez was prepared. "Thank you, Mr. President," she said warmly. "Our analysis confirms that Russia has significantly ramped up operations in the Arctic with an eye on Greenland, as you just said. Over the past year, they've increased their military presence, including the deployment of more Yasen-class submarines to patrol Arctic waters. Satellite imagery shows the construction of airbases and missile defense systems on islands within the Arctic Circle. At the top of the list is Alexandra Land, which is the westernmost island in the Franz Josef Land archipelago. Additionally, Russia has resumed large-scale military exercises likely intended to assert control and deter Western presence."

As she paused, Taylor thought about how much of an asset Elena had been to his administration for the past seven years.

She continued, "Economically, Moscow is prioritizing the Northern Sea Route as a commercial shipping lane. The NSR could become a key choke point under Russian control, giving them leverage over global trade since it's the shortest shipping route between Europe and the Pacific. Their efforts are also linked to securing access to untapped oil and gas reserves, which could potentially alter the global energy landscape."

Seeing an opportunity to add to the conversation, and never one to hold back, Secretary of Defense George Mitchell said, "From a military perspective, Russia's activities are concerning. They've modernized their Arctic fleet, including nuclear-powered icebreakers. This gives them year-round regional operational capabilities, which we can't match. The risk is twofold. First is their ability to deny access to the Arctic and control key shipping lanes. Secondly, they have access to our undersea cables, which are crucial for global communications and financial transactions.

"Because of this, we need a proactive Arctic strategy in which the United States and our NATO partners are not afraid to define the rules and laws governing the north. I disagree wholeheartedly with the critics of this approach who claim that taking a more vigorous position in the Arctic will further antagonize Russia and divert important resources from the Indo-Pacific region and China. This is simply not the case. Russia and, at times, China, have already taken steps to claim and militarize the Arctic. By acting now, the US and NATO will be better positioned to counter the threat posed by Russia in the Arctic and beyond."

Chairman of the Joint Chiefs of Staff General Troy Kincaid said, "To piggyback on what SecDef said, we also see enhanced interoperability between Russia's Arctic and conventional forces. Their exercises aren't just for show. They're simulating scenarios involving NATO contingencies. If hostilities were to break out, their Arctic bases could act as forward operating positions for strikes into Europe or North America.

"We've already increased our presence with Freedom of Navigation operations and joint exercises with NATO partners like Norway and Canada. However, we must invest more heavily in Arctic-specific capabilities, particularly icebreakers, long-range surveillance, and Arctic-resilient forces. Currently, Russia continues to build up its Arctic coastline with fifty-five icebreakers, thirty-seven surface vessels, eight nuclear submarines, and numerous aircraft of differing capabilities."

The general was accustomed to having the floor in meetings, and it didn't seem to matter that he was sitting among civilians, not subordinates. He continued, "Furthermore, we must ramp up our response to Russia's provocation in the Arctic. A few months ago, the North American Aerospace Defense Command intercepted Russian and Chinese bombers flying just 200 miles from Alaska's coast. More recently, NORAD launched US and Canadian fighter jets to track and intercept two Russian Tupolev TU-95s and two Chinese Xi'an H-6 bombers. As we talk, we're tracking a civilian cargo ship that we believe is loaded with Tsirkon hypersonic cruise missiles and is headed for Alexandra Land. If our hunch is correct, this is a considerable escalation."

"Thank you, General," said Taylor. "Let's now hear from SecState."

Secretary of State Brad Kelly was a two-term cabinet member, trusted and respected by everyone in the room.

"You already know this, but it's worth repeating that the Arctic includes territory belonging to eight nations: Norway, Sweden, Finland, Denmark, and their control of Greenland, Canada, the US, Iceland, and Russia. All except Russia are NATO members. The alliance offers an opportunity for us to strengthen our position in the Arctic region without having to go it alone.

"If we allow Russia to dominate the Arctic, we risk undermining international norms and setting a precedent that could embolden similar actions elsewhere. We must work closely with our allies to maintain a united front and emphasize the Arctic as a region of shared governance."

The president lifted his hand. Everyone turned to him. "All good points. Let's consider our options. First, we could increase our military presence and conduct joint exercises with NATO allies to counter Russian aggression. Second, we could invest in long-term Arctic capabilities, such as additional icebreakers, surveillance assets, and Arctic-trained forces, which are very long-term but necessary to get started now. And lastly, a more aggressive posturing by our forces in the Arctic would demonstrate to Russia and China our intent with the points you've made."

SecDef was the first to reply. "I support all three points, but we need to prioritize. Our current force posture in the Arctic is insufficient. We're relying too heavily on partnerships with allies like Canada while Russia operates unchallenged in large portions of the region. Increasing our military presence will send a clear message. However, these moves must be coupled with investments in long-term capabilities."

SecState added, "We also need to consider the optics. A purely military response risks escalating tensions and alienating Arctic states such as Finland and Sweden. We should strengthen alliances and promote multilateral governance frameworks that isolate Russia diplomatically."

The CJCS said, "With respect, we can't afford to ignore the operational reality. Russia isn't waiting for diplomacy. We need to pre-position forces and build infrastructure now. We should also expand our presence in the GIUK Gap and in the Aleutian Islands to ensure freedom of navigation and to make it clear to the Russians exactly how serious we are regarding the Arctic. And most importantly, increase our presence in Greenland and our military base at the Pituffik."

Since the room remained quiet after Elena's remarks, Taylor said, "Greenland isn't just ice and rock, it's a cornerstone of our national defense and a gateway to the Arctic. We can't afford to treat this as a distant problem. What happens there will shape the balance of power in the north for decades. Let's develop an integrated approach that balances military preparedness with a stronger presence, diplomatic engagement, and economic investment. We'll need to secure congressional support for long-term initiatives, particularly for funding icebreakers and Arctic infrastructure. I want a detailed action plan from each of your departments by next week. This isn't just about the Arctic; it's about maintaining global stability in the face of strategic competition."

The meeting continued for another hour with one clear consensus: The US would no longer react to Russian moves but would become more proactive. Taylor only hoped it could be done peacefully.

Chapter 13

USS IDAHO
0803 Hours, 19 July
Arctic Ocean

Captain Blake Stanton leaned back in his chair, his unpolished boots propped on the edge of the briefing table. He was deep in thought, considering his course of action against the Russian submarine that had given the slip to a P-8 crew. It appeared to him that the submarine was protecting a Russian civilian ship headed in the direction of the Franz Josef Land islands. His only conclusion was that the ship was carrying cargo so crucial that the Russians deemed it necessary to have a submarine escort. And that meant it was headed to the island of Alexandra Land, which has a Russian military base.

Sitting across from the captain was his XO, Lieutenant Commander David Harrington, who was contemplating what the heck, he didn't swear, his CO was doing with his feet propped up on the briefing table and his eyes closed. He had to say something.

"Captain, this is a high-stakes mission. Our intel puts the Kazan near our operating area. We should be doing something."

Stanton opened one eye slightly as Harrington interrupted his planning. "And what might that be, XO?"

"Well, I'm not sure, sir, but I wish you would at least say something."

"Give me a minute. I'm working on it." With that, the commanding officer of the *Idaho* closed his eye and returned to what he was doing.

Sitting behind her sonar screens and listening intently with her Sony headset, Submarine Chief Petty Officer Emily Reyes, a sonar technician, loved challenges like this. The seventeen-year veteran from Echo Park, a suburb of Los Angeles, thrived on the challenges presented by the newest and quietest Russian Yasen-class submarines. The faint sound of *Idaho*'s machinery was a constant background, but she had trained herself to filter it out. Instead, she focused on the subtle symphony of underwater noise: the crackling of shifting ice, the distant calls of marine mammals, and the rhythmic hum of shipping traffic.

She had two big pluses as a senior sonar operator. One was her God-given hearing, which was simply exceptional, and the other was her ability to recognize acoustic signatures. Complementing these traits was her ability to concentrate and maintain focus for extended periods in high-pressure environments, precisely like this patrol. She had an unyielding dedication to her profession and to success, which made her an especially vital sonar operator.

"Sonar, report," the XO's voice crackled through the intercom.

"Still scanning, sir," she replied in her always steady voice, no matter the seriousness of the situation.

Her eyes darted to the waterfall display, a cascade of acoustic data streaming across the screen. An anomaly caught her attention, a barely perceptible oscillation in the lower frequencies. Reyes carefully adjusted the gain to isolate the signal. It was faint, almost entirely masked by the ambient noise of shifting ice. But something about it felt artificial and deliberate. She had enough to make the call.

"Control, Sonar. Possible contact, bearing two-seven-zero," she announced. She adjusted the gain again. "Low-frequency propeller noise consistent with Yasen-class sub. Computer assist ID is the Kazan."

The captain snapped up, startling everyone in the control room. "I got this, XO." He toggled the intercom. "Good work, Reyes. Let's confirm. Helm, adjust course to one-eight-four. All stations, quiet running. Contact designated as Victor 3-2. Maintain track and log all movements. Tactical, prepare a full threat assessment based on its current course and speed."

"Aye, Captain. Assigning Victor 3-2 as a priority contact. Updating combat systems now."

Idaho shifted course, and its systems were dialed down to minimize noise. Tension was building in the control room as the crew waited for Reyes's next update.

Minutes began to tick by, seeming like an eternity to the crew. The XO reached for the mic. Stanton shook his head, stopping Harrington's movement.

It was so quiet that they could hear each other's breathing.

Reyes's pulse quickened as she tracked the faint signal and hoped she wouldn't lose it. But there it was again, moving slowly but deliberately and weaving through the underwater terrain. The *Kazan* was using geography to mask its movements, a classic tactic used by any submariner worth their salt.

"Control, Sonar. They're hugging the seafloor," she murmured. "Probably using the thermal layer to their advantage."

"TAO, Control," said Stanton, "plot trajectories. Pay close attention to the cargo ship designated as Alpha 2. Where it goes, Victor 3-2 will be nearby. I want a box on the sub without revealing our position."

"Roger that, Captain, computing now," said the Tactical Action Officer.

Suddenly, there was a new sound in Reyes's headset. It was faint but unmistakable. The *Kazan* had detected something and was searching for its source.

"Control, Sonar. They're pinging," Reyes said. "But their range is limited. We've still got the advantage."

Stanton had an idea. "FCO, launch Mark 3."

"FCO aye, sir."

The ADC Mk 3 decoy was a small, unmanned device designed to mimic the acoustic signature of a submarine and confuse enemy sonar or torpedoes. The fire-control officer fired it with help from the OOD.

Chapter 14

KAZAN

0836 Hours, 19 July

Arctic Ocean

Captain Ivan Gromov sat in the command chair of his Yasen-class submarine, his gaze locked on the glowing tactical display. He had his submarine hugging the seafloor to make it more difficult for enemy sonar to spot him. Above him, Alexandra Land loomed in the distance, Russia's icy stronghold in its northern bastion. The *Kazan* was here to protect the ship carrying some of the most potent weapons in the world to fortify the base's arsenal.

Above them was the *Vologda Star*, commanded by Commander Colonel Koltsov.

Gromov's mission was clear: ensure the *Vologda Star* reached its destination without incident. The orders from Northern Fleet Command emphasized the need to avoid detection and confrontation.

"Sonar, Captain. Status of *Vologda Star*."

"Captain, Sonar," said the senior petty officer, Viktor Sokolov, "holding steady on route, making ten knots."

"Roger, Sonar. I want to be notified immediately of any deviations."

"Aye, Captain."

Sokolov was working hard to isolate the noise from the cargo ship so he could perform his primary task of searching for adversaries. He ran another passive sweep to focus beyond the ship's noise envelope and narrowed the frequency band. He pressed against his headset, making for a tighter seal. Using the best sonar system the Navy had to offer, the MGK-600 Irtysh-Amfora, he listened for the hum of propulsion systems, transient mechanical clicks, or even the pressure disturbance of a sub moving through the water.

A half hour later, Sokolov said, "Captain, I have something faint at bearing one-eight-five. It's almost nothing, a transient noise, possibly mechanical."

Gromov walked over and stood behind his trusted sonar operator. "Sokolov, are you sure it's not biological?"

Sokolov was used to that question. Anyone who listened for other submarines tended to hear things that weren't there, because sometimes their mind played tricks on them. Sokolov wasn't one of those people, and the captain knew it. But Sokolov also knew a good captain always verified information.

Without taking his eyes off his screens, Sokolov answered, "Negative, sir. The frequency and pattern are inconsistent with marine life. It's too faint to classify, but it could be propulsion."

"Focus on the thermal layers, Sokolov," Gromov ordered. "If they're using a layer to hide, we might detect distortions from their movement." The captain knew that if he were being stalked, the adversary, most likely a Virginia-class American attack submarine, would have to move close enough to the *Vologda Star* to use that ship's noisy acoustic shadow to hide.

"And extend the sweep beyond the Vologda Star's noise bubble," Gromov said. "Overlay its signature with the background. Look for anything that doesn't match."

"Aye—wait, transient noise detected again. Short burst, low frequency. Bearing consistent with the first contact."

The sonar team worked meticulously, using *Kazan's* advanced signal processing algorithms to isolate the faint contact with their digital passive sonar, which could separate even the faintest traces from background noise.

It worked. "Sir, contact confirmed," Sokolov said at last. "Bearing one-eight-five. Distance approximately 7,300 meters. Propulsion signature matches a Virginia-class submarine."

Gromov nodded. "Well done, Sokolov." The captain knew the Americans were trying to stay hidden, but they'd come too close to the *Vologda Star*. Your first mistake, captain, thought Gromov.

"Contact," Sokolov called out. "New signature, bearing one-eight-zero. Acoustic profile similar to a Virginia-class."

Gromov hesitated before giving a command. There was no way there would be two Virginia-class submarines in the same area. He considered his options. A decoy was designed to mimic a real submarine and pull attention away from it. If he took the bait, it would expose *Kazan*'s position to the real threat. "Sonar, focus on inconsistencies in acoustic patterns to isolate which is the decoy."

Sokolov quickly isolated the decoy's faint hum. "Confirmed, Captain. It's a Mark 3 decoy."

"Nav, maintain position and speed," Gromov said. "Crew, we are taking no action. Stand down."

For two more hours, the two killers of the sea engaged in a silent battle of wits. The *Kazan* remained resolute in shadowing the *Vologda Star*, and the *Idaho* followed with a fire solution for the Russian sub if needed.

As the *Vologda Star* neared Russian territorial waters, Gromov said, "Sonar, active ping. Let the Americans know it's over and that we know their location."

Sokolov emitted a powerful *ping*. The sound reverberated through the depths.

Onboard the *Idaho*, they all heard the ping shortly after Reyes called out, "Active ping from the Kazan."

Grinning at his XO, Stanton said, "Well, that's the game. They know we're here, and they're telling us to back off."

Harrington said, "And we will, right, Captain?"

"Of course," Stanton said, his grin fading into a thoughtful expression. "This time."

"Helm," said Harrington, "plot a course away from the Kazan."

Chapter 15

NAS Whidbey Island
19 July
Oak Harbor, Washington

Hampton was airborne at 25,000 feet in his F-35, giving an extra tug on his seat straps until he felt the pressure for the exact tightness he preferred. It was as much of a habit as brushing his teeth. Behind and beside him were nine other F-35s and six EA-18G Growlers, including one with his new buddy Razor, who liked to dish out BS as much as Jessie did. He respected that in a man. It was weird that he didn't even know the dude's first name. To him, he was just that smart-ass Razor.

Today was unique because the 18th Aggressor Squadron from Eielson Air Force Base in Alaska was in town for a training exercise. The permission briefing had been clear: A simulated Russian Flanker-E squadron would intercept Blue Forces as part of a large-scale exercise.

The Air Force pilots playing the bad guys were flying F-16C/D Fighting Falcons, specifically Block 30 models, which are versatile and capable of replicating the performance of Russian fighters. For exacting realism, their fighters were painted in the latest Russian gray, white, and blue digital camouflage with pixelated patterns decked with a prominent red star on each wing.

As the Growlers and F-35s taxied to the runway, Razor's voice came through the comms, sharp and focused. "All flights, Shadow 11. Intel confirms Red Force Su-35 sims are airborne. They'll be looking to intercept and deny us access to the target area. Stay sharp. We're going right into their backyard."

Simulated or not, every pilot felt their pulse quicken with an added shot of adrenaline thrown into the mix. This was why they existed: to protect America and take down anyone who thought otherwise.

"Shadow 11, Raven 21," said Jessie, the flight leader for the F-35s. "Copy all. Break. Raven flight, check weapons status. Stealth protocol is a go. Keep it clean until we engage."

Soon after taking off, all aircraft formed up per their prebrief, and the Growlers began electronic warfare operations.

"All flights, Shadow 11. Jamming active in three—two—one. Bubble is up. Maintain formation and stay in the envelope. These Flankers are no joke, so don't give them a clean shot."

The Growlers' AN/ALQ-99 Tactical Jamming System pods created a powerful electronic shield, scrambling enemy radar and missile guidance systems to keep surface-to-air missile systems at bay. The F-35s followed closely, their passive sensors feeding critical data into the shared network.

"All flights, Shadow 11. SAM sites are active at ten o'clock and forty miles. They've got their teeth out early."

"Shadow 11, Raven 21. Copy and keep the SAMs blind. Break. Raven flight, hold formation. No one goes until radars are down."

Six of the F-16s approached at speed, simulating Russian tactics.

"All flights, Shadow 11. Bandits inbound. Six, bearing zero-eight-five, angels twenty. They mean to crash our party."

Jessie acknowledged, then said, "Ravens, stay weapons tight."

The Aggressors flew a pincer maneuver, splitting into two groups to flank the Blue Force formation. From the lead Red Force aircraft, the Aggressor commander issued his orders. "Red Team, spread out and engage. Prioritize the Growlers. They're the backbone of this formation."

The Aggressors fired simulated Vympel NPO R-77 beyond-visual-range air-to-air missiles in staggered volleys, targeting the Growlers' positions. Razor's team responded to the BVRAAMs immediately.

"Inbound missiles," Razor said. "Growler flight, deploy countermeasures. Jam hard, stay tight."

The EA-18Gs emitted a blanket of electronic interference, forcing the simulated missiles to lose their locks.

"Shadow 11, Raven 21. What's your status?"

"Raven 21, we're holding. Those birds are still closing. They're switching to close quarters."

With the Blue Team's attention focused on the Aggressors, the simulated SAM sites launched a wave of surface-to-air missiles.

"All flights, Shadow 11. SAMs are lighting us up. Break. Raven flight, switch to SEAD package. Launch HARMs." Razor's voice remained calm but urgent.

The EA-18Gs fired their simulated AGM-88 HARM missiles, neutralizing the SAM sites. Then Jessie heard what he'd been waiting for.

"Raven 21, Shadow 11. SAMs suppressed. Swagger, you're clear to engage the Flankers."

"Shadow 11, copy that. Break. Shadow flight, shift to combat spread. Let's take these bandits down."

The Aggressors transitioned to a dogfighting range and used aggressive Flanker tactics. One performed a simulated Cobra maneuver to get a good angle for a missile lock on an F-35. Jessie got on the radio.

"Raven flight, watch your angles. Bandits are trying to box us in. Maintain situational awareness."

Jessie locked onto an Aggressor, fired a simulated AIM-9X Sidewinder, and said, "Fox Two." Seconds later, he added, "Splash one."

Meanwhile, Razor found himself targeted by an Aggressor. His radar warning receiver screamed as the F-16 dove into pursuit. Razor banked hard, forcing his Growler into a high-G turn.

"Shadow 11, I've got one on me, defensive maneuvers. Don't wait up," he snapped, trusting his team to press on while he evaded the tailing fighter with tight turns, rapid dives, and anything he could think of to shake it.

As he came out of a tight 6-G turn, he forced the Aggressor into an overshoot. Razor rolled into position and took the shot, saying "Fox Three." When he got confirmation of the simulated AIM-120D AMRAAM kill, he couldn't help himself. "Bandit down. Tell me again how Growlers can't dogfight."

"Not bad, Razor," said Jessie. "Now, get back in the bubble before you break your own rules."

Chapter 16

USS Idaho
2103 Hours, 19 July
Arctic Ocean

It had been more than twelve hours since the *Idaho* had made contact with the Russian *Kazan*. During that time, Stanton had sent his intelligence report up the chain of command, which eventually reached the Commander of Submarine Forces Atlantic, who forwarded it to the Commander of Submarine Forces. What flagged Stanton's report to eventually make it to the NSC was the intel that a top-shelf Russian sub was protecting a civilian cargo ship headed for one of Russia's most strategically important bases. That was crossing a red line.

Three hours after the NSC got the report, the *Idaho* received orders to move within the twelve-mile Exclusive Economic Zone of Russia's Alexandra Land and determine precisely what the *Vologda Star* was carrying. Other intelligence reports indicated that the cargo could be Tsirkon hypersonic cruise missiles, which the US had little in its arsenal to shoot down. The Mach 9-capable missiles could carry conventional or nuclear warheads. Washington needed to know if the Russians were upping the ante in the Arctic.

Idaho perched at the edge of the EEZ, close enough to observe but just shy of violating Russian waters. Stanton knew this assignment was tough. They were twelve miles from the *Vologda Star*, and because of the earth's curvature, he needed to be within five miles to see everything the Russians were unloading. All he would be able to see from twelve miles out would be higher objects, such as cranes.

"OOD, raise Number One photonic mast," Stanton ordered. He knew he had to give it a try first. The Operator of the Deck repeated the command, and the photonics operator brought up the latest-generation mast, guiding it with a joystick and displaying the feed on a high-definition monitor.

Stanton studied the grainy image on the periscope monitor. The *Vologda Star* was tied up to a pier while cranes were unloading something. Stanton couldn't make out what.

While he was sneaking a peek, *Idaho*'s state-of-the-art systems intercepted bursts of encrypted radio traffic from the *Vologda Star* and its escort vessels. Patterns emerged: heightened security, rapid crane movements, and unmistakable military coordination.

Whatever the cargo was, it was big.

"Control, Sonar," said STSC Reyes, "I'm picking up infrared activity. Heat signatures consistent with the handling of missiles."

"Roger, Sonar," said Stanton, "keep your ear to the ground for the Kazan. We know it's out there."

Missiles. Stanton's body tightened up with that thought. If the Russians were unloading missiles at a military outpost this far north, it wasn't just routine logistics. This was a potential escalation, one that could have global ramifications. But from twelve miles out, the details were vague.

"Captain," said Harrington, "I know what you're thinking, but if we enter their territorial waters and get caught, that would be their red line and one that Moscow would not tolerate. We could start World War III."

Stanton knew his XO was right, but the stakes were too high to be so close without confirming what the Russians were up to. He circled back to his original thoughts. If the *Vologda Star* was unloading nuclear-capable missiles, that intelligence could change everything. The orders had said to move within the twelve-mile zone and to determine precisely what was on the cargo ship. The word within was up to interpretation, he reasoned.

"XO, what do we have if we just sit here?"

"We have a thermal signature indicating missiles, but nothing to confirm it."

Stanton's mind raced through the scenarios. A Yasen-class submarine could be lurking nearby and waiting for them to make a mistake. Russian destroyers were already patrolling the region, sweeping the area with their radar. Moving closer meant risking detection, confrontation, and potentially an international incident. But only if you got caught.

"XO, we're moving in seven miles. From five out, we can do what our orders said and determine precisely what the Russians are up to."

"Sir, I must respectfully object. That puts us in their territorial waters, a clear violation of international law."

"I'm aware," Stanton came back sharply. "But if they're unloading missiles, we need to know. I'll take the heat for this, but I won't let this slip through our fingers."

The XO just stared at his captain. Stanton had made his point that it was time to follow orders and make this work, or else.

"Helm, take us to zero-eight-five at 10 knots, depth 300 feet," Stanton ordered.

Idaho began its slow, deliberate advance. Stanton felt the weight of his decision settle over him like a lead blanket. Every foot closer brought them into more dangerous waters, both literally and figuratively. His career, the safety of his crew, and possibly the stability of the region hinged on what they found or didn't find aboard the *Vologda Star*.

Chapter 17

KAZAN
2333 Hours, 19 July
Arctic Ocean

While the Virginia-class *Idaho* was one of the world's quietest submarines, the Russians with their *Kazan* were barely one step behind in technology, if that. Captain Gromov stood in the *Kazan*'s command center, his eyes fixed on the sonar operator's screen. The faint signature of the *Idaho* had been visible on their sensors for hours. The Americans were careful, but even the best submarines left breadcrumbs for those skilled enough to find them.

"Sonar, update."

"Captain, they're holding at the edge of our waters. Twelve nautical miles out, barely detectable."

Gromov nodded, his suspicions confirmed. The Americans were watching the *Vologda Star*. They knew something important was being unloaded, and now they were debating their next course of action. Gromov could feel it. He'd played this game too many times not to recognize the pattern.

Suddenly, the sonar operator's body language changed. "Captain, the Idaho is moving. Bearing zero-eight-five, speed 10 knots. They're moving in."

You idiot, Gromov thought, you just made a fatal error.

"It's violating the twelve-mile boundary, Captain," the XO said, interrupting Gromov's thoughts about his next move. "It's heading directly toward the Vologda Star. Shall we notify the surface fleet?"

Gromov casually raised his hand, silencing him. "Not yet. The Americans think they are invisible, but they forget we, too, are unseen. We will handle this ourselves. Helm, close the distance but prioritize staying undetected. They don't know we're here, or they would not have committed such an aggressive act."

The *Kazan* glided with the precision of a predator stalking its prey, closing the gap to the *Idaho*. Through the sonar display, Gromov could see the American sub edging closer to the *Vologda Star*.

"Look at them," he said quietly, his voice almost amused. "So bold. They think they can slip in, take what they need, and leave without consequences."

"What are your orders, Captain?" asked the XO.

Gromov's mind raced. A direct confrontation would escalate the situation beyond control. Yet, letting the Americans get too close would allow them too much intelligence. I need to respond, he told himself.

"Prepare a torpedo," Gromov ordered.

0041 Hours, 20 July

Arctic Ocean

The *Idaho* pressed on, every creak of the hull amplified in Stanton's mind. He was taking a huge risk with his submarine and, most importantly, all 132 souls aboard. But the risk was eclipsed by the need for intelligence.

Approaching five miles out, the *Idaho* slowed to a crawl.

"OOD, raise the photonic mast to surveillance depth," ordered Stanton. "Verify ice clearance and confirm mast integrity before deploying. CCC, I want a full 360-degree sweep, then stay sector-specific to the Vologda Star."

A reply came seconds later. "Control, CCC. Sweep complete, all clear." High-resolution cameras with infrared imaging provided an immediate, detailed view of the *Vologda Star*. As the cameras focused, all the monitors in the control room showed cranes lowering specially made containers into military trucks. Stanton zoomed in, identifying the distinctive markings of Tsirkon missile crates.

"Helm—"

"Torpedo in the water!" Reyes shouted. "Bearing two-one-zero, distance 6,000 yards."

"All hands, brace for evasive maneuvers," ordered Stanton. "Helm, hard to starboard, 30 degrees down angle, put us below the layer. WEPS, launch two ADCs set for maximum acoustic decoy. And get me a firing solution on that launch platform."

The *Idaho* banked hard, engines adjusting to minimize noise while countermeasures were prepared. The torpedo's high-pitched whine, captured by passive sonar, echoed through the control room's speakers. The intensity of the sound increased as it drew closer.

"Control, WEPS. Have firing solution to the Kazan."

"WEPS, load—"

"Control, Sonar. Torpedo has passed us. It's not circling back, distance 1,700 feet."

Just then, the crew heard an explosion followed by a sharp jolt.

"Control, Sonar. Explosion confirmed 1,700 out."

A stunned silence filled the control room. Stanton knew Russian torpedoes were capable of tracking and reacquiring targets. A torpedo missing and not re-engaging was highly unusual. But he couldn't dwell on that. It was time to get back to international waters.

"Control, Sonar. Active sonar ping, bearing zero-one-five. It's the Kazan."

Harrington sounded nervous when he said, "Captain, they now know exactly where we are. I recommend we fire on them now." All eyes in the control room shifted to Stanton.

"And start a war? No, if they wanted us dead, they could have put their torpedo right up our ass. They're just sending us a message. Deploy countermeasures and launch a decoy northeast. Helm, dive to 600 feet and change course hard starboard to heading zero-nine-five. Let's use their aggression against them."

The crew responded, all aware their lives depended on their captain and his choices. The decoy was sent out to emit an acoustic signature designed to mimic *Idaho*'s movements as the submarine dove deeper.

"Control, decoy active," Reyes reported. "They're pinging again, sir, tracking northeast."

Good, thought Stanton, they took the bait.

As the *Kazan* chased the decoy, the *Idaho* slipped away, moving southward toward international waters. Stanton kept a steady eye on the tactical display.

"Sonar, status," Stanton said.

"They're still tracking the decoy, sir," Reyes replied. "No sign they've reacquired us."

Stanton nodded. "Good. OOD, maintain silence and put as much distance as we can between us and *Kazan*."

An hour later, the *Idaho* was in international waters. Stanton stood in the control room watching as the encrypted transmission containing their findings was sent to the Pentagon.

"With Tsirkons confirmed," said Harrington, "I guess the Russians weren't bluffing."

"They rarely do, XO," Stanton replied. "We got what we came for, but we've stirred the pot. Things are going to get much more hostile out here, I guarantee you that."

Far away beneath the icy waters, Gromov brooded over the encounter as he returned to patrol. Knowing the Americans had gained valuable intelligence, he considered that perhaps he should have programmed the torpedo to sink the American submarine. But *Idaho's* skipper had revealed his audacity in combat, and in the game of Arctic dominance, boldness could be a double-edged sword. He would look forward to their next encounter with pleasure.

Chapter 18

Ellsworth Air Force Base – 28th Bomb Wing
20 July
South Dakota

The high plains of South Dakota stretch in every direction, encompassing several Native American reservations, including the Lakota Sioux. Situated near their historic lands sprawls Ellsworth Air Force Base, the home to the sleek, matte-black B-21 Raiders loaded with the latest in stealth technology. It's a US top-secret, long-range bomber designed to carry both conventional and nuclear weapons.

Major Logan "Hawk" Carter was one of the chosen. As the B-21 pilot stood on the observation deck of the base operations building, he buried his hands deep in the pockets of his brown leather jacket against the chill in the air. As he took in the long line of Boeing B-1B Lancers, soon to be replaced by the B-21s that, unlike the Bones, would remain securely tucked away in climate-controlled hangars.

"Hard to believe we're entrusted with the first two," said Colonel Ava Richmond, as she glided up next to Carter. She was his former mentor and now the base commander. Her silver hair caught the midday light as she leaned against the railing.

"For right now, it seems perfect," said the athletic six-foot-one major. "Our feedback from real-life missions will go a long way in final development."

Richmond turned and smiled. "Always the pragmatist, aren't you?"

Carter looked at his mentor. "I guess that's why I'm still here as the lead pilot. I live for this."

After a few moments, the two went inside and entered the briefing room. The first airman to see them hollered, "Room, ten-hut." The noise of twenty people rising from their seats echoed through the room as everyone stood at attention.

"As you were," answered the colonel in a very relaxed tone. She continued to the front of the room while Carter took a seat in the front row.

Before speaking, the colonel scanned the room, appreciating the men and women who were pilots, operations support staff, and specialized technicians, entrusted to develop the cutting edge of America's state-of-the-art long-range bomber. It was all very exciting to be a part of America's newest weapon.

"Since idle BS is not in my DNA," she said, "let's get started." She hit a button on the remote, and a vintage picture of a prop-driven bomber popped onto a large screen.

"Folks," she continued, "as you should know, the B-21s in our hangars are named Raiders for a reason. During World

War II, the Doolittle Raid wasn't just an airstrike. It was a statement. At a time when the enemy thought we couldn't reach them, we showed them we could."

She gestured to the photo of the USS *Hornet*'s flight deck bursting with North American B-25 Mitchells. "Imagine for a moment being sent on a mission with no way back, a one-way trip into a war zone. Those crews knew it but still followed their leader, Lieutenant Colonel James Doolittle. Today, we honor the legacy of those Doolittle Raiders by taking a different kind of risk. We'll push our Raider aircraft to their limits, knowing what's at stake if we fail."

On their prearranged cue, Carter stepped up to take over the briefing while the colonel took her seat. "Our mission today is a surveillance and strike simulation in the Arctic Circle. We'll test the Raider's endurance, stealth, and targeting systems against a simulated adversary. But understand this isn't just a test. If the mission succeeds, it'll prove that the Raider is ready for operations much sooner than announced."

Chapter 19

PITUFFIK SPACE BASE
20 July
Greenland

As the hatch opened on the Boeing C-17 Globemaster III, Lieutenant Commander Sarah Freeman instantly felt the sharp Arctic wind bite at her exposed cheeks. She pulled her hood tighter over her head, but the cold still managed to snake around her body.

Shit, are you kidding me? She said to herself. This is summer.

Stepping onto the tarmac of Pituffik Space Base, her arctic boots crunched on the ice while she watched her breath get blown away by a strong wind. As she tried to adjust to the bitter cold, the next thing that caught her attention was the silence. It was so quiet it was almost deafening not to hear anything but the wind blowing through some nearby equipment. She immediately felt isolated.

Sarah had seen many bases in her career, but this one was unlike anything else. She adjusted the duffel bag slung over her shoulder and headed toward the nearest building. Walking with her head down against the wind, she had to admit she was proud to be among the first E-2 pilots assigned here. She was acutely aware of the responsibility that came with the assignment. This wasn't just about her skills as a pilot, but about charting the unknown, about being part of a forward-thinking Navy, and a new role for the Hawkeyes.

While she approached the building, a ground crewman bundled in layers jogged over, his breath clouding his glasses. He saluted her, and she returned it.

"Lieutenant Commander Freeman, welcome to Pituffik. You've got a briefing in thirty minutes." He pointed to a building a little further away.

She thanked him, her mind already shifting to what lay ahead. As she kept her head down and continued walking, her mind turned to Jessie and how much she missed him. After finally reuniting at the same base and even in the same house, this happened. The Navy sure wasn't kidding when they said the needs of the Navy came first. And even though both she and Jessie got it, it didn't mean they had to like it. As usual, she pushed those thoughts aside. She had a job to do.

After entering the building, she found the conference room. When she walked in, fifteen heads turned toward her. She felt like a spotlight had just lit her up, so she found the closest seat in the back and took it.

"Thank you all for assembling," said a man with eagles on his shoulders. "Today, we formally welcome the Navy's first land-based E-2 Hawkeye squadron to the Arctic. Lieutenant Commander Freeman, a special welcome to you," he pointed to her, "I'm sorry we didn't let you unpack, but the timing of this meeting is important. Your deployment here marks a critical evolution in how we secure this part of the world."

Leaning his chair back against a wall, a man with crossed arms and a toothpick hanging out of the corner of his mouth interrupted the colonel, which Sarah thought was a pretty ballsy move. "With all due respect, Colonel Grayson, Pituffik already hosts some of the world's most advanced space and missile tracking systems. What exactly do radar planes bring to the table that our satellites can't do better?"

"They bring perspective, Major Keller," Colonel William Grayson answered sharply. "Satellites give us the strategic view, but they can't track a TU-142 Russian bomber flying at low altitude through Arctic valleys. Remember, the E-2 is an early airborne warning and control aircraft, and its crew acts as a mini-operations center in the sky. Commander Freeman's squadron of three E-2s will fill the tactical gap. Of course, if that's all right with you, Major."

Major Keller looked down and didn't say a word.

"Colonel, if I may?" said Sarah.

"Sure, go ahead, Commander," said Grayson.

"Our E-2Ds are equipped with radar and communication systems designed for real-time threat detection and battlefield management. While satellites provide a broad overview, we specialize in coordinating responses to fast-moving, unpredictable threats. Think of us as the bridge between strategic intelligence and tactical action, or like the quarterback on a football game."

"Thank you for that," Commander. He displayed a PowerPoint slide showing the GIUK Gap, which served as a natural barrier and a critical passageway for naval forces moving between the Arctic Ocean and the rest of the world. As I was going to say, "Russia has been increasing its activity here by deploying submarines and long-range bombers to test US and NATO defenses. They're also leveraging electronic warfare to blind our systems. The Pentagon thinks that the E-2s will be critical in countering those tactics."

Sarah jumped in again. "Positioning our squadron here in Greenland allows us to monitor key choke points and to detect and track Russian bombers and fighters in real time while coordinating with P-8s, fighters, and other allied forces."

Rocking down from his perch against the wall, Keller said, "And what happens when those radar domes freeze over, when Russian jammers start targeting your planes, or better yet, when you can't even get to where we need your radar because you ran out of gas?"

"We're aware of the challenges, Major," Sarah said, "but this squadron was handpicked to handle them. Our radar systems are hardened against jamming, we've been working with engineers to adapt our aircraft for Arctic conditions, and our aircrews are qualified for aerial refueling from all AR platforms. We're not here to test the waters. We're here, like you, to counter Russia's aggressive moves in the Arctic."

The colonel displayed another slide showing Russian military assets near the GIUK Gap. He said, "Your first mission, Commander, will be a joint operation with our Space Force assets, a P-8, a flight of Air Force F-22s, and some tankers. We've detected increased Russian submarine and icebreaker activity in this area and eastward, likely tied to resource exploration or, as most believe, tied to expanding their military infrastructure. You will maintain airborne surveillance and ensure we know exactly what they're up to."

Leaning forward in her chair to get a better view, Sarah said, "Understood, sir. What kind of support can I expect from Space Force?"

Grayson looked at Keller, who answered, "We'll provide satellite intelligence and monitor for ballistic missile launches or hypersonic threats. Just don't expect us to babysit your radar coverage."

Sarah smiled. "Don't worry. We'll have the skies covered."

A short time later, Grayson again emphasized the strategic importance of the E-2 squadron's presence. "This isn't just about Greenland, folks. It's about the future of Arctic security. If we lose control of this region, we cede the high ground on Earth and in space. Commander Freeman, your team is the spearhead. Let's make sure it hits the mark."

Sarah nodded, the weight of the mission settling on her shoulders as the room started to clear after Grayson left. She glanced at Keller, who muttered under his breath as he walked out the door, "Let's see if the Navy can handle the Arctic."

Sarah, unshaken, replied, "We're not here to try. We're here to win."

Chapter 20

Ellsworth Air Force Base – 28th Bomb Wing
20 July
South Dakota

To conclude his brief, Major Carter went over the big picture. "First, we'll both approach Russian-controlled airspace, then stay just outside their 12-mile territorial boundary. From there, Raider 92 will use its advanced sensor suite to gather intel on a convoy moving toward the Russian forward base on Alexandra Land and then head to Pituffik. Finally, Raider 91 will simulate a precision strike to test targeting systems.

Standing at the back of the room, Colonel Ava Richmond added, "Let me clarify, we're not crossing the line. This mission is about testing the B-21's ability to operate undetected and to collect critical data. However, if anything goes wrong and they suspect we're there, you'll need to execute your egress plan immediately. We're not going to provoke a shooting war. And since the world doesn't know the Raider is operational, we need to keep it that way. As you've been briefed, upon completing the mission, you'll land at Pituffik Space Base and continue operations from there. You saw cargo and personnel already airlifted out of here, and you're the last to go. Those who've

"

already departed understand they're to catch and turn the aircraft when your mission's complete."

Carter's Mission Systems Officer and co-pilot was an inquisitive soul and asked more questions than a ten-year-old on a road trip. Today was no different. 1st Lieutenant Megan "Pixie" Alvarez raised her hand. "Major Carter, what's the risk of detection from their radar systems, even outside their airspace?"

Carter said, "As you know, the Raider is optimized for this type of mission. Their high-frequency radar won't pick us up unless we give them a reason to look. Stay cold, stay high, and stay clean. That means no sudden altitude changes, no prolonged emissions from our systems, and no visible contrails. If there aren't any more questions, then let's do this."

Hours later, over the Arctic Ocean, Carter and Alvarez began their test protocol after hearing the other crew had successfully completed their simulated run near Alexandra Land.

Even though it was summer, a vast expanse of ice and snow stretched below the sleek B-21, a glittering patchwork of white and dark open seas under the moonlight. They were cruising at 50,000 feet, the stealth systems fully engaged. Inside the cockpit, the two pilots monitored their instruments.

"Approaching the 12-mile boundary, Hawk," Alvarez reported.

"Maintain altitude," Carter replied.

The B-21's advanced sensor suite operated like an electronic black hole. Instead of emitting signals, it absorbed and analyzed everything in its path, including communications, radar pings, and atmospheric anomalies.

"Got a convoy on Alexandra Land," Alvarez said. "Eighteen vehicles. Looking closer."

"Copy that. Keep gathering data. We're maintaining flight path at 12.5 miles out." Even at this distance, the Raider's sensors operated at peak efficiency, providing a detailed picture of the convoy moving across the distant icy terrain.

On their tactical display, a translucent line marked the twelve-mile boundary. Well beyond it lay the convoy, a cluster of vehicles identified by satellite reconnaissance and confirmed by the Raider's sensors.

"Passive sensors have locked on the convoy," Alvarez said, her voice steady despite the tension. "Multiple vehicles, trucks, mobile radar, and what looks like a short-range SAM system."

Carter pressed against his harness, his eyes scanning the display. The B-21's advanced passive sensor suite silently collected electromagnetic emissions from the convoy below. The radar pings from the mobile unit, encrypted communications from the trucks, and even faint thermal signatures from the different vehicle engines were all captured, processed, and displayed in crisp detail.

"Focus on that radar unit, Pixie," Carter said. "We need every detail. No emissions, though. Keep it passive."

Alvarez worked the controls, directing the Raider's long-range optical and infrared sensors to analyze the convoy. Even at 12 miles, the aircraft's advanced electro-optical targeting system operated precisely, identifying equipment types and configurations and constantly providing a firing solution.

On the tactical display, the convoy appeared as a series of icons, each tagged with a designator. Supply trucks formed the bulk of the group, but two vehicles got their attention: a mobile radar unit and a self-propelled SAM launcher.

"Looks like an SA-21 Growler," Alvarez said, using the NATO designation for the Russian-made S-400 Triumf SAM system. She zoomed in on it and reminded them both, "Yeah, it has a range of 250 miles."

Carter studied the display. "Simulate targeting on the radar unit. Just one JASSM profile."

Alvarez tapped a command, and the B-21 systems calculated a precision strike using a simulated AGM-158 Joint Air-to-Surface Missile. The targeting software accounted for every variable: wind, terrain, convoy vector, and speed.

Carter liked the way this was going.

"Target locked," Alvarez reported. "Simulated JASSM impact in fifteen seconds."

Carter let the moment pass in silence, imagining the strike in a real-world scenario. The radar would be gone, the SAM would be blind, and the supply trucks would be left exposed. The Raider wouldn't need to fire a second shot.

"End simulation," Carter ordered. "We've got what we need. Let's—"

The cockpit alarm chimed softly.

"Low-frequency radar sweep," Alvarez said while glancing at her displays. "Looks like they're probing farther out than usual."

"How far?"

"Thirteen miles. Close, but they're not picking us up."

Carter adjusted the Raider's heading, ensuring they stayed well beyond the boundary. The aircraft's active stealth system countered the radar's signals, subtly altering its electromagnetic profile to blend into the natural background noise.

"Still clean," Alvarez said after a tense moment. "They're scanning, but it's like they're blind."

"Good," Carter said. "Let's keep it that way. Maintaining current course and altitude."

Suddenly, a sharp tone cut through the cockpit.

"Incoming fast-mover," Alvarez said. "Not ours."

Both pilots' heads were on swivels to check their instruments and scan the skies.

Alvarez said, her voice rising, "Radar ID as one MiG-31 at two o'clock, heading this direction. It's 4 miles out and closing fast."

Carter's hands unconsciously tightened on the controls. "Confirm heading."

"Two o'clock high. Vectoring this way. Mach 2-plus."

Carter didn't waste time scanning the sky because he knew he wouldn't see it. "Initiate evasion profile. Go cold. Dump to the deck. Now."

Although the Mikoyan MiG-31 Foxhound wasn't a direct threat, its high-speed capability and advanced optics made it a serious problem.

"Deploy countermeasures," Carter added as Alvarez worked her controls as he'd ordered. "Keep it passive." He adjusted the aircraft's altitude to get lost in some clouds.

The Raider's countermeasures suite activated, flooding the air with decoy signatures that mimicked an Arctic weather phenomenon. To the MiG's sensors, it would look like a faint shimmer of polar winds, so there would be nothing to investigate.

After a few minutes, it was all clear.

"Nice work, Pixie," Carter said. "It's all yours now. Take us to Pituffik." Alvarez took the controls, and the B-21 made a gentle turn.

Carter was pleased with how well the bomber had accomplished its simulated mission, even in the unforgiving Arctic. The unanticipated visitor had further demonstrated the aircraft's unparalleled stealth and precision capabilities. He had to admit that the B-21 was indeed the future of American airpower, and he kicked back with a very contented feeling about what had transpired.

Chapter 21

BOEING P-8 POSEIDON
1025 Hours, 21 July
Arctic Ocean

Cruising at 25,000 feet, Maddox had his crew especially vigilant as they flew near the Nagurskoye Military Base. The Russians were super sensitive to the Americans getting too close to the strategically important installation. But Maddox was careful and ensured they were outside the twelve-mile exclusion zone. It was a point made for years, but the US had to remind the Ruskie's that this was international air space, not sovereign airspace as they claimed. So here they were. The crew was tracking another convoy of cargo ships, corvettes, and one nuclear-powered icebreaker headed to Nagurskoye.

"Okay," said Maddox, his eyes on the convoy, "we're picking up some strong emissions from radar. Looks like Bastion-P coastal defense systems are live. I want it recorded with all frequencies and power outputs."

"Copy that," said his Electronic Warfare Officer, EWO, Lieutenant Karen Parsons. "Bastion-P is active. It looks like they're scanning our position, and data logging is in progress."

"Going to 15 angels," said Maddox.

The radar warning receiver blared an alert. Maddox's head snapped to the threat indicator on his screen.

TACCO came on their internal comms, "Contact! Fast movers inbound from the northeast, two bogeys, closing fast."

Maddox looked at the blips that were converging rapidly toward their position.

"Ghost, we've got inbound Russian interceptors," said co-pilot Lieutenant Robert Johanson to Maddox. "ETA two minutes."

"TACCO," said Maddox, "are we anywhere near Russian airspace?"

"Negative, Ghost. We're thirty miles outside the exclusion zone, well within international waters."

Maddox was not reassured, as the blaring radar warnings suggested that the Russians didn't care about international boundaries.

The fighters came into view through the cockpit windows. One flew alongside the P-8, the pilot visible in the canopy with his visor reflecting the sunlight. It was bizarre to look out and see the Russian fighter pilot, who looked at Maddox like he was saying, You've got balls entering my backyard.

Maddox stared back. Suddenly, the MiG rolled slightly to one side, dropping one wing lower than the other. At the same time, his RWR blared, signaling the P-8 was being targeted. A digital display in his cockpit and mission cabin showed a graphic representation of the radar threat, marked by a large, glowing icon indicating the MiG getting closer to the center of the screen. A steady tone from the RWR became a higher-pitched, urgent signal as the MiG switched from general radar tracking to a fire-control radar, indicating a potential missile launch.

While Maddox was deciding what to do, the second MiG-31 blasted across his nose, rattling his aircraft and the crew.

"Returning to base," said Maddox as he gently pulled the yoke to turn the P-8 away from Russian airspace and toward Pituffik. The two Russian fighters rejoined and followed alongside them, maintaining contact at all times. Suddenly, both went to afterburners and were gone. Everything in the cockpit returned to normal except the ringing in his ears from the warning alarms.

Maddox thought that this crap was getting way out of hand. He also realized that the Russians could have blown them to pieces, even though they were in international airspace. The whole experience was not pleasant. Even though his aircrew was alive, he knew the confrontations had just ratcheted up a notch.

Chapter 22

Northrop Grumman E-2D Advanced Hawkeye
0718 Hours, 23 July
Arctic Ocean

Freeman thought it was interesting that today's mission to the Arctic Ocean was between the Franz Josef Land archipelago and the Greenland EEZ. Years ago, the islands were best known for their rare bird species. Now nesting in their place was the ever-expanding Nagurskoye Military Base on the Alexandra Land island, just six hundred miles from the North Pole.

It was early morning, but during her short time at Pituffik Space Base, Sarah had noticed that orienting time to morning or night didn't matter. The sun just moved around the sky, always seeming to be in her eyes.

"Pituffik Tower, Picket 11," she said. "Preflight checks complete. Request clearance for takeoff."

"Pickett 11, Pituffik Tower. You are cleared for takeoff, runway zero-four, winds at 12 gusting 20 at zero-four-five. Maintain your heading on climb to two-five thousand feet. Contact departure on frequency two-four-five-point-seven."

Sitting in the left seat as the commander of her E-2, Sarah thought it strange not to be taking off from the deck of an aircraft carrier. But times were changing, and she felt fortunate to be commanding the fleet of three E-2s at this remote base to analyze the feasibility of stationing them in the Arctic.

Sarah glanced over at her new co-pilot, Lieutenant Chase "Phantom" Northcott, whom she was still sorting out. When reading his personnel file, she'd noted several references to his ability to remain calm under fire and stay focused on the mission, but everything between them had been straight-up-by-the-book communication; there was no idle chatter, and thus no way to know more about him.

After refueling from a tanker just before reaching the coast of Greenland, Sarah and her crew were monitoring 282,000 square miles of the Arctic Ocean. They got started as soon as Sarah got the aircraft over the water.

"Radar, report the status of assets," Sarah said.

"Raptor 21 flight is maintaining CAP at angels thirty-five, 15 miles northeast of Alexandra Land. No fuel or weapons issues reported. One Poseidon, Stalker 11, is on station seventy miles to the west of Alexandra Land conducting ASW and surface scans. They've deployed sonobuoys, and no subsurface contacts confirmed."

There was a short break, and then Radar added, "Systems are green across the board. Datalink feeds from Raptor and Stalker are stable, with real-time updates on threat vectors. Currently, no anomalies in our airspace."

"Good report, Radar," Sarah replied. "All right, team, listen up. This mission brings us close enough to Alexandra Land that we're operating in the shadow of a significant Russian military base. They know we're here, and they'll be watching us as much as we're watching them. We're here to do a job, and we're damn good at it. Let's prove why this squadron got sent to Greenland in the first place."

It was all business, as Sarah preferred, and the crew closely monitored their AN/APY-9 radar. Sarah noticed a blip on the radar just inside their area of operation, and she reported it to her fighters.

"Raptor 21, Pickett 11. Maintaining grid sweeps at 40,000 feet. Radar is clear but with anomalies on the edges of the AO. Could be weather clutter. Stand by for confirmation."

"Radar here, ma'am," her operator said. "I'm picking up a faint contact. Bearing zero-six-five, range 300 miles. Speed indicates strategic bombers, now confirmed, not weather."

"Copy that. Confirm type." Seconds ticked by, and Sarah got more anxious.

"Two Tu-95 Bears," Radar reported. "They're heading southwest and skirting the EEZ. Likely testing response times."

Sarah toggled her comms to the F-22 flight again. "Raptor 21, Pickett 11. We have two bogeys, Tu-95 bombers, bearing zero-six-five at 300 miles. Nearing the Greenlandic EEZ. Recommend intercept to identify and deter."

"Raptor 21 copy, moving to intercept. Maintain overwatch." The two F-22s peeled off from their position, kicking in their afterburners as they streaked toward the Russian bombers.

"Additional contacts," Radar called, "three escort fighters, identified as Su-35s. They're shadowing the Bears."

Sarah's pulse quickened. The Russian bombers had fighter escorts, which meant they weren't on a routine probe. It was a show of force. "Raptor 21, Pickett 11. Three Su-35s are in escort formation with the bombers. Maintain caution during intercept. We're painting them for you."

"Roger that, Pickett 11. Eyes on the Bears. Adjusting course to avoid direct engagement with the fighters. If they close in, we'll respond."

Sarah glanced at her tactical display. The two Tu-95s were heading toward Greenland with their fighter escorts, and the two F-22s were flanking them. The Bears had the range to strike key American sites.

"Radar, does Reykjavik Control have the Russian aircraft?" Sarah said.

A minute later, Radar responded, "Ma'am, neither Reykjavik nor Nuuk Information has traffic control of the aircraft."

"Raptor 21, Pickett 11. Civil ATC doesn't have control of the bogeys. We should assume they're hostile."

Positioning themselves just outside missile range, Raptor 21 broadcast over the international emergency radio channel, "Unidentified aircraft, this is the United States Air Force. You are about to enter Greenlandic airspace. Identify yourself immediately and state your intentions, or we will take further action."

The aircraft didn't respond. Adjusting their course, the Su-35s edged closer to the EEZ.

"Raptor 21," said his wingman, "I've got a bogey on my six, closing fast."

Sarah said to her crew, "Keep those tracks clean and feed them directly to the Raptors. I want continual updates."

"Roger," said Radar, "the Bears are holding steady at flight level three-five-zero, maintaining heading zero-seven-zero. Speed constant at 400."

Seconds later, Radar added, "New data. Su-35 escorts are adjusting position. Looks like they're shifting into a defensive posture, bearing zero-seven-five, 20 miles ahead of the bombers. They're forming a wall."

"Raptor 21, bogeys are at—

"Pickett 11, we see it."

"Raptor 21," Sarah said, "they're 15 miles from EEZ boundary. The fighters are spreading out to flank you. Watch your six."

"Copy that, Pickett 11, adjusting to compensate."

After what seemed like minutes, Sarah added, "Raptor 21, bandits have crossed into Greenland airspace. Maintain shadow and prepare for escalation if they ignore warnings."

"Pickett 11, Raptor 21. Roger that. Switching to active radar."

Both fighter pilots switched their Northrop Grumman AN/APG-77 active electronically scanned array radars to active mode. Instantly, the AESA radars' powerful beams painted the lead Tu-95. Both pilots confirmed that the targeting data for their missiles had lit up in their HUDs. Each had a lock.

Raptor 21 decided to give one more warning before engaging with their AIM-120 AMRAAMs.

"Unidentified aircraft, this is the United States Air Force. You are inside Greenlandic airspace. Turn back immediately, or we will take defensive action."

Both F-22 pilots designated their targets using their Hands-On Throttle and Stick control, selecting the Multi-Function Display. The system instantly confirmed the target with a lock-on tone.

Raptor 21 put his finger on the weapon release trigger on the control stick and said, "Two-two, fire one

AMRAAM on the target designated Alpha-1 in ten seconds. On my command, ten—nine—eight…"

"Ma'am," Sarah's radar specialist said, "Bombers are banking left, new heading zero-eight-five. They're pulling back."

"Four—" continued Raptor 21.

"Raptor 21, Pickett 11. Bandits are turning away." Sarah said.

"Two-two, do not fire, repeat, do not fire," Raptor 21 said.

"Two–two copy. About time. Guess they didn't like the thought of being blown to shit."

"Two-one, roger that. Maintain course and speed and disengage targeting radar."

Minutes later, Sarah said, "Raptor 21, Pickett 11. Confirmed, Russian aircraft heading back toward Alexandra Land. Maintain CAP until planned return to base. See you at the debrief. You made them think twice about pushing further."

"Pickett 11, copy maintain CAP until planned RTB. We couldn't have done it without you keeping the big picture. You're the reason we didn't have to flip the switch today."

Chapter 23

USS IDAHO
1824 Hours, 23 July
Arctic Ocean

Captain Blake Stanton was a natural risk-taker. Ask anyone aboard the USS *Idaho*, and they would all agree. And his crew would also tell you without hesitation that they would follow him into any battle anywhere, a testament to their unwavering trust in his leadership. Harrington was the lone exception. An Annapolis graduate, he'd earned the prestigious distinction of Class Honor Graduate, ranking first among 1,121 midshipmen in academics. He was destined for great things, but would do it prudently and by the book, the way most did.

Even as *Idaho* put distance between it and Alexandra Land, Harrington questioned his captain's decision to take the sub within Russian territorial waters, a clear violation of that country's sovereignty and international norms. If he were the captain, he would have stayed outside the 12-mile limit per his orders, no matter the outcome. Orders were orders, even if you couldn't make out exactly what the Russians had been unloading.

But Stanton had followed the intent of the orders more so than the wording of the orders, and Washington was now hopping mad at Russia's escalation by deploying a missile the US had little or more honestly, no capabilities to shoot down. In the Department of the Navy, some brass considered Stanton a genius, while others thought him a reckless captain who needlessly endangered his crew. If anyone were to ask Stanton about it, he would have given a short answer: "I got the job done." End of conversation.

Well below the surface of international waters, Stanton stood in the command center of America's newest Virginia-class fast attack submarine, the fifth of the Block IV variant. This generation incorporated stealth measures, refined sonar and surveillance systems, and the Navy's most advanced combat suite to date. It was the most formidable hunter the US had yet sent to sea.

"Sonar, report," Stanton said, breaking the silence around him.

"Still clear, Captain. No sign of the Kazan or any other threats," came the reply from Emily Reyes. Stanton knew he was fortunate to have her as his sonar operator. Her attention to detail regarding acoustic differences was unmatched.

Stanton also knew that the *Kazan* was searching for him because he'd violated their territorial waters to confirm the unloading of Tsirkon hypersonic cruise missiles. Game on.

1830 Hours, 23 July

Arctic Ocean

Captain Ivan Gromov was pacing the floor in his command center. The Americans had slipped away with valuable intelligence, and his job was to prevent such an act. He unconsciously clenched his fists as he moved around, periodically staring at the sonar operator's screen as though sheer willpower could force the *Idaho* back into his grasp. He, too was depending on his sonar operator, who had picked up nothing on the American sub.

Screw it, Gromov thought. It was time to go all in and get this asshole.

"Sonar, full sweep," Gromov ordered.

The operator nodded and adjusted his controls. "Active ping ready, Captain."

Gromov knew that if he played this card, he might not only find the *Idaho* but would also let the *Idaho* know precisely where he was. He reasoned it was worth it.

"Do it," Gromov growled.

The sharp, unmistakable ping of active sonar echoed through the depths.

"Captain," the sonar operator called out, his voice tense, "contact bearing zero-nine-zero, range 14 kilometers. Sound signature identifies it as the Idaho, sir."

An active ping echoed through the *Idaho*, the sound deafening in its clarity. But the dread it brought to many did not affect Reyes, who continued to do her job. "Control, active sonar contact, bearing one-one-five, range approximately 2 miles. Ping source matches Kazan. They're sweeping."

"Targeting?"

"Not yet, sir," Reyes replied, scanning the updated returns. "This ping is a narrow-beam search to refine their tracking solution. They're moving in our direction."

"They're attempting to provoke a reaction," said the captain. "Helm, reduce speed to 3 knots and hold depth beneath the thermal layer. Minimize our acoustic profile."

"Captain, second active ping detected. Same bearing, range decreasing, now 2,800. Speed 12 knots."

Stanton had a decision to make. Releasing decoys too early would reveal his position. But since everything pointed to the fact that they knew exactly where he was, it seemed the right thing to do. His adversary was getting bold. At their current speed, they would refine their firing solution within minutes. He turned to his weapons officer.

"WEPS, prepare two acoustic decoys. Deploy on my command, one northwest at heading three-one-zero and another to the southeast at heading one-four-five. Set them to simulate our acoustic signature at varying depths."

The weapons officer worked his keyboard, then nodded. "Decoys ready, Captain."

"Deploy the northwest decoy," Stanton ordered. "Let's see if they bite. Helm, adjust course 10 degrees to starboard and hold steady at 600 feet. Stay under the layer."

The decoy launched with a muffled hiss, its acoustic signal mimicking the *Idaho* as it drifted northwest. Stanton watched the sonar display, waiting for Reyes's analysis.

"Captain," she said, "Kazan has bypassed the decoy and continues in our direction."

"WEPS, release Decoy Two."

"Decoy Two away."

Suddenly, Reyes said, "Captain, thermocline shift detected with a new layer forming at 400 feet. Currents are intensifying near our depth."

That wasn't good with two submarines in such close proximity. A thermocline shift could compromise both stealth and maneuverability, and also distort sonar readings, creating unpredictable conditions.

"Helm, adjust depth to 400 feet. Stay under the new layer," Stanton commanded.

"Aye, sir. Adjusting depth to 600 feet," the helm officer confirmed.

The *Kazan*'s sonar operator, Sokolov, said urgently over the comms, "Captain, thermal shift detected, a new layer forming above us at 500 feet. Currents increasing. Idaho*'s* signature is fluctuating."

Gromov made a snap decision. "Helm, they'll adjust to maintain stealth, so match their depth changes and hold position below the layer. Let's keep the pressure on them."

"Aye, Captain. Adjusting to match."

The two submarines, each maneuvering to adapt to the shifting conditions, were essentially blind since both sonars were too distorted to obtain accurate bearings. Both captains now relied on instinct, their only remaining option.

On the *Idaho*, Reyes called out, "Control, the Kazan*'s* bearing has shifted range, now 2,000 yards. They're closing faster, speed at 13 knots."

If submarines had a front window, neither captain would have liked what they saw. The two killers were on a collision course.

Stanton said, "They're using the thermocline shift to cover their approach. Helm, reduce speed to 2 knots and adjust heading 5 degrees to port."

In *Kazan*, Sokolov gave an equally concerning update, "Captain, the Idaho's signature has shifted again. Range now 900 meters. They're altering course."

Gromov said, "Hold steady on our heading. Let's watch for their next move."

Each captain was attempting to outthink the other, and neither realized how close they were. The Arctic waters, always unpredictable, had now become an area of shifting currents and distorted acoustics.

Idaho was the first to see it. "Contact directly ahead," said Reyes. "Range 300 yards. Collision imminent!"

Stanton fired off, "Helm, emergency stop, all back full."

Idaho's engines roared to reverse their course, but the distance was too short. A sharp metallic screech echoed through the hull as the two submarines collided. Several standing crew members, including the Stanton, were thrown to the deck, some smashing into equipment. The sonar officer flew hard against a metal column, gouging his forehead in a two-inch gash. Blood splattered everywhere.

Stanton found himself on the floor. He shook it off and was up on his feet in seconds. "Damage report." Stanton barked, gripping the console to steady himself.

After several moments of checking with the different stations, Harrington said, "Captain, there are no breaches. The ballast tanks are intact. There are some injuries. We're still receiving reports."

On the *Kazan*, a similar scene unfolded as the submarine jolted violently. Gromov steadied himself against the command console and demanded, "Damage report."

After a few moments, his XO reported, "Hull is intact, no leaks. No critical systems affected. No ruptures, and four injuries."

The turbulence from the collision and the chaotic currents made it impossible for either submarine to maintain proper depth control. Both captains quickly reached the same conclusion.

"Helm," Stanton said, "find us a break in the ice and surface so we can assess the situation."

Moments later, the *Idaho* burst through the ice in a dramatic explosion of frozen ice slabs, its black hull gleaming under the pale Arctic light. The *Kazan* surfaced with equal force less than a mile away, jagged ice clinging to its angular conning tower. As the massive submarine settled, its conning tower rose above the shattered ice, steam hissing from the vents as the frigid air met the residual heat of the reactor systems.

In *Idaho*'s control room, Stanton turned to the XO. "I'm going topside to do the visual inspection."

Harrington hesitated before saying, "Captain, are you sure? The conditions—"

"I want to see it with my own eyes," Stanton interrupted, his tone leaving no room for debate. "If there's any real damage, I need to assess it firsthand, and we need to know what the Kazan is doing."

Minutes later, Stanton stood by the ladder leading to the bridge access hatch, dressed in heavy white thermal gear and a Neoprene face mask. The OOD and two sailors were ready beside him, similarly outfitted and equipped with binoculars, LED lights, and a compact inspection kit.

"Open the hatch," Stanton ordered.

The sailors braced themselves, then the hydraulics hissed as the hatch swung open. A blast of icy wind whipped through the opening, sending a chill down their spines despite their heavy gear. Stanton was the first one topside.

One by one, the sailors followed onto the bridge. The bitter cold stung their faces, and frost quickly formed on their gear as the sub's warm interior air met the freezing temperatures outside.

The first thing Stanton noticed as he stepped onto the conning tower was the absolute stillness of the Arctic. The shattered ice surrounding the *Idaho* glistened under the faint glow of the sun, creating a surreal alien landscape. He pulled his binoculars from a pouch on his chest and quickly scanned the horizon.

"There," he said, pointing toward the distant silhouette of the *Kazan*. Less than a mile away, the Russian submarine had also surfaced, its conning tower rising starkly against the jagged ice. Steam rose from its vents as figures emerged onto its bridge."

"Looks like they're also doing a visual inspection," Stanton said. As he scanned the area around the Russian submarine, he focused on the bridge. Then he saw him, the *Kazan*'s captain, looking back at him through his binoculars.

"Message from the Kazan," the OOD said, handing Stanton a laminated card with a light signal decoded. Stanton read it silently, "Captain of the Idaho, watch yourself. You're skating on thin ice."

Stanton smiled faintly behind his mask, then turned to the OOD. "Send: Captain of the Kazan, thanks for the weather report. Hope your dry suit is rated for deep water."

With the inspection complete and *Idaho* showing no significant damage other than a long paint scrape down the stern, Stanton gave the order to return below deck. One by one, the team climbed back through the hatch, and then the hydraulics sealed it shut with a hiss.

Harrington met Stanton as he came into the control room. "Any damage, Captain?"

"Minor scrapes and nothing to interfere with our mission," Stanton said, removing his gloves. Turning to the helmsman, he said, "Prepare to submerge and resume silent running, speed 5 knots. Course one-nine-five under the layer."

As *Idaho* disappeared beneath the ice, Stanton glared at the tactical display, his mind lingering on the encounter. This clash with the *Kazan* was only the beginning, and a question loomed in his thoughts: How far would this dangerous game go?

Chapter 24

Pravda
22 July
Moscow, Russia

Throughout modern history, Russia has developed the ability to control the narrative of any international occurrence, framing itself as the victim of a belligerent act by blaming whatever country it chooses.

It was an age-old scheme. By controlling the narrative, they could shape global perceptions and influence public opinion worldwide while advancing their geopolitical agenda. Within hours of the incident, they broke the story in their state-owned paper, the *Pravda*:

American Submarine Provokes Collision in Russian Waters

In a brazen act of recklessness, an American nuclear-powered submarine violated safe navigation protocols and collided with a Russian vessel in the Arctic Ocean, perilously close to Russian territorial waters. This incident, which just occurred, has drawn condemnation from senior officials in Moscow, who described it as an unprovoked act of aggression.

According to sources within the Russian Navy, the Russian submarine Kazan was conducting routine patrol operations in the Barents Sea when the American submarine made an unexpected and dangerous maneuver, leading to the collision. Russian sailors reportedly acted with exemplary professionalism, preventing a more catastrophic outcome.

Defense Minister Natalia Romanova condemned the United States' actions, stating, "This is yet another example of Washington's disregard for international norms and safety at sea. The United States continues escalating tensions in the Arctic, where stability is paramount to Russia and the world."

The Kremlin has confirmed that six Russian sailors were injured, and substantial damage was suffered by the Kazan, which had to be towed to the base. Meanwhile, officials have noted that the American vessel offered no assistance and immediately retreated from the scene, an act many see as an admission of guilt.

As we have reported, the Arctic has become a growing point of contention as Western nations seek to expand their military presence in this vital region, pushing aside Russia's claim to the area as its own.

"This reckless behavior demonstrates that the United States is not interested in fostering stability or respecting the boundaries of other nations," said Admiral Viktor Bondarenko, a leading figure in Russia's Arctic naval strategy. "The Arctic is a region of peace and cooperation, but Washington's actions are a threat to global security."

The Russian Foreign Ministry has filed an official protest with the U.S. Embassy in Moscow, demanding a full investigation and assurances that such incidents will not occur again. Kremlin officials have also suggested the possibility of expanding naval patrols in the Arctic to prevent further provocations.

As the world watches, it is clear that the United States must answer for its dangerous actions, which have once again highlighted its unwillingness to respect international norms and Russian sovereignty.

A doctored photograph of a submarine with a torn side, reportedly the *Kazan*, accompanied the article.

Headlines of the collision became the lead story for days in papers worldwide:

North Korea

"Aggressive U.S. Naval Maneuver Endangers Arctic Peace"

China

"Clash of Superpowers in Arctic: U.S. and Russia Risk Global Stability"

United Kingdom

"Cold War Tensions Resurface Beneath the Ice"

United States

"Near Miss in Arctic Waters: U.S. and Russian Subs Collide in Strategic Region"

India

"Arctic Incident Highlights Risks of Militarization in Polar Regions"

As the world speculated and alliances whispered behind closed doors, the true story of what happened beneath the icy Arctic waters remained locked within the halls of power. The headlines became weapons in their own right.

In Moscow, the Kremlin celebrated the effectiveness of its pre-emptive narrative strike, using it to rally allies and stir nationalist fervor. Meanwhile, neutral nations weighed the cost of Arctic militarization against their own political interests, unsure whether to condemn it, align themselves with it, or remain silent.

The collision quickly became more than an isolated incident. It was now a global symbol of the fragile peace in one of the world's last contested frontiers. Publicly, the blame game raged on, but privately, the leaders of both nations wrestled with where this was leading. Russia made plans to upgrade its Arctic bases further.

Chapter 25

THE WHITE HOUSE
25 July
Washington, DC

What the world was told about the collision between the US and Russian nuclear submarines in the Arctic never explained the why. But it was the why that prompted President Mark Taylor to call an emergency meeting of his NSC.

There was standing room only in the Situation Room as all statutory and non-statutory members were seated. Filling the seats behind the large table were the officials' top aides.

The president wasted no time. "Ladies and gentlemen, thank you for assembling on such short notice. We're facing a crisis that demands our full attention and strategic coordination. Let's get to the facts." Before continuing, he scanned the room to make sure he had everyone's attention.

He did.

"As we're all aware, a US Navy submarine collided with a Russian Sub in the Arctic Ocean. The details aren't finalized, but initial reports indicate this wasn't an intentional act of aggression by either side but rather the result of tactical maneuvering in contested waters. While no casualties have been reported, this incident serves as a stark reminder of the growing tension and risk in the Arctic. I want an update on Idaho's status, the extent of the damage, and any potential risks to classified technologies by the end of the day.

"One of the underlying factors of the incident is that the Idaho was on a critical mission to verify if the Russians were secretly bringing in hypersonic weapons. In that, Idaho was successful, and I can report that Russia has been caught in the act of deploying these missiles to Alexandra Land. This is a direct violation of all international agreements and a blatant escalation of their military posture in the Arctic. When presented with this, the Kremlin will undoubtedly deny or spin this as a defensive necessity against an expanding NATO. Our job is to counter their narrative with indisputable evidence. I expect options on the table for how we will respond diplomatically, economically, and militarily should the situation escalate further."

The president glanced down at his notes about the hypersonic missiles that the US would struggle to intercept. "Let's not be naive. Russia has been systematically expanding its military footprint in the Arctic while the world has been distracted by the wars in Ukraine and Israel. From advanced radar systems to nuclear-capable bombers operating from their Arctic airfields, Russia is making a determined move to dominate the Arctic. Their recent naval exercises, coupled with the deployment of hypersonic weapons, make it clear they're probing our resolve. Our era of complacency is over. Inaction is no longer an option."

"Sir, if I may," interrupted SecState Brad Kelly, "we need to consider that by taking a more assertive position in the Arctic, we run the risk of further antagonizing Russia. We'll have to divert critical resources from the Indo-Pacific region to the Arctic."

SecDef George Mitchell stood up, which was outside the standard protocol. He looked right at SecState. "With all due respect, Russia has already militarized the Arctic by massively expanding its icebreaker fleet, reopening Soviet-era bases, and, as we just discussed, deploying hypersonic weapons. If we fail to assert our presence now, we cede strategic ground to Moscow and allow it to control critical shipping routes, thereby allowing its power to be projected unchecked. Furthermore, this isn't just about Russia. China has declared itself a near-Arctic state and is increasing its regional footprint. If we don't act decisively, we risk losing both the Arctic and the Indo-Pacific."

Not waiting for others, including the president, to reply, CJCS General Kincaid backed up his boss. "Russia's 2022 invasion of Ukraine provides evidence that Moscow will not adhere to the current global order and will continue to challenge Western international norms wherever possible, including in the Arctic. Moreover, NATO has expanded with the accession of Finland and Sweden, and now seven out of the eight Arctic nations are NATO members. The alliance offers an opportunity for the United States to strengthen its position in the Arctic region while not having to go it alone."

"Thank you, General," said the president. "Having read over the recommendations to increase our force position in the Arctic, I want the Ford carrier strike group deployed to that region. I also want to move forward with the directive I issued to develop our missile system in Greenland. You are aware of my priorities, but to reiterate, these include THAAD and Aegis Ashore. On the radar side, rush the completion of our Upgraded Early Warning Radar.

"Finally, this is a pivotal moment for our country. Russia is probing us, testing how we respond when confronted. They're betting that we'll waver and avoid confrontation at all costs. We cannot afford to appear weak, but we must act with calculated precision. Our goal is deterrence, not escalation, but let me be clear: If Moscow believes it can use the Arctic as a chessboard for unchecked military expansion, it is gravely mistaken.

"I expect updates every six hours. We need real-time intelligence, strategic recommendations, and a coordinated response. This team has existed for moments like this, so let's get to work."

Chapter 26

USS FORD

26 July

Naval Base Kitsap, Washington

Naval Base Kitsap's dockyard was hectic. The USS *Gerald R. Ford* had been preparing for deployment since the president's order. Now that the execute order was in hand, every sailor and civilian was scrambling to complete last-minute tasks. The towering carrier, the most advanced warship in the world, loomed like an iron fortress over the gray waters of Puget Sound.

For some, the order could not have come soon enough. One of those was Captain Dick "Mad Dog" Johnson, the carrier air wing commander referred to as the CAG. After his carrier's eight months in drydock for emergency repairs from two Iranian drone strikes, he and his command were more than ready. As he strolled the deck of the warship, he took in the mammoth flight deck and thought of his responsibilities. He loved the challenges they presented, just as when flying the F-35 in two wars.

He was in command of Carrier Air Wing Eight, including a list of state-of-the-art aircraft. As he scanned the flight deck, he noted the F-35s and the Boeing FA-18 E- and F-model Super Hornets near Catapults 1 and 2 in the forward section. At mid-deck were the EA-18G Growlers, and keeping them company were the E-2D Hawkeyes. Aft were the MH-60 S and R-model Seahawk helicopters. But not all aircraft were on deck. Back on Whidbey Island were some high-alert fighters ready for rapid response.

Having been stationed on two other carriers, Johnson appreciated the redesigned flight deck. The more aft-positioned island created significantly more open space, allowing for increased sortie rates and easier aircraft handling. To cap it off, the Electromagnetic Aircraft Launch System was a first. With EMALS, carrier launches were quicker and more efficient.

Looking around, he couldn't help but get lost in his thoughts of the war with China. It felt like a lifetime ago instead of just a few years ago, and so much had changed.

Feeling a tap on his shoulder from behind, he turned to see a pilot standing there with a shit-eating grin. It was his top gun, Lieutenant Commander Jessie "Swagger" Hampton.

"Hey, Mad Dog, what brings you to these parts?" Jessie loved to tease the CAG, whom he respected as much as his own father. Mad Dog was a legend in naval aviation circles, renowned for pushing his pilots to their limits and beyond, which was precisely how Jessie lived and flew.

"Considering this is my turf, Swagger, I should be asking that of you. How's the onboarding into the new unit going? You ready to be back in my command?"

Jessie's smile increased in size. "Too late to back out now, I suppose."

"Yeah, right, like you would ever miss an opportunity for a fight."

"I must admit," said Jessie, "I look forward to mixing it up with the Russians. They think they're hot shit."

"Just don't make me have to fish you out of the sea, like what happened to you against that Chinese fighter pilot."

Jessie rubbed a hand over his heart. "Ouch, that hurts. One mistake, and I hear about it for the rest of my career."

Just then, the loudspeakers blared, "Attention all hands, prepare to get underway. Set material condition Zebra throughout the ship. All departments make final preparations for sea. Standby to take in all lines."

"Well, son, I guess we'd better get with it," said Johnson. The two did a fist pump. Stepping back, Jessie popped a salute, which Mad Dog returned. Jessie then made an about-face and trotted off.

Johnson couldn't help but see in Jessie what he had been ten years ago. After the inevitable scuttlebutt had spread about a deployment, Jessie had come to his office asking to join one of his squadrons. Mad Dog didn't need a lot of convincing to make the necessary phone calls to get Jessie out of his shore duty assignment. Jessie had the experience and skills needed for the upcoming cruise. Besides, he liked the man, everything that is, except his swagger.

As the *Ford* and the ships comprising Carrier Strike Group 12 maneuvered out of Puget Sound, three Arleigh Burke-class destroyers and a fast combat support ship moved ahead in a protective formation.

The buzz aboard the *Ford* was that CSG-12 was embarking on a historic mission, an Arctic deployment through the Aleutian Islands to the Bering Strait, then along the Northern Sea Route in the Arctic Ocean and over to the GIUK Gap, a strategic choke point where Russian submarines often prowled. Everyone knew this was in response to the escalating activity throughout the Arctic and the recent collision between the *Idaho* and a Russian submarine. Many also knew traveling so close to Russia on the NSR would ruffle some Russian feathers.

Chapter 27

NOVOSIBIRSK

0233 Hours, 31 July

Baffin Bay, Greenland

Aboard the *Novosibirsk* submarine, Captain 2nd Rank Igor Romanov had spent years honing his skills in dry deck shelter delivery of special forces. This was his first DDS delivery operation within NATO territorial waters on the northwest coast of Greenland. He was ready.

"Captain, arriving at the designated area just outside the detection zone," said the XO. "Sonar reports no activity."

Romanov ordered, "Make depth 30 meters, all stop."

As the *Novosibirsk* slowly rose to the ordered depth, the naval Spetsnaz team moved methodically inside the lock-out compartment located aft of the sail. The red lighting cast long shadows as they secured their equipment and checked each other's suits and rebreathers. The mission clock counted down to the designated insertion time.

"Lock-out chamber, prepare for flooding," the dive officer said over the internal comms.

When the red light blinked green, Captain Viktor Sergeev gave a silent nod. The inner hatch sealed, and the first two divers entered the flooded compartment, pressure equalized with the surrounding sea. The outer hatch unlocked with a hydraulic groan, and the divers slipped out into the blackness, disappearing toward their rendezvous point beneath the hull.

The chamber cycled again. Sergeev, calm and precise, oversaw the rotations as each pair exited. Four cycles. No wasted motion. No words.

"Last pair away," came the call over the internal circuit.

"Deploy swimmer delivery vehicles," Romanov ordered.

The dive officer activated the release sequence. Two compact underwater craft, matte black and acoustically shielded, unlatched from external mounts and glided silently into the water. Each carried two Spetsnaz operators who had regrouped with their SDVs near the forward section of the hull.

Armed with APS underwater rifles and waterproof assault packs, the teams formed up and pushed toward the Greenlandic coastline, their profiles nearly undetectable to sonar or satellite.

"SDV teams clear," the dive officer confirmed.

Romanov turned back to the tactical plot. "Seal the lock-out chamber. Rig for silent running. Make depth four-zero meters, course zero-one-five. Hold position and monitor for NATO movement. Sonar, report."

"Nothing, captain."

The SDVs skimmed just above the seabed to avoid detection by enemy sonar. The two-man teams remained silent as they monitored their heading, keeping a precise distance from one another. Quick hand signals from Sergeev indicated minor course corrections every few minutes.

As the advance landing party neared the shore, the divers scuttled their SDVs and swam the last meters. The team surfaced slowly, only their eyes breaking the waterline as they scanned for threats. The shoreline was quiet, aside from the rhythmic lapping of waves against the jagged rocks.

Sergeev gave the signal, and the Spetsnaz team moved onto land in synchronized movements at one-minute intervals. Their dry suits clung to them as they emerged from the icy depths, and their APS rifles swept the terrain in front of them as they moved.

Sergeev motioned at Sergeant Lebedev, who quickly deployed the ZALA 421-08M, a compact reconnaissance drone. Within minutes, the drone fed real-time imagery to Sergeev's tablet, confirming what their initial reconnaissance had suggested: There were no immediate threats in the area.

Using GPS coordinates, the team headed for the hidden horde of supplies that had been dropped in the higher elevation snowpack by a Russian cargo aircraft a week earlier during a snowstorm. The four GPS-guided supply pods, each the size of a coffin, carried arctic sleds, weapons, communications gear, and survival rations.

Coated to absorb any radar waves, when the plane dropped the pods, a small controlled-release parachute guided them to 60 meters above the surface. Then, a small charge severed their chutes. The pods plummeted into the snowpack, their aerodynamic design allowing them to penetrate and bury themselves deep into the ice upon impact. Once settled, a thin layer of snow covered them, further camouflaging them. Inside each pod, a small heating unit activated for a short time to melt and then allow the surrounding snow to refreeze and ensure they would remain firmly encased until recovery.

Searching for the pods, Sergeev stopped his eight-man team while he used his portable receiver to check for the signal. He triangulated the position by broadcasting on an encrypted low-frequency burst to avoid detection by NATO surveillance.

Soon the men were digging away at the hardened snowpack. Finally, one of the Spetsnaz operators heard a loud metal clank as his entrenching tool struck one of the pods. Within hours, the team unpacked weapons, ammunition, food, white ghillie suits, backpacks, collapsible carts, and encrypted radio units.

Moving inland was a calculated effort. The Arctic summer's continuous daylight provided no natural cover, forcing the team to rely on shadows from ridges, rocky outcroppings, and glacial overhangs. Their approach followed a narrow meltwater stream, allowing them to use the flowing water to mask their tracks.

The ascent from the bay to their search for a high-ground observation post took them across glacial moraines and rocky valleys. The air was crisp, and the silence stretched for miles. The only disturbance was the distant sound of US aircraft cycling in and out of Pituffik Space Base.

By the second day, the team was near their target overlook site, a granite ridge 9 kilometers from the US base. The ridge was 750 meters high, offering a panoramic view of the surrounding area. It provided excellent cover and concealment in crevices and rocky outcrops. Sergeev had also chosen it because the terrain was tricky, meaning the Danish forces were less likely to sweep the area randomly. Even the granite, with its high metal content, interfered with some low-frequency sensors, allowing them some passive cover against long-range ground-penetrating radar sweeps.

Upon arrival at their observation site, the men unpacked their thermal camouflage net, specially made with radar-absorbing material. The net would not only hide them visually but would also scatter radar waves, keeping the overlook indistinguishable from the surrounding granite.

Next, they set up optical scopes with enhanced digital zoom for 24/7 daylight observation. Lastly, they set up comms using a directional burst transmitter with a pencil-thin signal beam and encrypted numerical bursts.

Russia had now taken its first physical step in making Greenland part of the Motherland.

Chapter 28

BOEING P-8 POSEIDON
1205 Hours, 2 August
Arctic Ocean

It was fast becoming a perfect morning. The sun was a constant companion in the Arctic, like it or not, and Maddox loved it. He was in the left seat of his P-8, with one hand on the yoke and the other around a cup of coffee. He took another sip, hoping it would taste better than the last.

"Jesus, Jackson, what did you do to this coffee?" Maddox asked while glancing back at his TACCO, Lieutenant Norm Jackson.

Jackson didn't even look up from his console. "That, sir, is premium Navy issue. Tastes like burnt jet fuel because it probably is."

The crew chuckled. Lieutenant Robert Johanson, the co-pilot, was still smiling as he adjusted a switch on the overhead panel. "Just be glad we're not on a submarine. I hear those guys drink coffee that could peel paint off a bulkhead."

"Well, the caffeine's kicking in, Han, so I guess it's doing its job." Maddox exhaled, shaking off the fatigue. "How we looking, TACCO?"

"Got the same movement below us. The Russian naval group consists of a Slava-class cruiser and two escorts. I doubt that the Yasen-class submarine we've been looking for is with them. Nothing's irregular, but they're sticking close to Alexandra Land."

"Standard BS," said Maddox.

Aircrewman Operator Petty Officer First Class Jason "Gordo" Gordon, a sensor operator, twisted in his seat. The twitchy kid was on his first tour and seemed a little jumpy. "You think they'll buzz us today? You know, just for fun?"

Maddox sighed. That was the last thing they needed. "I hope not, but given the way things are going—"

"We got company," Jackson cut in.

"Talk to me, TACCO," Maddox replied to Jackson as he set his coffee down.

"Two Su-35s just popped up on radar, bearing two-eight-four and closing fast, distance 40 miles, altitude 30,000. They're at Mach 1.2 and accelerating."

"Picking up intermittent radar locks from their fire control system," said the EWO. "No missile tracking yet, but they're testing us, Ghost."

"They're playing games," replied Maddox. "I'm going to keep a steady course and altitude."

Better get the word out to the *Ford*, thought Maddox. "TACCO, inform fleet we're being painted by Russian fighters. Request immediate support."

"Roger, transmitting alert." On secure comms, Jackson keyed in:

"Strike Control, Trident 21. We are locked up by two Su-35s. Request fast movers."

On secure comms: "Copy Trident 21. Vectoring two F-35s to your location. Stand by. ETA fifteen minutes."

"Trident 21, Hudner. We have you on radar. Russian Su-35s maintaining lock. Holding SM-6s for now."

Maddox flipped a switch on his comms panel, "Russian aircraft, this is a US Navy P-8 operating in international airspace. Maintain safe separation."

Seconds passed, and nothing.

"They're coming in, Ghost," Johanson said, peering out of the cockpit. "This is going to be close."

SUKHOI SU-35 FLANKER-E FLIGHT

1216 Hours, 2 August

Arctic Ocean

Running combat air patrol for a convoy of ships carrying additional advanced weapons to Alexandra Land, Major Viktor Zhukov was the flight leader of two Su-35s. His wingman, hanging a few hundred meters to his right. As they stayed close to their convoy, Zhukov pondered the orders he had received this morning. The CO had explicitly said, "Any aircraft that gets near our convoy, I want them pushed back. Make them feel unsafe. Do whatever it takes, but force them to leave the area." His orders were no problem for two of the most aggressive pilots the Russians had flying Su-35s. And their aggressiveness was precisely why they were chosen for today's CAP.

As if almost on cue, a target popped up on Zhukov's Heads Up Display, HUD.

"Rusher 52, you seeing this?" asked Zhukov.

"Rusher 51, confirmed."

"Standard intercept protocol," said Zhukov, since they were close to visual range. "We will force the Americans to acknowledge our presence. Let them know we control these skies."

Zhukov adjusted his throttle, feeling the subtle shift as the twin turbofans responded to his input. He wanted to come in slower so there would be no mistaking who was buzzing them. This would be about intimidation, not shooting the Americans out of the air.

His passive electronically scanned array radar displayed the P-8's exact range as 59 kilometers, bearing 310 degrees, and speed of 402 km/h. His radar warning receivers showed that the Poseidon was running its surface-search radar but wasn't actively scanning for threats.

"Rusher 52, go to line approach," Zhukov said over the secure frequency.

His wingman responded immediately, "Understood, closing to 500 meters." He slid slightly behind Zhukov and lower, a typical Russian tactic. One pilot watched the target and forward air space while his wingman monitored for hostile reactions or third-party aircraft.

At 18 kilometers, both pilots switched to electro-optical sensors and visual acquisition, focusing on Poseidon's large fuselage for target confirmation.

So predictable, Zhukov thought. The Americans were sticking to their course, playing the long, safe game.

"Rusher 51 to Control, we are engaging in a close pass maneuver," Zhukov transmitted back to Rogachevo Air Base on a secure UHF channel.

"Affirmative, Rusher 51. We see you. Execute. Push them out of our airspace."

The phrasing made Zhukov pause. Technically, the P-8 wasn't in Russian airspace but in international skies. But he reasoned, the Arctic was shifting. Russia controlled these waters, and everyone needed to get used to it.

Zhukov flicked his comms switch to an open frequency. "American aircraft, this is a Russian Su-35. You are approaching a restricted flight zone. Adjust your course away from the area immediately."

A response came after a few seconds. "Russian aircraft, this is a US Navy P-8 operating in international airspace. Maintain safe separation."

At 9 kilometers, Zhukov adjusted his approach vector. The Su-35 angled left, rolling 10 degrees, which would bring its wingtip close to the Poseidon's fuselage. Zhukov knew this was the most effective way to disrupt the target's route.

As the P-8 grew larger and larger, Zhukov called out his distance to himself. "500 meters—good, 100 meters still good."

His digital flight control system responded smoothly as he made micro adjustments to his lateral position. He could now see the faint outlines of the American crew through the cockpit windows, both pilots staring at him.

"Don't overdo it, Rusher 51," his wingman warned over the intercom."

"Relax, Sorkin, I've done this before."

Piloting his P-8, Maddox couldn't believe it as his radar warning receiver sounded again. The Su-35s were cycling their radar locks, surely testing them and ensuring they knew they were being watched.

Maddox steadied himself as he watched out of his cockpit window as the Su-35 approached and flew close alongside them.

"You believe the balls on this asshole?" yelled Johanson.

Maddox had been buzzed one other time, but that encounter was not nearly as dangerous as this one was becoming. The Russian pilot was so close that Maddox saw his dark visor reflecting the Poseidon's fuselage.

Maddox felt adrenaline shoot through his body as he mumbled, "He's too close."

Johanson said, "He's going to get caught in our wake, Ghost."

Maddox toggled the open frequency. "Russian aircraft, you are too close. Back off."

A sudden jolt of clear air turbulence rocked the P-8. Maddox watched as the fighter wobbled for a split second, then veered away a few yards. But he was helpless when the Su-35's right wingtip suddenly came toward his plane. He instinctively moved the yoke.

But the fighter was too close. Its momentum was exacerbated in the turbulence, and as it decelerated and fell back, a wingtip ripped the right horizontal stabilizer off the P-8.

Alarms blared in Poseidon's cockpit.

"Impact!" yelled Johanson.

The P-8 pitched violently. Maddox fought the yoke, but the aircraft wouldn't respond as it rolled hard to the right.

Maddox shouted as he applied full opposite rudder, "I'm losing control! Engine two's out. Han, transmit Mayday."

Maddox fought heroically as the P-8 began a violent spiral toward the Arctic Ocean below. Screams filled the air the whole way down until the aircraft slammed into the sea, ripping it into thousands of pieces of metal and body parts.

Trying to control his Su-35, Zhukov responded to the sudden turbulence by decelerating and pulling away sharply from the P-8. But he'd gotten battered by the plane's wake. He fought to gain control of his fighter, panic on his face that no one saw but he felt.

His wingman yelled, "You hit them, you hit them."

Zhukov paid him no attention as he continued to fight his controls, which didn't respond to his actions. He saw the P-8 spiraling toward the sea and resolved that he wouldn't suffer the same fate.

Slamming on the left rudder pedal and using his stick, Zhukov worked hard as the jet rolled to the right. The highly responsive Su-35's control surfaces began to steady the roll, pitch, and yaw. He pushed the nose down slightly to regain control with fresh airflow over the wings. Carefully adding throttle, he brought both engines back to full power while pulling back the stick, finally bringing the Su-35 out of its spin. He was just 90 meters from the surface of the Arctic Ocean.

Gaining altitude, he headed home and ignored the screams of his co-pilot as he tried to fathom what had just happened.

"I didn't mean to kill them," he kept softly repeating.

Chapter 29

DEBRIEFING ROOM

1411 Hours, 2 August

Rogachevo Air Base, Russia

It had only been six hours since Major Viktor Zhukov had been flying over the Arctic Ocean, and all he could do now was stare at the wall. He had no idea how many generals and staff were filling the room. Many were talking simultaneously, but he wasn't hearing anything. He was reliving the harrowing experience of sending nine Americans to their watery grave. Granted, he was an aviator trained to kill the enemy, but there was no war, and he hadn't meant for that to happen.

He felt a finger being jammed into his chest. He looked up and saw a sweating, fat man with more brass on his shoulders than he had ever seen. "So I will say it again, Zhukov. The American aircraft suddenly maneuvered erratically and struck your aircraft. Unfortunate, but not your fault. Is that correct, Major?"

Zhukov stared, frozen. He had never killed anyone before, and the confusion clouded everything until something clicked. His Type A instincts kicked in, clearing the fog like a flipped switch. Sitting up straight, Zhukov looked the general in his beady eyes and said, "You are correct, General. If that dumbass American had stayed on course instead of veering toward my aircraft, we wouldn't be having this conversation. This was entirely the fault of the Americans. Yes, their deaths are unfortunate, but those are the facts."

He reached for a pen and signed an affidavit stating just that.

THE WHITE HOUSE
1900 Hours, 2 August
Washington, DC

Little did the Russian authorities know a Norwegian fishing trawler had caught the entire collision on camera. Much of the footage was shaky and faint, but experts from the National Geospatial-Intelligence Agency were able to piece enough footage together to highlight the Su-35 turning into the P-8.

However, the most incriminating surveillance came from satellite reconnaissance, which showed the collision had been deliberate. Imagery showed the Russian Su-35 making an aggressive maneuver moments before the impact. This was enough for President Mark Taylor to address the American people. Sitting behind the Resolute desk, he looked straight into the camera.

My fellow Americans,

Tonight, I come before you with a heavy heart as we mourn the loss of nine brave servicemen and women who asked for nothing more than to serve their country.

Yesterday, our country faced an unprovoked and reckless attack by the Russian military. While conducting a routine reconnaissance mission over international waters, the crew of a US Navy P-8 Poseidon was deliberately targeted by a Russian fighter jet. The collision that followed killed every member of the crew.

To the families of our fallen heroes, your sacrifice will never be forgotten. We stand with you, ensuring that your loved ones' memories will always live on, and we will support you in the days, weeks, and years ahead.

America is united in our grief, but we are also united in our strength. We will not be intimidated by those who seek to spread division or terror. The ideals that our brave men and women defend are what make this country great: freedom, justice, and the rule of law. We will not allow anyone to take those from us.

We hold Russia responsible for their deaths. This was no mishap. The Russian fighter made a dangerous maneuver that caused the crash of our aircraft. I repeat, this was no accident. We have classified evidence to substantiate it.

Let me be clear: The United States will not tolerate attacks on our service members. We will not stand idly by while our forces are put at risk. We will always act to defend American lives, and we will do so with our military's full force and resolve.

As your Commander-in-Chief, I am committed to holding Russia accountable for its actions. Under my orders earlier, our Navy deployed the USS Ford battle group. Other American assets are being put in place as we talk. While my administration will always look to diplomacy first, we will be prepared for any situation.

In the coming days, we will discuss our response with our allies and work together to ensure that Russia's actions do not go unanswered. But tonight, let us focus on what is most important:

remembering the lost lives, honoring their courage, and ensuring their sacrifice is never in vain.

Thank you, and may God bless our fallen heroes, their families, and the United States of America.

Chapter 30

2ND BRIGADE, 11TH AIRBORNE DIVISION
0545 Hours, 3 August
Joint Base Elmendorf-Richardson, Anchorage, Alaska

Everywhere he looked in the vast hangar, soldiers were in constant motion checking weapons, tightening rucksack straps, and loading duffel bags onto pallets that would go onto waiting aircraft. Captain Robert "Frosty" Shepherd's focus remained on one group amid the organized chaos, the 160 men and women of Bravo Company, 1st Battalion 501st Infantry Regiment, his command.

Standing alongside him was one of his platoon leaders, 1st Lieutenant Dani Mercer. Shepherd trusted her like few he had ever served with in his six years in the Army. He figured her upbringing in El Paso, Texas, as the only child of a hard-assed Command Sergeant Major father, made her who she is today, one tough SOB. Shepherd knew she had grown up always fighting the doubters, including her dad. But she had proved them all wrong.

"So, Captain, who's involved with this NATO exercise?" she said.

"It looks like the Danes and Canadians."

"Sounds like fun," she said with a big smile.

What Shepherd wasn't revealing was that OPERATION ARCTIC SHIELD was a pretext to rapidly reinforce Greenland in response not only to the downing of the P-8 but, more importantly, to the intelligence that the Russians might be making a move on the sparsely but strategically important island, much like the tactic they used on Ukraine. Shepherd figured the Russians were becoming more aggressive because of what President Taylor had been saying lately that the acquisition of Greenland by the US was an absolute necessity for the security of the free world. The president had never ruled out taking it by force.

The DOD had issued information to the press about a joint exercise with Denmark, Canada, and a sprinkling of troops from Finland, Sweden, and Norway. But Shepherd had learned in his intel briefing that the real mission was to secure key infrastructure, establish defensive positions, and monitor Russian activity around Greenland.

Additionally, should Russian forces attempt to probe or make an unannounced presence on Greenland's substantial coastline, the 11th Airborne's rapid response units would already be positioned to intercept and deter. If tensions escalated, NATO forces would immediately shift from exercise mode to real-world operations, turning Pituffik Space Base into a staging ground for Arctic confrontation.

As Shepherd was getting ready to join his company, which had finished loading the baggage pallet and was heading out to the aircraft, he saw his battalion commander, Lieutenant Colonel Mark Callahan, approaching. Shepherd snapped to attention and saluted sharply.

After Callahan returned the salute, he said, "Are you and your company ready?"

"Yes, sir," said Shepherd, "the last of the company is boarding now."

"Just one more thought for you, this isn't Afghanistan, and this isn't Iraq. No mountains, no deserts. If things go sideways out there, there's no quick extraction. No friendly villages. Just ice, wind, and whatever's waiting for you in the dark."

"Roger that, sir. That's why they're sending us, right? We're Arctic-trained and don't need any stinking roads."

"Just remember the rules of engagement. The first shot can't come from us."

Shepherd exhaled, glancing toward the C-17, now firing up its engines. "Understood, sir. But if they pull anything, I won't hesitate."

Callahan looked satisfied. "I know you won't." He clapped Shepherd's shoulder. "See you in Greenland."

Chapter 31

USS Thomas Hudner
0605 Hours, 3 August
GIUK Gap

Lieutenant Commander Brett Jansen couldn't help but notice that he seemed to be continually tested as the newest officer aboard the ship. Whenever he entered a room, talk ended abruptly, and all he got were blank stares. Certain officers like Lieutenant Commander Nate Holloway, the ship's operations officer, often discussed orders instead of simply doing them. Jansen had heard through the grapevine that some people on the *Hudner* questioned Jansen's experience, especially since he'd been on a minesweeper that was shot out from under him during the war with Iran. It didn't seem to matter that he'd gotten this job because of his heroics saving his ship and had been hospitalized for his injuries doing so.

Then last week, when he was in the CIC looking over the shoulder of the ship's senior chief sonar operator, Mike "Gator" Gatlin, he got the comment, "Sir, minesweepers are about patience, but this here's about aggression. The Russians play dirty up here, and the ice will kill you just as fast as a torpedo if you don't respect it."

Jansen realized right then that rank and position had no bearing on being a leader. He would have to earn their trust, just like he'd always done as a junior officer.

A broadcast came over the 1MC. "This is the captain. All department heads and senior leaders report to the wardroom immediately."

Jansen headed to the wardroom. As the last of the ten senior staff took a seat around a long rectangular table, Captain Don Reynolds stood at one end. Everyone understood this had to be important because this meeting and his demeanor were out of his routine.

Cutting right to the point, the captain told the officers about the situation. "I just got off the line with the admiral." Reynolds looked down at the document with the written orders from CSG-12's commander, Rear Admiral Lower Half Michael Graves. "Intelligence reports that the Ford is being shadowed by at least one Russian Yasen-class submarine. The Hudner will take point on ASW operations. All other assets are out of range, so if that sub gets too close, we are to neutralize the threat." He looked back at his gathered officers. "These aren't just routine patrols anymore, not since the downing of the P-8. Washington can't risk another situation, so we must protect the Ford at all costs."

Reynolds set the document on the table. "The admiral also stated that one or more of these subs would test our defenses, response, and readiness. Well, guess what. They're about to find out just how good we are. XO, you're leading the CIC. I want a full ASW sweep pattern to be established and maintained around the clock. Use passive first, and if we lose them, go active."

"Yes, sir," said Jansen.

"TAO," said the captain, "load the tubes. We'll keep our Mark 54s ready to fire at a moment's notice, but we won't engage unless we confirm hostile intent. Holloway, get us a P-8 on station as soon as possible. Gator, your team is my early-warning system. If the Russians even sneeze down there, I want to hear about it."

Gatlin couldn't resist saying, "Hell, Captain, we'll hear 'em before they even know they got a cold."

A few chuckles passed through the room, easing the tension.

"It's time to put your training to work," Reynolds said. "This is not a drill, and this is not an exercise. We're playing the most dangerous game in naval warfare, and we don't get a second chance if we get it wrong. Dismissed."

For *Hudner*, the sonar of choice for this mission was the Lockheed Martin AN/SQR-20 Multi-Function Towed Array, which streamed behind the ship to detect acoustic anomalies. It was the most advanced passive and active sonar system in the Navy's Arleigh Burke class destroyers. The MFTA was towed far behind the ship, isolating itself from self-generated noise. Another significant advantage was that it could penetrate deep into thermoclines, which submarines often sought to hide under. Additionally, the MFTA's long-range capability in passive mode exceeded 50 nautical miles.

Gatlin went to work at his sonar station, and Jansen stood near him. The senior chief was slowly getting used to the new kid on the block, whom most didn't trust yet.

An hour passed, but Gatlin still had nothing, which wasn't unusual when searching for Russia's quietest submarines. Finally, he said, "XO, I've got something faint. Below the thermocline but moving fast."

"Give me a classification," said Jansen.

"My best guess right now is Yasen-class. Bearing two-one-five, range approximately 10,000 yards. Sir, he's moving in."

Turning to Lieutenant Rachel Kim, Jansen ordered, "TAO, have the P-8 deploy a passive sonobuoy net. I want a firm track."

A few minutes later the P-8 was over the sector dropping a widespread sonobuoy field. They reported back quickly.

A comm line chirped open on Jansen's headset. "XO, update from the P-8," said Kim. "They've got a confirmed Yasen-class contact bearing two-one-five. Speed increasing to 15 knots."

Gatlin jumped in, "It just did a non-standard maneuver and is pushing the reactors. Look at that cavitation. This bastard's not sneaking anymore. He's running fast."

Concerning, thought Jansen. "TAO, update on its course."

Kim looked at a red arc on her screen. "Two-four-zero, direct line to the Ford, sir."

Jansen immediately keyed the comms to Reynolds on the bridge. "Captain, the Yasen-class sub is making a direct approach to the Ford. It's not slowing."

Reynolds came back calmly. "Then we put ourselves between it and the carrier. Helm, hard starboard. XO, get me firing solutions."

The destroyer heeled sharply, its bow cutting deep as the stern swung wide and left a huge foaming arc in its wake. Onboard, the crew braced unconsciously as the ship tilted through the turn.

"TAO," said Jansen, "plot torpedo solutions for the Yasen-class sub. Ready tubes, but don't fire until I give the command."

"CIC and WEPS confirm Mark 54s are hot. All systems green."

"TAO," said Jansen, a little more animated, "active ping. Let them know we're watching."

"Active ping sent, no response. It's locked onto the Ford."

Gatlin added, "Sir, it's accelerating. 20 knots, now 25. XO, contact is at 28 knots. Still closing."

Jansen heard Holloway say, "What's your call, XO?"

Jansen was all over it, and he toggled bridge comms. "Captain, the Russian sub is increasing speed toward the Ford."

Without hesitation, Reynolds said, "Engage."

"TAO," Jansen said, "Fire one Mark 54, direct path."

After the TAO relayed the order, WEPS said, "Weapon away."

As the Raytheon Mk 54 lightweight torpedo raced toward the Russian sub, TAO reported, "Torpedo is tracking. Impact in seventy seconds."

Jansen now had two choices. If the sub turned, he could redirect the Mk 54. If the Russians didn't change course, Jansen would do everything in his power to sink the sub.

"XO," Gatlin said, his eyes locked on his scope, "The Yasen-class sub is turning and dumping countermeasures."

Jansen could see the sub was continuing to turn away from their location. "Good, that's the move we wanted. TAO, cut the torpedo off and redirect it wide."

TAO came back immediately, "Wire command sent, torpedo adjusting course away from the target."

Gatlin added, "Tracking torpedo has lost the lock. Russian sub is peeling away. He's running."

In those final moments, Jansen hadn't seen the captain come into the CIC and stand beside him. Jansen only knew it had happened when the captain put his hand on Jansen's shoulder and said, "We gave the bastard a way out, and he took it. Nice job, XO."

Jansen stood a bit straighter and turned to acknowledge the address, but the captain had already turned to everyone else in the CIC. "Great job today."

After the captain left to return to the bridge, Holloway approached Jansen and offered his hand to his XO. "I didn't think you had the ice water for it, but I guess I was wrong." With that, he turned away and went back to his station.

Even though earning the crew's respect would be a slow process, Jansen knew he'd taken a giant first step.

Chapter 32

THE KREMLIN

3 August

Moscow, Russia

Soon after President Andrei Petrov's secret meeting, Admiral Mikhailovich of the Northern Fleet directed Colonel Alexander Popov of the GRU Spetsnaz to lead a team in planning the Russian move into Greenland. The admiral's one stipulation to Popov was to avoid direct confrontation with a NATO country that could invoke Article 5 and bring all the NATO countries against them. Article 5 had only been declared once, and that was after 9/11. Russia didn't want to be the second cause for a full-blown NATO response.

Although Greenland operated as an autonomous territory, it remained a part of the Kingdom of Denmark. However, Denmark retained control over Greenland's foreign policy and defense matters, which meant Greenland fell under NATO's collective defense obligations, including Article 5.

Consequently, within a few weeks, Colonel Popov's team had developed a multifaceted plan, involving economic infiltration and covert operations in preparation for hybrid warfare. To kick off the first phase of the plan, Russian state-owned corporations began investing in Greenland's rare earth mining projects, securing footholds under the guise of economic cooperation. Simultaneously, Spetsnaz teams, composed of elite military and intelligence personnel who trained for high-risk and specialized missions, were stationed at Russia's northernmost bases awaiting orders.

The plan hinged on exploiting political divisions within Greenland. Popov directed his agents to infiltrate the growing independence movement that had evolved, fueled by dissatisfaction with Copenhagen's governance. Many Greenlanders resented Denmark's tight control over their economy and natural resources, feeling that profits from mining and fishing were being drained away to Copenhagen while local communities saw little benefit. Additionally, Denmark's restrictive policies on foreign investment, including limitations on partnerships with non-Western companies, had created resentment among Greenlandic business leaders who saw Russia as a viable economic partner.

Russian intelligence operatives also carefully cultivated relationships with key figures in the Greenlandic independence movement, providing financial support and political consulting to shape their messaging. Moscow-backed media outlets quietly pushed narratives emphasizing Denmark's colonial history, highlighting perceived injustices, and framing Russia as a partner in Greenland's economic self-determination. Simultaneously, Russian diplomats lobbied for direct trade agreements to bypass Danish oversight and reinforce the idea that Greenland could thrive independently with the right alliance.

Popov even went to Nuuk, the capital of Greenland, and home to the Greenlandic Parliament. Under the guise of the Arctic Council, of which Russia was one of the eight members, he went to discuss energy cooperation and scientific collaboration. Secretly, he was there to lay the groundwork for Russia's deeper infiltration by winning over key leaders.

As he met with Greenlandic organizers and business figures, Russian nuclear icebreakers, armed and carrying electronic warfare suites, were dispatched to survey the island's coastline under the pretense of climate research. The EW suites were designed to jam radar and communications, disrupt drones, and counter guided missiles while creating a base for cyberattacks. Meanwhile, Russian submarines patrolled the waters, mapping potential access points for military deployments.

Additionally, covert Russian teams posing as civilian researchers and contractors quietly established "climate research" outposts in Greenland's remote regions. While officially non-military, these sites were strategically placed near airstrips and fjords that could, if needed, support aircraft and sealift operations. Danish and American authorities grew suspicious, but the cover story remained intact.

While the Russians had been setting up their covert infrastructure to take over Greenland, the US had been preoccupied with the rhetoric of the presidential candidate vying to replace President Taylor on his party's ticket, as Taylor was being term-limited out of office.

That candidate, Senator Samuel Preston, was a no-nonsense hawk from Texas. In an interview on *Meet the Press*, he riled many people when he said matter-of-factly, "If we don't secure Greenland now, we'll be fighting for it in a year against powers that don't have our best interests in mind."

The Greenland prime minister immediately posted, "We don't want to be Americans."

The comment didn't faze Preston. He made it clear that he was also troubled that Denmark had refused to negotiate with the US regarding the takeover of Greenland's governance. He argued that doing so was in the best interest of the United States and suggested that US economic and military leverage should be applied to bring them to reason, a theme he repeatedly used on the campaign trail.

European nations, particularly Denmark, continually criticized his statements as imperialistic. NATO was concerned that Preston's aggressive stance could destabilize alliances. Even his own party was split. Some viewed him as a strategic genius, while others feared his rhetoric could lead to a diplomatic backlash. Meanwhile, the Russians celebrated his remarks as they drew Greenland's independence movement more under their control.

Russian officials used Preston's blatant statements to continue their disinformation campaigns to spread propaganda among discontented Greenlanders, to push narratives of self-sufficiency and anti-Danish sentiment, and to divide the country's 52,000 residents.

After eight months, the preparation phase of Popov's plan was complete. It was time to move.

Chapter 33

PITUFFIK SPACE BASE

3 August

Greenland

The first indicators surfaced in the command center at Pituffik Space Base, the cornerstone of US military presence in Greenland and the Arctic. Satellite imagery picked up unusual movement of Russian naval assets off Greenland's eastern coastline. The vessels, mostly icebreakers with a few support ships, weren't just conducting routine Arctic operations. Their trajectories and coordination suggested a deliberate maneuver aimed at increasing Russian presence in this strategic region.

At the same time, US intelligence noted a sharp increase in Russian diplomatic efforts in Nuuk, the capital. Pro-American insiders reported that Russia was involved in high-level talks and substantial payoffs with personnel from the independent movement, certain Greenlandic officials, and elite business owners. Russia was successfully stoking anti-American sentiment.

President Taylor and his NSC had been sending directives that this trend had to stop immediately. Officials said Greenland was not just some icy, mostly empty expanse, but was vital to the defense of the Arctic and beyond. They reemphasized to naysayers that Pituffik Space Base was the key to American missile defense. The base housed early-warning radar systems critical to detecting intercontinental ballistic missile launches, which made the base indispensable to NORAD. Orders were explicit that Russian military posturing had to be countered swiftly and decisively.

The Pentagon responded accordingly, ordering surveillance flights by the Boeing RC-135 Rivet Joint reconnaissance aircraft based in England and increasing P-8 Poseidon maritime patrols, both to monitor Russian naval activities and to gather any additional intelligence they might be able to pick up. CSG-12 had also arrived in the GIUK Gap area.

The State Department ramped up efforts to reinforce the weakened US-Greenlandic ties in response to Russia's political and diplomatic moves. Washington emphasized its support for Greenlandic self-determination within the framework of the Kingdom of Denmark, countering Moscow's efforts to drive a wedge between Nuuk and Copenhagen. A high-level delegation, including representatives from the Department of Defense and the State Department's Bureau of European and Eurasian Affairs, was dispatched to Nuuk to shore up American influence and reassure local leadership.

Meanwhile, in the Pentagon, senior defense officials considered more assertive measures. The 11th Airborne Division was sent to Pituffik Space Base with other NATO units under the guise of OPERATION ARCTIC SHIELD. Included were troops from Denmark, Canada, and a sprinkling of soldiers from Finland, Sweden, and Norway. Leaders were briefed on potential deployment scenarios, including airlifting forces to Greenland's remote airstrips in the event of a situation escalation.

The American response was clear: Greenland would not be exposed to Russian encroachment. Whether through diplomatic maneuvering, military presence, or intelligence operations, Washington was prepared to counter any attempt to shift the Arctic balance of power. All were aware that this stance left little room for maneuver. Greenland had become a potential battleground between the US and Russia for control of the Arctic.

Chapter 34

2ND BRIGADE, 11TH AIRBORNE DIVISION
1301 Hours, 3 August
Pituffik Space Base, Greenland

The wheels of the first of three C-17s no sooner stopped than Captain Shepherd had his company on the move. Paratroopers dressed in Arctic combat gear surged from the aircraft to their assigned perimeter area. The soldiers were armed with the latest Army weaponry, Sig Sauer's XM-7 rifle and XM-250 automatic rifle. Both chambered the new 6.8mm round, improved for accuracy, range, and most importantly, lethality.

Lieutenant Dani Mercer was on comms within minutes. "Perimeter secure. No contact."

Damn, how Shepherd loved precision.

He scanned the horizon. The sun hovered stubbornly above ice-crusted peaks, a midnight sun with no shadows and nowhere to hide. Always expecting the enemy to be watching, he said, "EW, establish defensive positions on the eastern ridge. Get those jammers online. I want their eyes blind and their ears ringing."

The electronic warfare team scrambled to the rise to quickly assemble their jammers. Antennae shot skyward, and a reconnaissance drone whined upwards to sweep the area for anything out of place.

After offloading from the second C-17, it didn't take long for satellite terminals and secure radios to hum with activity in the battalion's mobile tactical operations center. Digital maps flickered with live feeds from Space Force assets. A ground-based E-2 had airspace overwatch and was taking care of everyone's six. Efficiently encrypted comms were set up with higher command and coordinated with Allied assets. A redundancy protocol satellite feed, plus HF and mesh networks, was soon operational. The TOC lit up with multi-channel chatter relaying troop movements and airspace conditions.

Total elapsed time from wheels down totaled fifteen minutes. It was only the beginning.

NORTHROP GRUMMAN E-2D ADVANCED HAWKEYE
1311 Hours, 3 August
Airborne near Pituffik Space Base, Greenland

Freeman was still adjusting to land-based operations and her dual role as a pilot and commanding officer of the three E-2s temporarily assigned at Pituffik Space Base. Busy writing a new set of operational instructions for E-2 aircrew, she'd had little time to think of Jessie. She'd heard from him that he was back in an operational squadron on the *Ford*, and she had felt how they both had ended up in the Arctic was just weird. The Navy was clear; husband-and-wife teams didn't exist, the keyword being *teams*, meaning two married pilots flying off the same carrier. But no one said they couldn't be serving in the same area. And even though they'd both shown up in Washington state, both on shore duty assignments, here they were, both deployed into a hot zone. Again.

Damn, she thought, too bad they couldn't get an apartment on Pituffik.

A radio call brought her back to her cockpit. "TOC, Pickett 11. Reporting radar online, commencing full ISR sweep."

The tactical displays in the E-2 pulsed with the feeds from the plane's powerful Lockheed Martin AN/APS-145 radar, painting a vivid picture of everything within a 300-nautical-mile radius. The CICO and their back-end crew worked with brisk, been-here-before efficiency.

"Link established with Space Force assets," reported the radar operator. "Satellite overlays coming in."

"Bravo 6, Pickett 11," Sarah transmitted over a secure channel that linked her directly to Shepherd on the ground. "Radar is coming online and commencing initial wide-area sweep."

The AN/APS-145 radar spun above the fuselage, noting every contact, friendly, unknown, surface, or airborne. Each was classified, tracked, and relayed to the TOC.

"Pulling live imagery and thermal overlays from Space Force," CICO said. "Feeding it to Bravo 6."

Sarah kept the E-2's orbit steady, adjusting altitude slightly to optimize radar coverage.

"Ma'am," the radar operator said, "Picking up intermittent low-power emissions. Could be a recon drone or a ground radar trying to paint us."

"Roger that, RO. Don't light up the EW suite just yet," Sarah ordered. "If they're fishing for us, we'll wait until they bite and get them then."

The radar pulse came again, this time a tighter, more focused beam briefly sweeping across the Hawkeye's fuselage.

"Deliberate sweep," the RO reported, getting closer to his screen. "Someone's not just scanning, they're searching."

Sarah toggled Shepherd. "Bravo 6, we're picking up active radar emissions from the northeast. Nobody should be out there."

"Pickett 11, copy," Shepherd said. "We'll stay low. Can you blind them?"

"Stand by, Bravo 6," Sarah said, then said on aircraft intercom, "CICO, light them up."

Coordinating with an airborne Growler, the E-2 vectored in EW support. Within seconds, powerful, deceptive signals flooded the battlespace. On enemy radar, what would have been a single contact now fractured into a dozen ghost signatures, which would confuse any operator.

Several minutes passed with no info. "RO, what's going on?" Sarah said.

"Signal lost, ma'am. No taper, no drift."

"Bravo 6, Pickett 11," Sarah said. "Be advised, whatever was out there just went dark. No emissions, no movement. It's just gone."

"Roger, Pickett 11," Shepherd replied. "If they pop up again, I want to know."

As Sarah looked out her cockpit window at the vast expanse of the Arctic, she realized the place was never truly empty.

Chapter 35

Spetsnaz Unit
1322 Hours, 3 August
Granite Overlook, Greenland

The elite Spetsnaz unit had been observing the area around Pituffik Space Base from their granite overlook for three days and was gaining significant intelligence. Captain Sergeev had provided Moscow with detailed locations of radar arrays, aircraft counts and types, force compositions, and locations of network nodes. Currently, Sergeev and Sergeant Lebedev were setting up to disrupt US comms to assist in a planned move on the east coast of this frozen island. Above his team, blinking silently, was a US tactical microwave line-of-sight relay node, whose purpose was to extend communication over terrain and obstacles. The remaining six of the Spetsnaz unit were spread outward and provided cover.

Sergeev had taken off his gloves as he finished working on a cable box. "Ready, Lebedev. Hand me the signal disruptor."

The sergeant pulled a matte-black rectangle from his parka and handed it over. Working quickly, Sergeev connected the device that, once armed, would introduce a timed data lag across the entire encrypted feed, delaying orders, masking sensor returns, and confusing response coordination.

"This will work, Captain?" Lebedev asked.

Sergeev adjusted his SR-3M Vikhr assault rifle on his shoulder to better work with his hands. "Yes, comrade. It's a delayed loop so that the Americans won't notice until things don't work."

Suddenly, Sergeev heard a noise that didn't fit the environment.

2ND BRIGADE, 11TH AIRBORNE DIVISION
1328 Hours, 3 August
Near Pituffik Space Base, Greenland

Shepherd held his fist in the air, signaling the nine others in his combat patrol to halt. He dropped to a knee, using the icy lip of a shallow depression for cover. Three hundred feet ahead, tucked between jagged granite slabs, he'd spotted the faint orange glow of a heat source through his thermal monocular. The signature was just enough to confirm a presence but not a shape.

He handed the scope to Lieutenant Mercer. She peered through it and, after making some adjustments, said, "I got eight signatures. Six low-profile. Two are working on something with a blinking light."

Shepherd took the scope back and swept the terrain. He spotted them too, eight figures moving near the site of a known unmanned communications relay. It was one of several low-profile nodes used to route secure data between Pituffik Space Base and US early-warning systems in Canada. The relay wasn't hardened, just a camouflaged structure with satellite uplink capability. But its role in transmitting command-and-control data made it a high-value soft target.

"Two are working on a box of some sort," he said. "Mercer, take Alpha team and flank them on our right. I'll stay with Bravo team and push forward slowly. Move out."

Mercer took her four men, making up Alpha, and they carefully went right. Shepherd and his team moved forward. Staying undercover was necessary, even though it was 3:28 a.m. The sun was still visible on the horizon, casting covering shadows. They stayed in them the best they could.

At 150 feet out, Shepherd could make out the two people under the relay node. They wore white camo slick suits that blended well into the ice and snow.

He heard Mercer say in his earbuds, "Alpha in position, have six hostiles."

"Execute on my mark. I have the two working on the device." Shepherd signaled his intent to his team, and they readied their rifles.

Dropping to a knee, Shepherd raised his suppressed M7 and settled the reticle just below the shoulder blades of the man hunched over the open relay box. The cold air held still for a heartbeat.

"Execute."

Shepherd squeezed the trigger. The target jerked, collapsing face-first into the snow. In one quick motion, the target's partner grabbed the rifle from his shoulder and fired back. Shepherd heard the rounds smash into the rocks just above his head. Before he could fire again, he saw the man take one in the chest and go down under the relay station. He motioned for Alpha team to follow him forward.

When Shepherd had given the execute command, Mercer and Alpha team had fired simultaneously and rushed in, taking down the six identified hostiles. Both teams converged, then split up to check that each hostile was either dead or wounded. Only one of the eight was still breathing. Mercer put cord cuffs on the man and searched him as he lay in the snow. She confirmed that he was Russian.

Shepherd called it in. He figured correctly that this might be just the tip of the iceberg.

Chapter 36

MV Petropavlovsk
1021 Hours, 4 August
Scoresby Sound, Greenland

The Russian civilian cargo ship MV *Petropavlovsk* rode low in the frigid Arctic waters. The ship's published manifest stated that it carried scientific equipment in response to an urgent geophysical event, which Russian officials had labeled a seismic anomaly on the southwestern coast of Greenland. The officials had failed to mention that the anomaly was caused by their deep-sea explosives. To support the narrative, the Russian press was going all out, labeling the anomaly as a previously undiscovered tectonic movement that could significantly impact the Arctic shipping lanes used by ships worldwide.

The Russian press portrayed their countrymen as heroes coming to the rescue of the Arctic. The problem was that the anomaly was technically in Danish waters and that the Russians had been told that under no circumstances should they proceed. The Russians politely apologized and said their response was in the interest of the safety of the eight Arctic states, of which Russia was one. Thus the anomaly had to be investigated. Besides, they were already there and could quickly take action.

Two weeks earlier, under the cover of Arctic fog and flagged as a civilian freighter, the *MV Obelisk* slipped into Scoresby Sound, citing mechanical failure. Its log showed a cargo of foodstuffs and drilling components bound for Svalbard. No one asked questions.

Once anchored near Cape Brewster, the crew worked fast. Cranes lowered two drab-green shipping containers onto the ice-hardened shoreline. Inside: a disassembled P-18 "Spoon Rest" radar array and its generator system. A five-man technical team, dressed as Arctic researchers, drove the crates inland on tracked utility vehicles and vanished into the frozen interior.

By dawn, the radar stood near a ridgeline overlooking the fjord, its VHF array camouflaged beneath white netting and frost. The crew kept it cold and dark, powered down, silent, watching. A Spetsnaz security element dug into the rocks nearby, their orders clear: hold the site until Vasiliev arrived.

Now, with the BK-10Ms en route and boots about to hit the ice, the radar powered up. Its dish swept the upper atmosphere, hunting American surveillance birds.

Major Aleksandr Vasiliev was preparing for a different type of action as he stood at the stern of the *Petropavlovsk*, not as a scientist but as the commanding officer of his twenty-four Spetsnaz operators. He swept the Scoresby Sound again with his thermal binoculars, searching for movement. As expected, there was none in the isolated fjord, the largest in the world. It was time, and he descended into the ship's cargo hold.

Once in place, he yelled over his radio, "Launch."

Instantly, two bay doors opened, and two Kalashnikov Group BK-10M high-speed assault combat boats revved their engines, causing the large fans to push them out to the sea. The hovercraft can reach extremely high speeds, with a top speed of 117 km/h.

Standing at the helm of the lead boat, Vasiliev continuously scanned one of the few flat areas where they would drive up onto the rocky shore. He heard the hovercraft pilot say over comms, "Five minutes to the landing area." Behind him sat his highly trained Spetsnaz troops with rifles slung across their chests. Several were checking suppressors. Others double-checked the crates of surface-to-air missiles.

Tonight, this part of Greenland would be under Russian control.

BOEING P-8A POSEIDON
1031 Hours, 4 August
Above the Greenland Sea

Lieutenant Commander Alex "Seeker" Hayes adjusted the throttle on his P-8. At cruising speed of 390 knots, he kept his aircraft on a steady course at 32,000 feet as his crew worked through pre-surveillance checks. They were to investigate the Russian scientists who had reported that they were responding to seismic activity near Scoresby Sound.

Yeah, right, Hayes thought. They were probably working for the same assholes who sent his buddy Ghost and his crew to the bottom of the sea and then had the balls to call it an accident. Bastards.

"Seeker," said his co-pilot, Lieutenant Katie Reynolds, "coming up on target area."

"Thanks, Katie. All stations report in, TACCO first."

"Nothing on radar."

"EWO, any RF signals going on?" Hayes said.

"Negative, Seeker, which is strange. Civilians would be using open comms, but I haven't heard a peep."

"Seeker," TACCO said, "picking up multiple heat sources near reported position. Confirming now. Radar shows a cluster of smaller structures with two vehicles near the shoreline."

"Confirm type."

"Shit," TACCO said, "I mean, Seeker, the vehicles are hovercraft. Russian BK-10s."

"Those are military-grade," Reynolds said, "which scientists don't use."

"I'm with you on that, Katie," Hayes said.

He wasted no time and toggled his radio. "Pituffik control, Trident 11. Negative on RF signals. EO/IR scan shows multiple thermal sources where there shouldn't be any on Scoresby Sound shoreline. Small structures and two BK-10 hovercraft. Appears military and not a research camp. Stand by for imagery confirmation."

"Copy, Trident 11. Maintain surveillance. Pickett 11 is inbound for tactical coordination."

Events were ramping up, thought Hayes.

NORTHROP GRUMMAN E-2D ADVANCED HAWKEYE
1032 Hours, 4 August
Above the Greenland Sea

Flying at 25,000 feet, the large radar dish of the E-2 spun steadily, sweeping the Arctic for things that didn't belong. Sarah repositioned herself in her seat for what felt like the umpteenth time. It wasn't easy to stay comfortable during quiet times. She was still adjusting to the continuous daylight, which resulted in different shades of colors throughout the twenty-four hours of sunshine. But radio traffic made her perk up.

"Okay, crew, let's be on alert," she said. "A P-8 is reporting Russian military activity."

"Running full-spectrum sweeps, stand by," the RO said. After a pause, he said, "Nothing."

As they neared the area, Sarah checked all her instruments again, a good habit she'd picked up during the Chinese War after she'd had to ditch in the China Sea, killing her co-pilot.

Don't go there, she scolded herself. She reminded herself that the event was the same time she'd met Jessie, who'd been shot down and was picked up by the same rescue crew. The memories of being in that helicopter were very faint since she'd had a severe concussion. But Jessie had told her that—

"I've got something, Danger," said the RO.

Meanwhile, the P-8 had something too. "Seeker," TACCO said, "are you seeing this? It's definitely too much heat for a civilian operation. There's a power system running along the area, which is anything but temporary."

"For sure, TACCO," Hayes said. "They're hiding something. Let's get a closer look." He adjusted the flight path of his P-8 to optimize the angle of the electro-optical high-resolution camera.

"Seeker, they're using camouflaged nets. Wait a minute, I have a radar trailer under one with antennae above the net."

"Confirm type."

"Mobile radar station, looks like a Russian P-18 Spoon Rest D," TACCO said. "And there's something long and rectangular near the shoreline. Shit, that's a containerized missile launcher."

The cabin went silent momentarily as they all realized this was not a scientific exploration of earthquakes but the beginning of a military incursion.

"Pituffik, Trident 11," Hayes said, voice clipped. "We have a military radar system and possible SAM launchers at the Russian site. This is a military camp."

"Copy, Trident 11. Get clear and report. We're sending in additional assets."

As the P-8 flew out of the area, Major Vasiliev watched the sky through his high-powered binoculars from the ground at the Russian site.

His intelligence officer stated the obvious, "The Americans have found us."

Disregarding his comments, Vasiliev said, "Are we ready?"

"Yes, sir. The jamming suite is online and ready for your orders."

"Then let's make it official," said Vasiliev. "Activate EW. Blind them."

Flying away as ordered, things went from bad to worse on the P-8.

"Pickett 11, Trident 11," Hayes radioed, his voice tight. "Russians are jamming us hard. We're losing radar clarity, and comms are going intermittent."

"Trident 11, Pickett 11, understood," Sarah said. "We're picking up the jammer. Stand by."

Her EWO said, "Ground-based source likely from the Russian camp. Getting a bearing now."

A moment later, the plane's Lockheed Martin AN/ALQ-217 Electronic Support Measure suite isolated the signal. "Danger," EWO said, "ESM's got it. Russian EW system geolocated on the north side of their camp."

Sarah jumped on secure comms. "Pituffik, Pickett 11. We have confirmation of a Russian electronic warfare site in Greenland. Request immediate suppression."

"Pickett 11, copy priority tasking to neutralize jamming system. Support en route."

Chapter 37

1036 Hours, 4 August
Scoresby Sound, Greenland

"Raven 21, pushing to station." Jessie Hampton adjusted his throttle and his F-35 roared toward Scoresby Sound, Greenland. His wingman, Lieutenant "Cutter" Nolan, Raven 22, was close behind.

A mile off his left wing, two EA-18Gs from the USS *Ford* were part of the on-call strike package that Jessie was leading. His new buddy and F-18 Weapons School graduate, Lieutenant Ronnie "Razor" Harper, sat in the lead Growler as Shadow 11. Behind him, his wingman was preparing for their jamming assault.

"Raven 21, Picket 11. We need their jammers disabled to expose their false flag operation. Russian radar and EW assets are located on the north side of the encampment. Coordinates are on your MFD."

Jessie recognized the voice the moment it came through his headset. It was Sarah. She was directing him into battle as casually as if she were telling him to set the table for dinner. To say it felt surreal wouldn't do his feelings justice.

"Copy that, Pickett 11," said Jessie. He toggled to his strike package's frequency. "Razor, you got the target info?" he asked his Growler lead.

"Already locked, Swagger," Harper responded, going hot on his extended range Advanced Anti-Radiation Guided Missiles. "Ready to light 'em up on your command."

"Do it," Jessie said calmly.

The Growlers unleashed four AGM-88G missiles, which streaked toward the Russian radar and jamming systems. "Fox Three, Fox Three," came over comms.

Immediately, both pilots activated their jamming pods, sending high-energy pulses across the spectrum to disrupt Russian fire-control radar and blind their missile defenses. The "scientists" had no place to hide.

Flying her E-2, Freeman was watching the horizon to monitor the impact of her husband's airborne command. A bright, red-orange ball on the surface of the water at the mouth of Scoresby Sound caught her attention instead.

"What the hell?" yelled Sarah over her internal comms as she watched massive explosions rip through the MV *Petropavlovsk*. The Russian cargo ship had just been blown to smithereens.

"Holy shit," Sarah's co-pilot yelled. "They blew up that ship."

Seconds later, four anti-radiation missiles hit the Russian radar site. Huge balls of fire shot skyward. Sarah saw the explosions and noted the slight delay between them.

The E-2's TACCO said, "Distress call in the clear." He put the frequency on intercom for everyone to hear.

"Mayday, Mayday. To all Russian forces, we have been attacked by American aircraft. The *Petropavlovsk* has been hit. NATO is attacking our scientists!"

Chapter 38

SUKHOI SU-35 FLANKER-E FLIGHT
1046 Hours, 4 August
East of Scoresby Sound, Greenland

As part of its Arctic plan, Russia put phase two of Greenland's seizure into operation. Before the cargo ship MV *Petropavlovsk* came to rest at the bottom of the mouth of Scoresby Sound, Russian forces were already airborne in four Ilyushin IL-76s out of Olenya Air Base located on the Kola Peninsula, not far from Finland's northeast border. Flying cover were four Su-35s and two MiG-31BMs. In support were one Beriev A-50 for airborne warning and control, and one refueling tanker. They were all headed for Constable Pynt's civilian airport to set up a base of operations.

The remote airport was devoid of any military presence. It was operated by a small contingent of fifteen civilians whose job was to keep the runway open to serve a nearby remote village. One of those fifteen supported the independence movement and had received a significant payoff from his Russian "friends." He was to ensure that there would be no problems from his coworkers if Russian aircraft approached to land.

That wasn't the same case with Jessie.

1047 Hours, 4 August

Above the Greenland Sea

As the smoke was still rising from the Growler strike on the Russian portable missile site, Hampton heard his Sarah again.

"Raven 21, Pickett 11. New contacts inbound from the east."

"Raven 21, copy. Numbers?"

Orbiting to the west, Sarah's team gathered the data quickly because, in battle, any delay could prove fatal.

"Raven 21, looks like a transport wave. We have four IL-76s escorted by four Su-35s and two MiG-31s at a higher altitude. They're all heading straight for Constable Pynt Airport, coordinates being pushed to you. ETA ten minutes."

"Raven 21 copies all. What info do we have on that airfield?"

"Raven 21, single 4,000-foot runway, recently paved. No taxiways, small gravel parking area. But the Russian transports can land there."

Jessie switched to the strike frequency. "New mission is to deny the IL-76s from landing at the coordinates already pushed to us. Raven 22, we will intercept and get between the transports and the airfield. If they continue, we increase pressure, but do not fire unless we take fire first."

"Raven 22 rodger," said his wingman to acknowledge.

As Jessie gave the orders, he flew toward the airport, letting the other pilots follow him. "Shadow flight, jam the Flankers' radar and comms. If they attempt to engage, jam their missile radar. You heard the ROE."

Just then, comms came onto the Strike frequency. "Raven 21, NATO Command. You are authorized to deny access to the airfield by all available means short of direct engagement. Do not fire unless fired upon."

"Raven 21 copy," said Jessie. "Raven 22, move to intercept."

Jessie jammed the flight stick forward, initiating a 60-degree nose-down trajectory toward the runway. He noted his speed was 500 knots. As he got in the vicinity of the runway, he pulled back on the stick, bleeding speed and transitioning to level flight in just the right spot.

Inside the lead Russian cargo plane, the pilot recognized what the Americans were doing. The F-35s were flying in front of and just below their flight path. "American fighters are blocking my approach," he radioed. "What are my orders?"

Su-35 flight leader Major Viktor Zhukov knew he had seconds to reply. From his eighteen years in the military, he understood the importance of getting feet on the ground. "Proceed. If they don't move, they will be responsible for the consequences."

The transport pilot shook his head and thought about how easily a decision had been made that could get him and his crew killed.

Jessie heard an alarm from his RWR, indicating that a weapons radar had locked onto him. He rolled the dice. "Raven 21 to Russian IL-76, you are attempting to land at a NATO-controlled airfield. Abort your approach immediately."

There was no response, neither vocal nor by a changed flight path. Jessie continued his blocking maneuver to prevent the aircraft from landing.

Inside his EA-18G, Lieutenant Ronnie Harper made a snap decision and deployed a string of infrared flares along the Russian aircraft's descent path. They didn't work.

Jessie tried one last time. "Russian aircraft, this is your final warning. Abort immediately, or you will be intercepted."

Inside the IL-76, the co-pilot yelled as the altimeter got closer to zero, "Break away. We are going to crash!"

The pilot knew if he aborted, he would fail his country. As he saw the American fighter fill his cockpit window, he was determined not to let that happen. He put the large aircraft into a steeper descent. The F-35 rolled left, coming within feet of his transport but opening up the runway approach. The transport plane slammed hard onto the runway, but, accustomed to short takeoffs and landings, the pilot maintained control. Braking hard, he came to the end of the runway and was able to turn onto the hard-packed earth to park. The other three transport planes landed in quick succession behind him.

As the first transport parked, its cargo ramp lowered. Troops from the 76th Guards Air Assault Division stormed out and set up a perimeter. Following them was a Spetsnaz team that split up to take control of the main operations building and other smaller facilities. Ready to kill anyone who resisted, the men were surprised to see airport workers waving at them with big smiles.

Following the troops, specialists quickly debarked the vehicles of the Pantsir S-1 air defense system along with twelve surface-to-air missiles. In no time, they had the SAM systems operational.

Two Russian Kamov Ka-52 attack helicopters, loitering at low altitude, swooped in, providing immediate air cover.

Sarah, flying her E-2, summed it up. "Raven 21, Picket 11. Airfield is compromised. Russian forces are securing the site. They've set up SA-22 Greyhounds."

"Copy, Picket 11. We're pulling back."

Chapter 39

THE KREMLIN
1155 Hours, 4 August
Moscow, Russia

An hour later, President Andrei Petrov sat at the long conference table, thinking it was probably not much different from what the Americans used in their Situation Room. The significant disparity, he thought, was the man sitting at the head of the table and how much shrewder he was than President Taylor.

Petrov's cabinet members and select military leaders filled all the seats. They were viewing the near-total destruction of their scientific headquarters on Scoresby Sound and the sinking of the *MV Petropavlovsk*. The Americans had killed all but three souls in an unprovoked attack. Once again, it was time to let the world know how Russia would respond.

"The document is ready for you, Mr. President," his foreign minister said.

"You all have had the opportunity to assist with the writing and, more importantly, the input. Do all of you approve?"

Sixteen hands shot up in the air, each person wanting to be the first to show their commitment to Petrov.

"Thank you, comrades. Release it."

The Russian leaders remained seated, waiting for the next part of their plan to be put into action. Minutes later, a technician switched the feed, and on the screen appeared a solemn-faced news anchor whom Petrov himself had chosen. The man was wearing a dark suit with a prominent Russian flag pinned to the lapel.

Good evening, citizens of Russia and our brothers and sisters around the world. We have just received tragic news from the Arctic region. American fighter aircraft have launched an unprovoked attack on a Russian research facility in Greenland, which is housing scientists investigating the recent tremors in the area. This blatant, unprovoked attack resulted in significant casualties. Additionally, the civilian cargo ship MV Petropavlovsk, carrying humanitarian and scientific supplies, was ruthlessly sunk by NATO aircraft. This act of barbarism has shocked our nation and the world.

The screen cut to footage showing smoke rising from the sinking cargo vessel. Three people could be seen jumping into the water. The narrator, well-trained in presenting the news that Petrov had approved, spoke again, this time with controlled rage.

This brutal aggression, initiated by the United States and NATO, is an act of war. It is the same pattern of American imperialism we have seen time and time again. Today, they do it in Greenland. Tomorrow, it could be Moscow itself.

Let us be clear. This attack cannot go unpunished. Russian citizens have been murdered in cold blood by American forces. Our peaceful scientists, our sailors, and our humanitarian workers are all victims of NATO aggression.

The camera cut to a Russian survivor, wrapped in a blanket, who had studio blood smeared on his face. His voice shook and tears formed in his eyes as he recounted his rehearsed story.

I was on the ship when the first missile hit. There was no warning. I heard the screams of my friends, the scientists, and the doctors. They were burning alive. The Americans gave us no warning. They wanted to kill us all.

The camera cut back to the news anchor.

The Russian people will never forget this hideous crime. The families of those lost today will not be

ignored. President Petrov has vowed swift and decisive action.

For the next act, the camera showed a live feed of the president sitting at the table with his council. His rage was evident to the millions worldwide watching this developing story. Petrov's expression was grave as he spoke.

The Russian Federation has always stood for peace. We have always sought cooperation, stability, and friendship among nations. But today, our patience has been tested beyond its limits.

Petrov leaned closer to the camera as if addressing each Russian citizen personally, something he had rehearsed many times.

The United States has lied to the world again. They have called us aggressors while they invade, destroy, and kill. They tell their people they are defending democracy, but today, their bombs have murdered our innocent civilians. This is an appalling crime against humanity.

The Russian news director, with years of experience working with the president, went to a split screen to show images of the *MV Petropavlovsk* burning in the Arctic waters, the bombed-out Russian encampment, and American F-35s and Growlers edited to make them look like they were attacking the ship.

This attack will not go unanswered. As of this moment, I have ordered immediate military reinforcements to Greenland to protect our scientists from further NATO aggression. We are deploying additional peacekeeping forces to ensure that such atrocities do not happen again as our scientists attempt to ascertain what caused the seismic activity affecting shipping lanes in the area.

Comrades, this was not just an attack on Russia. It was an attack on all nations that resist American imperialism. We call upon our allies and all countries that value sovereignty and peace to stand with us in condemning NATO's aggression.

The world now watches what the United States will do next. Russia will defend itself. We will not be intimidated. And if NATO chooses to continue this path of war, then the consequences will be theirs to bear.

The camera went black, and many watching wondered what else would go black.

Chapter 40

INTELLIGENCE OPERATIONS CENTER
2206 Hours, 4 August
Pituffik Space Base, Greenland

Greenland had long been a quiet outpost in the Arctic, but that changed with Russia's renewed expansionism in the twenty-first century, first evident in Ukraine and now pressing north.

Nobody knew that better than the team assembled in a large room at Pituffik Space Base to discuss what happened less than twelve hours prior when the MV *Petropavlovsk* sank. Large monitors displayed the recorded satellite imagery, electronic warfare logs, and infrared footage from the P-8 and E-2.

Captain Ryan McCallister, the Air Force intelligence officer assigned to Arctic operations, peered at a console where an Air Force signals intelligence analyst, Staff Sergeant Julia Gilbert, was filtering through an intercepted Russian radio transmission.

"This is the one flagged by NSA." Gilbert adjusted the audio settings of the transmission that the National Security Agency had indicated might be worth investigating. "They're still decrypting it, but they identified key Russian call signs matching a Spetsnaz ground unit at the encampment.”

McCallister nodded. “Anything useful yet?”

Gilbert pointed to a waveform analysis showing distinct voice imprints. “We’ve got a near-instantaneous spike in transmissions right before the Petropavlovsk exploded. This wasn’t a distress call. This was a detonation order. Here it is.”

She clicked a file, and the audio, now partially translated, played over the speakers. “All teams, prepare for final phase. Confirm sequence.”

A second voice said, “Final phase confirmed. Detonation in T-minus fifteen seconds.”

Then a new voice, urgent and almost panicked, said, “Wait. There are still men aboard.”

The original person quickly jumped in, “Execute. No delays.”

The recording then went to static.

“Great work, Gilbert. That’s our confirmation. The Russians sank their own ship and left their people aboard without giving it a second thought.”

Colonel William Grayson, commanding officer at Pituffik, walked up. “Do we have visual confirmation?”

Captain McCallister turned to the colonel and said, “Hell yes, I mean, yes, sir, we do. Airman Nash, please show him what you were able to uncover.”

Sitting at the adjoining workstation, Senior Airman James Nash said, "Yes, sir. You are about to see a high-resolution infrared and electro-optical video taken by the P-8."

He made a few strokes on his keyboard, and a video popped up on his monitor. The screen displayed a thermal image of the MV *Petropavlovsk* just moments before the explosion. The video progressed in slow motion, timestamped and geolocated to the exact coordinates of the Russian encampment.

"This was taken exactly 42 seconds before detonation," Nash said, zooming in. "You can see faint movement along the deck. Some crew members were still aboard."

As the video slowly advanced, Nash said, "Now, watch for an internal explosion." As he said this, a bright white flash suddenly erupted from deep within the ship's hull, the infrared sensors registering an immediate heat bloom.

McCallister pointed at the screen. "That's not an external impact from our missiles but an internal detonation aboard the ship."

Nash cross-referenced it with synthetic aperture radar data from the P-8. "The explosion began in the midsection, directly near the bulk cargo hold. If this had been a missile strike, we would first see a concentrated heat signature on the outer hull. Instead, this detonated from within."

He switched the screen to electro-optical footage, taken simultaneously by the P-8's cameras. This time, the explosion was in full color, with a rapid expansion of fire and debris tearing the vessel apart. Both officers exhaled in disbelief at the explosives' instant destruction.

They all knew this intelligence was critical for White House decision-makers, starting with President Taylor. Colonel Grayson said, "Get this packaged with the SIGINT find and send it to the NSA and the Pentagon immediately."

The world needed to see this.

Chapter 41

THE WHITE HOUSE
0550 Hours, 5 August
Washington, DC

President Taylor sat at the head of the Situation Room's conference table surrounded by his NSC experts. His eyes were fixed on the infrared and electro-optical footage taken from the P-8. The sequence was undeniable: The explosion originated inside the MV *Petropavlovsk*, and the ship broke apart without any external missile impact. Most of those in the room were seeing the footage for the first time. There were gasps as America's elite minds grasped the situation. Interpretations came fast and furious.

The first to speak was DNI Elena Ramirez. "This is an ironclad case. The Russians staged the entire thing, making it look like we were responsible."

SecState Brad Kelly nodded in agreement. "Moscow has already flooded their media with claims that we attacked their ship and bombed their research teams. China and Iran are backing them. France and Germany are calling for de-escalation. We need to get the word out."

"This is so Russian," said CJCS Kincaid. "They create the crisis, and we're the ones on defense. While we have infighting, they strengthen their position, all the while pointing the finger of guilt straight at us."

Ramirez said, "We need to take control of the narrative. I suggest we declassify everything: the infrared footage, the radio transcripts, and the timeline. We give it to NATO, the UN, and every major news outlet before Russia can solidify its version of events. We must show the world the liars they are."

Looking disgusted with being tricked, SecDef George Mitchell said, "It won't stop Moscow from denying it, but it'll put them on the defensive."

President Taylor interjected, "George, bring us up to date on what the Russians are doing at this moment." A staffer approached him and slid a note in front of him when he finished speaking.

"Yes, Mr. President, as of seven hours ago, we had multiple Russian IL-76 transport planes land at Constable Pynt Airport on Greenland's east coast. They were escorted by Su-35s. It's clear they are reinforcing their presence, making any removal operation much harder."

Kincaid jumped in, "Then we turn them—"

"Just a minute," said Taylor. "Denmark's on the hotline, saying they're going to invoke Article 5 immediately. We need to address that first. Brad?"

"From a State Department perspective," said Kelly, "not yet. Russia's move into Greenland is a military incursion based on an emergency response to seismic activity in the area. They fear that it could affect the shipping lanes. Additionally, there hasn't been a direct Russian attack on Denmark, and the Russians are now claiming self-defense after they falsely reported our attack on their civilian ship." He gestured toward the screen. "By proving Moscow orchestrated everything, we will gain more international support. I believe we can rally NATO to act under a coalition response without escalating to full-scale war."

"I would like to add," said Kincaid, "if we invoke Article 5 now, we're committing NATO forces to direct conflict with Russia and possibly China, which supports Russia in the Arctic. That means more than just air intercepts; it also involves deploying ground troops and naval forces and potentially engaging Russian forces directly in combat. Right now, I doubt European leaders will go for that without clear evidence that Russia initiated an unprovoked attack. That takes time and more proof than what we've got."

"Agree, this is more a NATO crisis, not a NATO war," said Ramirez.

Several other heads nodded. Mitchell added, "We still have military options short of Article 5. We can impose a NATO-enforced no-fly zone over Greenland, intercept Russian transports, and blockade their supply lines."

Kincaid said, "If the Russians fire on our aircraft, that's the game changer. If they shoot first, that provides us with legal justification under Article 5."

"Okay," said Taylor, "we push them back without pulling NATO into an all-out war. We expose their lies, enforce a blockade and no-fly zone, and make it clear that if they escalate, we will invoke Article 5. I'll speak with Denmark while you make it happen."

Chapter 42

HDMS EJNAR MIKKELSEN

6 August

Coastal waters of Jameson Land, Greenland

Commander Anders Nyholm peered through his binoculars from the bridge of the HDMS *Ejnar Mikkelsen*. He was an eighteen-year veteran of the Royal Danish Navy and had recently seen action against pirates operating in the Gulf of Guinea off the coast of Nigeria. In that action, Nyholm's naval forces killed four pirates and captured five others. Now he was patrolling off the east coast of Greenland, Denmark's territory, and this time his adversary was Russia.

"XO, status report," he said. "Any communication from Constable Pynt?"

"Negative, sir. Constable Pynt is dark. Radar has shown multiple aerial contacts descending inland. Most likely additional Russian aircraft."

Nyholm lowered his binoculars. "They're landing troops."

"Sir, the last message from NATO said that we are to observe, report, and not engage unless provoked."

"Such bullshit," Nyholm mumbled. Russian forces were invading Greenland, and he was ordered just to observe.

"Captain, contact bearing zero-eight-three, altitude low, speed climbing," the sonar operator reported, unable to hide the tension in his voice. "Looks like two fast movers."

The tactical officer glanced at the screen. "Russian IFF squawk, Su-30s. Probably from Nagurskoye."

On the bridge, Nyholm raised his binoculars as twin shapes emerged from the misty horizon, sun glinting off their twin tails. Painted in low-vis Arctic gray, the Su-30s dropped to just above wave height, banking sharply to cross the ship's bow at 400 knots.

"They're painting us," the EW officer said. "Kh-31 lock, probably a simulated targeting run."

Nyholm turned to his fire-control officer. "Bring the OTO Melara online. Do it quietly. Targeting solution only."

"Aye, sir. 76 is locking, bearing zero-eight-five."

Nyholm knew all too well that if this show of force by the Russians went sideways, he would be severely outmatched, and in combat, that means death.

Outside the bridge windows, the lead Su-30 swung around again in a wide arc, slower this time, as if daring them to react. The ship's gun servos tracked it silently.

The XO jumped in. "Captain, should we challenge them?"

Nyholm shook his head. "No open comms. No saber-rattling. They know we are here and ready to engage if necessary."

"Captain, "surface contact, bearing zero-two-one, hull up," Radar reported over the intercom. "Visual confirmation coming in now."

Nyholm stepped to the starboard bridge wing, lifting his binoculars. The ship on the horizon was coming into sharper detail, with a low-slung, squat profile, a square superstructure well forward, and an open deck in the stern. No flag, and the hull number looked deliberately obscured. The captain noted that it wasn't painted over hastily; it had been removed. There was no ensign, but the experienced captain didn't need one. "That's a Ropucha-class amphibious landing ship. Russian."

Nyholm grabbed the radio mic. "Unidentified Russian vessel, this is Commander Anders Nyholm of the Royal Danish Navy. You are in Danish territorial waters and conducting unauthorized military operations. Cease operations and withdraw immediately, or we will be forced to stop you."

There was no response.

After a couple of moments had passed, Nyholm figured that if the Russians were going to fire, they would have done so by now. He reasoned this was a scare tactic to get them out of the area.

The only man aboard the HDMS *Ejnar Mikkelsen* who could decide to reply to this infiltration on Greenland was him, but he could hear the words ringing in his ears—no first strike.

"Weapons, use the 76," Nyholm ordered. "Fire one warning burst off the bow of the Russian ship."

WEPS reported ready, and immediately the OTO Melara 76mm naval gun barked a short, thunderous burst, sending a shell into the water 200 meters ahead of the ship.

One of the circling Su-30s broke ranks. It roared down sharply, diving low across the *Mikkelsen*'s bow, followed by a warning shot from the Russian ship.

"Royal Danish Navy vessel," said a voice over the radio, "you are interfering in an authorized Russian scientific operation. You have fired without cause. This is a reckless and aggressive act. Withdraw immediately, or you will be held responsible for escalation."

Before he could answer, a radio transmission came through. "Ejnar Mikkelsen, this is the Danish Joint Arctic Command. Do not escalate. Record and report. Withdraw from the fjord."

The Danish crew watched as the Russian ship surged forward, its engines churning dark water beneath the bow. As it neared the shoreline, it slowed and beached itself with a heavy groan of steel on rock. Moments later, the ship's massive bow split open. A ramp dropped, and armored vehicles rolled down onto the frozen sand, followed by naval infantry moving in tight formation.

Nyholm contemplated his next move. His XO took notes, and just as the second-in-command was about to comment, the captain ordered, "Bridge, come about, plot a course to open water. Weapons, keep the gun hot."

Soon after *Ejnar Mikkelsen* left the area, Russian state media broadcast video footage of the Danish warship appearing to be firing its weapon at the Russians. What wasn't shown was anything related to the Russian ships and troops landing; it was just a looped video of the Danes firing on the Russian ship, making it appear as if several rounds were fired. The broadcaster reported exactly what he had been told to say.

Today, Danish naval forces recklessly opened fire on a Russian peacekeeping vessel delivering humanitarian supplies and medical personnel to Greenland. Thanks to the Russian crews' calm and professional actions, escalation was avoided. Russia demands accountability for Denmark's provocative actions in sovereign Arctic waters. And be warned. Russia reserves the right to defend its peacekeeping missions.

Meanwhile, at Constable Pynt Airport and along the fjord's shoreline, Russian forces were now dug in with no shots fired at them. The world remained silent.

Chapter 43

NATO HEADQUARTERS
August 7
Brussels, Belgium

It had been three days since Russia moved into Greenland, and NATO was still attempting to coordinate a response. Despite all the divisive arguing, a majority of nations had reached a consensus on how to deal with Russia.

Thirty-two NATO ambassadors and the Secretary General, with his senior staff, occupied seats at the oval table for the meeting of the North Atlantic Council. Large screens hung high at each corner of the room displayed satellite imagery, intercepted communications text, and a live feed from a US Northrop Grumman RQ-4 Global Hawk orbiting above eastern Greenland. They were all listening to Danish Prime Minister Henrik Hansen, who repeated the same points he had been making over the last three days.

"As I have said repeatedly, Russia has seized sovereign Danish territory. There is no ambiguity. There is no misunderstanding. Constable Pynt Airport is our land. The Russians have deployed troops, weapons, and missiles, and have established a base that will now be most difficult to dislodge. This is an invasion in every practical and legal sense. Denmark is calling on NATO to respond under the terms of our alliance. We ask for a declaration of Article 5."

He looked at the leaders seated around the table. "And yet, we hesitate. Three days have passed. What signal do we send to the world if NATO cannot respond to one of its signatory nations being invaded? Is this Ukraine all over again?"

Some murmurs broke the silence.

The US Ambassador raised his eyebrows and shook his head. "The United States shares Denmark's outrage. And we agree that Russia's actions are unacceptable. But we also understand what Russia is up to. This wasn't a blitzkrieg, as in Ukraine. They're occupying just enough territory to provoke a crisis that's just outside of the limits to trigger Article 5."

He stared directly into Hansen's eyes and made a point shared by many in the room. "They want us to strike first. They want the narrative to flip. If we launch a vigorous response now, we risk dragging the alliance and possibly the world into full-scale war. Russia wants us to act rashly. The moment NATO fires the first shot, Moscow floods the world with claims that we escalated, that we attacked peacekeepers, and that we're the aggressors. China, Iran, and half the Global South will side with them or at least remain neutral. We need to be smart, not fast."

The Polish ambassador stood next, her voice sharp and unapologetic. "Sharing a 232-kilometer border with Russia's Kaliningrad Oblast, my country has always been waiting for the next boot to drop right on us. We have warned this council for years that Russia doesn't need to fire the first shot. They take a little at a time and dare us to act, like in Crimea, Donbas, Abkhazia, and Ukraine. And now, like in Greenland. We draw red lines, and they draw new maps."

She directed her gaze to the ambassadors from the US and the Western European nations. "Every time we hesitate, they dig in deeper. Denmark has been invaded. If NATO doesn't respond now, the Article 5 guarantee is a myth, and every one of us along Russia's border knows what comes next. If you will not fight for Greenland, will you fight for Latvia? Or Estonia? Poland demands action now."

The chairman called on the French ambassador, who remained seated. "France does not question Denmark's claim nor Russia's intentions. But be honest, invoking Article 5 would escalate this into a conflict for which Europe is unprepared. We are still recovering from years of economic strain. We must consider proportional response before invoking mutual defense."

The German ambassador didn't wait to be called upon. "Germany stands with Denmark. But we must act deliberately. There are still diplomatic channels. There is still the UN. If we escalate now, we risk losing the support of our populations and further dividing this alliance. If we go to war, let it be on terms we choose, not those set by Moscow."

The British ambassador said, "The UK stands firmly with Denmark. But we must ensure NATO acts as one. A splintered response helps no one. If Article 5 is not supported, we are prepared to consider other means, such as coalition response, expeditionary deployment, sanctions, and cyber action. But most importantly, we cannot appear weak."

"Let's be realistic here," said the Italian ambassador. "My country has no strategic interests in the Arctic. We do not minimize Denmark's loss, but we must protect our interests in the Mediterranean. A war in the north could divert resources away from other obligations, such as those in Libya, migration, and the Balkans. We caution against hasty entanglement." Sitting next to him, the ambassadors from Spain and Greece nodded in agreement.

NATO Secretary General Marcus van Dijk, a blond-haired Dutchman, scanned the large room. "Distinguished colleagues, we have completed emergency consultations under Article 4. We have reviewed Denmark's request to invoke Article 5. We have heard the arguments, and we have deliberated fully."

As he paused, every eye was on him to hear what most expected. "As you know, the NATO treaty does not authorize formal voting procedures for Article 5. Consensus is required of all thirty-two nations. Currently, that consensus does not exist. Therefore, Article 5 will not be invoked."

Groans were heard from eastern-flank nations. Denmark's ambassador shook his head in disgust.

The Secretary General continued, "We will, however, continue operations under Article 4. We will increase joint reconnaissance patrols in the North Atlantic and Arctic airspace, accelerate regional force posture reviews, and establish a special working group to coordinate Arctic security. We will also reaffirm our commitment to Danish sovereignty and condemn the Russian Federation's unauthorized military presence in Greenland in the strongest possible terms."

He looked down. What he said next came from his heart and his feelings for Denmark. "Our strength is unity. And unity must endure even when our instincts diverge. But let me say this clearly, NATO cannot remain forever in a state of deliberation. The world is watching. Moscow is watching. Our enemies do not wait for the debate to finish. They exploit it. If we do not act, we must prepare for what comes next because this will not be the end. It's only the beginning."

Chapter 44

Constable Pynt Airport

August 7

East of Scoresby Sound, Greenland

Colonel Mikhail Barinov always chose the field over a desk in his twenty-three years of service. The broad-shouldered Russian with a buzz cut that was still completely black had fought in Chechnya, Syria, and most recently, Ukraine. He demanded everything from his peers and subordinates, and in return, he gave them respect, which to a soldier was all that mattered. He was the kind of leader few could rival, and there weren't many soldiers who wouldn't follow him into any fight. Barinov believed that the fighting moment could come at any time as he oversaw the takeover of Greenland from his foothold at Constable Pynt Airport.

It was day four, and reinforcements and defensive equipment couldn't arrive fast enough. As he stood in the filtered light shining through the window that was covered with camouflage netting, he unzipped his parka and turned to the makeshift operations table, which was a collection of crates. He studied the maps held down on the table by grenades. Just then, a junior officer entered, his boots covered in mud from the melting snow.

"Sir, our Orlan drone confirmed two heat signatures in the foothills north of Ridge Three. Likely Danish recon or a US scout team."

Barinov didn't bother to look up as he moved a red enemy token across the map. "Lieutenant, set a Spetsnaz ambush line behind the rocks east of the snowmelt basin. Also, deploy two snipers with suppressed VSS rifles. No firefights. Eyes only, unless they cross the ridgeline."

"Yes, Colonel," the young man said, saluted, and left.

Another man entered, this time a captain of a Spetsnaz team. "Sir, the Ka-52s are ready for their security patrol."

"Okay, Captain, I want them to fly low but make sure they're easily seen. I want NATO to see we are controlling the area."

"Yes, sir, on it now." He quickly left the tent.

Turning to his radio operator, Barinov said, "Comms, I want the status on the next transport aircraft."

"Sir, it's five minutes out," said the pimply nineteen-year-old kid.

As Barinov went back to studying the maps, he knew that every inch he gained today would be another NATO debate tomorrow, delaying their response even more.

Chapter 45

USS FORD

0600 Hours, 7 August

Greenland Sea

Sitting in his usual seat up front in the ready room, Jessie listened to the intel officer and liked her style of no bullshit and to-the-point, just like the way he flew his F-35.

"This morning," she said, "we're continuing full-spectrum ISR coverage along the eastern Greenland air corridor. Russian forces continue to expand their footprint at Constable Pynt, including the reinforcement of radar coverage and the probable deployment of S-400 Triumf surface-to-air missiles, also known as SA-21 Growlers by NATO. Expect Su-35s as air support."

All pilots sat up straighter, knowing that the SAM system was an ass-kicker. It had a long reach of over 200 miles and used VHF to identify stealth aircraft.

As intel sat down, the Operations Officer continued the brief. A slide showing aircraft call signs and dedicated frequencies appeared on the screen at the front of the room. "Hawkeye Echo-One, an RQ-4 Global Hawk, will begin its first racetrack pass over the northeastern surveillance arc at 0615Z. You're tasked with outer-layer security. Expect increased radar emissions and possible Russian interceptors, as with previous missions, but the last 72 hours have shown more aggressive posturing from their side.

"Raven 21, Hampton, is your flight leader. The flight will maintain a southern escort track, high and fast, approximately 20 miles south of Raven 31's flight path. This track will fly offset north at a slightly lower altitude and act as an early intercept or recovery path if Raven 21 is forced down. Maintain EMCON Charlie, and keep AESA radar passive unless a threat emerges. Pickett 21 will provide the battlespace picture. Questions?" There were none, so the CAG took over.

Captain Mad Dog Johnson was another no-nonsense guy. "Listen up. Here are your ROEs." A slide appeared on the screen. "Maintain Weapons Hold unless one of the following conditions is met:"

1. You are fired upon or you visually observe a hostile launch against your aircraft or any friendly asset.
2. You are locked up by a fire-control radar and believe a hostile act is imminent, then you report it immediately and prepare to defend.
3. A Russian aircraft crosses into international airspace and performs a hostile act such as threatening intercept behavior, warning shots, or unsafe maneuvers.

Mad Dog paused a moment to let the pilots review the words on the slide. "If any of these three conditions occur, then the ROE shifts to Weapons Free in self-defense. But do not fire pre-emptively. You are not authorized to enter Russian-claimed airspace without direct approval from the strike group commander via me or the Ford CIC."

The CAG nodded, and the screen went dark. "Okay, no cowboy shit. Just stay cool and safe. We're walking a razor's edge today. The Global Hawk is unarmed and legal under international law. If they hit it, it's not just an escalation, it's a declaration. Your job is to watch, deter, and survive. If the balloon goes up, don't hesitate. Just don't start it. Jessie, you're lead. Everyone else watches each other's six. Dismissed."

Chapter 46

0708 Hours, 7 August
Constable Pynt Airport

Colonel Mikhail Barinov stood inside the improvised command center, the back half of one of the airport's existing buildings fortified on the exterior with pallets of equipment still wrapped in plastic. Bare desks had been replaced with hardened consoles, and thick communication cables snaked across the floor. So far, so good, thought Barinov as he noticed his aide coming over.

"Colonel, the latest satellite pass confirms the Americans launched another Global Hawk out of Thule, or I should say, Pituffik."

"What is the route? Same as the first one?"

"Yes, sir, identical. High-altitude track at 60,000 feet. It's orbiting northeast of our position, roughly 30 kilometers offshore, loitering and transmitting continuously."

Barinov casually walked over to the window and looked at the makeshift parking ramp where aircraft were unloading pallet after pallet of supplies. Beyond that, rows of camouflaged tents stretched out. Armored vehicles dotted the area, including several Uralvagonzavod T-90M Proryv, his most advanced tanks. So many decisions made and so many more to make, he thought.

"Sir," said his radar operator, "the Global Hawk just made a slow turn, now running parallel to our southern flank. It's painting our Triumf site."

That made the decision easy. "Fire," Barinov said.

"Confirming—"

"You heard me. Take it out."

The launch command was relayed. On the outer perimeter, a 40N6 super-long-range surface-to-air missile surged from the S-400 Triumf launcher, and the sound penetrated the thick walls of the command center.

RAVEN FLIGHT
0709 Hours, 7 August
Patrol over the Greenland Sea

Jessie Hampton scanned the horizon from his F-35 as he flew according to the mission brief. It was a beautiful day in the Arctic, with clear skies, a bright sun, and shadows on the sea cast by the occasional iceberg. But on land, there were darker shadows because the Russians were taking advantage of the uninterrupted buildup of Constable Pynt Airport. He didn't like it; nobody did. He was a fighter pilot and ready to prove it.

He'd seen in the mission brief that there would be no Sarah today. Instead, he had a crew from *Ford* giving him eyes on the playing field. "Picket 21, Raven 21," Jessie radioed, "How's Global Hawk doing?"

"Raven 21, as you can see, flying at 60 angels in international airspace and traveling north–south along the Russian front. Be advised that we're collecting coverage of the SA-21 emplacement. They've been rotating radar modes with lots of emitter discipline, like they're trying to look innocent."

Just then, Jessie's threat receiver sounded.

"Swagger," Jessie's wingman, Lieutenant Jace "Cutter" Nolan said, "RWR just lit up. Long-range. SA-21's painting the drone, not us."

Jessie's eyes shot to his Distributed Aperture System screen. A thin red triangle flashed, indicating S-band lock, long track, and a range of 50 to 70 miles.

"Raven 21, Pickett 21. Missile in the air. Repeat, missile in the air. It's a 40N6, bearing zero-six-zero, range 60 miles."

Jessie twisted in his seat, eyes flicking to the upper-right quadrant of his helmet display. The RQ-4's transponder data and radar signature painted it clean at sixty thousand feet and holding a lazy figure-eight pattern above the coast. Then it was gone.

"Raven 21, Pickett 21. Global Hawk telemetry cut. Missile impact confirmed. No recovery signals."

"Swagger," said Nolan, "SA-22 Greyhound active."

Jessie knew exactly what the Russians were doing. They were using their SA-22 radar to identify aircraft that might target their SA-21 batteries. What his next move would be was a decision above his pay grade.

Jessie toggled his comms. "Ford Actual, Raven 21. We just lost the Global Hawk. Request guidance to hold or to RTB."

"Raven 21, fall back to Phase Line Bravo. No direct engagement unless fired upon."

Jessie acknowledged, but his hands flexed on the stick. Everything in him wanted to roll in low and fast to show them they couldn't fire without consequence. But orders were clear: no engagement. Not yet, anyway.

Chapter 47

USS Idaho
0735 Hours, 7 August
Greenland Sea

"Captain, 180 miles east of Constable Pynt," came the call from Navigation.

Captain Blake Stanton stood behind the conn, one hand resting on the back of the diving officer's chair as his thoughts focused on a plot against the *Kazan*. Around him, the crew was bathed in a dim red glow. It was tense. Every crew member knew they were inside contested waters, treading a fine line between caution and outright confrontation.

"Control, Sonar," came the calm voice of his principal sonar operator, Emily Reyes. "Contact acquired. Very faint. Bearing zero-eight-five. Intermittent screw blade harmonics, non-American signature."

"Classify."

"Stand by." Reyes adjusted the gain on her screen. "Profile matches Yasen class. Probable ID is the Kazan."

All those in earshot thought the same thing: they're back. This was the third time the *Idaho* had picked up the *Kazan* in a week. But this time was different. The *Kazan* wasn't shadowing a surface ship or guarding a known supply route.

It's hunting the *Idaho*, thought Stanton.

"Depth?" the captain inquired.

"Sir, level with us," said Reyes.

Stanton stood over the navigation plot. The water was deep but narrow, with ice to the north and a shelf to the west. The *Kazan* was herding them toward a dead zone.

"They're boxing us in," he muttered. "They think we're the eyes for a NATO strike package."

"Captain, FLASH message from COMSUBLANT. They've confirmed a Global Hawk was downed by an SA-21 battery near Constable Pynt about twenty minutes ago."

His XO came to stand next to him. "It seems to me things are escalating."

Stanton looked back at Harrington and said nothing.

He thought it was time to make things more difficult for the enemy and become invisible. "Helm, reduce speed to five knots. Take us under the thermocline to 800 feet."

As the boat angled downward, soft groans vibrated through the hull.

"Control, Sonar," said Reyes. "Active ping. Single pulse. Narrow beam."

That told Stanton the *Kazan* knew roughly where the *Idaho* was running. The Russian commander wasn't bluffing. His boat was closing fast, changing angles, sweeping with narrow-beam sonar—hunting, not warning.

The Idaho went deep, hidden from radar and silent on comms. But even a faint wake or a swirl of warmer water could betray her. In the Arctic, silence was always fragile.

"Deploy decoy," Stanton ordered, voice low but firm. "Noisemaker only. Push it to starboard and shallow."

The fire-control officer didn't hesitate. "Loading ADC Mk-4, preset depth one-twenty feet, offset bearing zero-two-zero."

Within seconds, the countermeasures tech entered the data. Hydraulic actuators engaged with a soft thump as the small cylindrical decoy was shunted into position.

"Tube Five ready."

"Launch."

A muted whoosh vibrated through the deck plates as the canister slid clear and the small expendable entered the water. The ADC Mk-4 activated almost at once, running a programmed noisemaker profile to mimic a fast-moving submarine at moderate depth. Screw harmonics, broadband machinery noise, and randomized cavitation pulses were emitted in patterns meant to confuse a homing torpedo's tracker rather than perfectly reproduce any single vessel. The sound signature bled into the Arctic black; the Idaho held her breath and slipped away.

"Decoy running," Reyes confirmed. "It's drawing attention. Kazan's bearing is shifting, a slight angle change."

Stanton stared at the sonar's plot. The Russian boat was reacting. That's good, he thought. Let them chase shadows.

He gave orders for the *Idaho* to turn toward the sea route the Russians were using to supply Constable Pynt.

Chapter 48

CHRISTIANSBORG PALACE

7 August

Copenhagen, Denmark

Around a large table, the elite of Denmark sat in an emergency meeting of the Foreign Policy Committee. Leading the discussion was Prime Minister Henrik Hansen. Held in a secure wing of Christiansborg Palace, everyone was behind reinforced doors and under the constant watch of armed agents from the Security and Intelligence Service. Deep inside the historic structure, away from tourists and the press, heavy drapes were drawn tightly, blocking the gray dawn in Copenhagen. A digital clock in the corner reminded everyone how long it had been since Russia had invaded Greenland and how long since they'd received no help except from the Americans.

The attendees had been discussing the lack of support from NATO, specifically their failure to invoke Article 5 after the Russian invasion, which cited unusual seismic activity as a pretext.

"The Americans won't commit fully," said General Henrik Lyhne. "Their focus is elsewhere. And since NATO isn't going to invoke Article 5, time is fast running out."

The prime minister nodded. "Let me add that I just got off the phone with the German chancellor, who urged strategic patience. Paris said nothing of value. Even the Brits were cautious, citing logistic limits and legal ambiguity about Greenland's status under NATO's defense clause."

The defense minister added, "Yes, they'll all hold meetings, issue statements, and do nothing. Meanwhile, the Russians are turning our airport into a forward operating base to take all of Greenland from us, exactly like they did in Ukraine."

The foreign minister added, "If we act without NATO, we risk isolating ourselves. We all know we can't win this alone."

"We're not trying to win a war," said Hansen. "We're trying to ensure there's still something left to defend when NATO finally comes to their senses."

He paused and scanned the room to emphasize his next point. "We have a window, maybe a week. Once the runway is extended, they can land anything they want. There will be armor, heavy artillery, maybe even long-range missiles. After that, no strike will succeed without a full-scale war."

The room was quiet. No one disagreed. All eyes were on him.

"Prepare our forces," Hansen said passionately. "We will go in hard, hit fast, and show the Russians and the world that we are not afraid to defend what is ours."

The decision was made. Denmark would act alone.

Chapter 49

PITUFFIK SPACE BASE
0400 Hours, 8 August
Greenland

Royal Danish Air Force Major Christian Olesen strapped himself into his F-35A, happy to have said goodbye to the F-16 he and others had been flying for years. Welcome to the twenty-first century, he thought. He knew today he would need all the technology and stealth of his fifth-generation fighter. As the flight leader for nine other F-35s, he was so ready to kick some Russian ass.

As he led his flight to the runway, he taxied over frost clinging to the tarmac and blew the white stuff into little vortices. Inside his helmet's heads-up display, he saw his planned flight route outlined in a cool green color. Their ingress track hugged the ice cap and weaved through the deep fjords of East Greenland. His weapons systems screen displayed his four Stand-in Attack Weapon air-to-surface missiles, armed and ready. Final confirmation for the mission came through a brief, coded datalink burst; all ten aircraft were green.

At 0417 hours, Olesen pushed the throttle forward and rolled. His jet lifted, disappearing almost immediately into the everlasting twilight of the summer night. The rest of his flight followed, spaced at precise intervals.

Once airborne, they all maintained terrain-hugging altitudes to stay below the Russian radar horizon. They flew under EMCON Alpha, meaning strict emissions control. There was no radar, external communications, or Multi-function Advanced Datalink or Link 16 chatter. Every aircraft followed prebriefed waypoints and precise timing, relying on inertial navigation and onboard systems.

Each F-35 carried four SiAW air-to-surface missiles to engage enemy radar, SAM sites, and command nodes. The SiAWs were hung in the internal weapon bays to maintain stealth and high-speed standoff attack capabilities. With a range exceeding 200 nautical miles and accuracy to less than a meter, the SiAWs were built to penetrate modern integrated air defense systems without compromising the F-35's low-observable profile.

As the pilots clung to their programmed routes, they carved through the sky above them the fractured landscape with surgical precision by diving into glacial valleys, vanishing behind jagged ridges, and staying low over the frozen earth. From above, they were ghosts. From below, they were shadows moving beneath Russian radar.

Their route took them east across the Greenland Ice Sheet, then down into the labyrinth of fjords west of Jameson Land. At under 500 feet above ground level, they passed over ice-covered rivers and narrow canyons where no human had set foot in decades.

Nearing the release points, Olesen's targeting overlay activated automatically. Russian radar emissions had been triangulated from a week-long array of signals intelligence. Radars, air surveillance arrays, and fire-control units were all buried in snow berms or mounted on mobile launchers around Constable Pynt. But each one was marked on Olesen's overlay. Each one was assigned.

At precisely 0444 hours, the bomb bay doors on the F-35As cycled open in perfect unison. Two SiAWs dropped cleanly from each jet, vanishing into the Arctic darkness on their strike trajectories." The missiles' solid-fuel motors ignited moments later in low-flash burns. The weapons accelerated to supersonic speed. Staying low, as programmed, they followed terrain and rode electromagnetic signatures like bloodhounds on the scent of a bear. Their guidance systems locked onto the enemy's emitters before the Russians even knew they'd been fired on.

Inside his cockpit, Olesen spoke for the first time, "ONE, weapons away. Clean release. Doors closed."

His wingman said, "TWO, same. All tracking."

The other pilots reported in sequence. Forty missiles were inbound to the Russians.

Olesen scanned his threat display. It was still dark, no emissions, no radar locks, and no comms bursts. The Russian defense net hadn't seen them—yet.

"Ghost flight, head home," he said. "Silent egress."

Reports of confirmed hits and secondary explosions momentarily lit up his HUD. He smiled under his helmet.

Chapter 50

CONSTABLE PYNT AIRPORT
0451 Hours, 8 August
Russian-occupied eastern Greenland

To Colonel Barinov, the first explosion wasn't loud so much as it was wrong and unnatural, a gut-punching crack in the stillness of a dim Arctic night. A radar trailer lit up in a flash of orange and shrapnel. The blast wave slammed into the adjacent support truck, flipping it onto its side in a burst of flame and torn canvas.

Inside the airfield's operations center, Barinov never saw that impact. He was thrown backward against the wall as the shockwave shattered the windows and blew out every light. Alarms blared, but too late. He stumbled outside, blood running from a gash across his scalp into his right eye. His ears rang, and his vision tunneled.

Thirty meters away, a missile slammed into a fire-control radar site. The targeting mast collapsed in a fireball, its electronics fried before it even registered the inbound threat. One of the defensive missiles caught the edge of the blast, and the site's crew was incinerated as their missile rack was mangled into scrap iron.

Another impact tore through a command van, splitting the chassis in two and sending flaming debris into the nearby fuel dump. A rapidly building fire started. A warhead struck the communications array. The base's long-range radio link, intended to coordinate with the Western Military District headquarters in St. Petersburg, disappeared in a blinding flash.

Thirty seconds later, only screams and secondary explosions pierced the air. From Barinov's vantage point, using his one good eye, it appeared that most of his defensive grid was gone.

Although his ears kept ringing, Barinov heard his aide yelling, "Colonel, Colonel, communications is reporting numerous direct hits. Radar, fire-control, command van, and the runway. It appears it was Danish F-35s."

Barinov clenched his jaw. He turned in a slow circle, surveying the carnage. The airfield perimeter was lit in strobing pulses from secondary fires. The main radar dish lay crumpled like foil, and orange flames rose over what had been the SAM battery.

A medic ran up to him and grabbed his arm to get him to sit down on the ground. "Just a minute, Doc." Barinov pushed the man away. "Don't I look a little busy?"

"Sir, that's a nasty cut. Let me take a look." The medic pulled a large, thick dressing from his med kit.

"It can wait." Barinov grabbed the dressing and held it against his forehead.

He turned to his aide. "Sound perimeter alert. Tripwire sectors one through four. Post anti-armor teams on the northern slope. There's a trail there, shallow grade, so the enemy will probably come from there."

"Sir," the medic said, "I must insist—"

"Doc, shut the fuck up while I try to save what's left of our encampment." The medic took a few steps back as the colonel turned back to his aide. "Get the Mi-24s airborne now and the VDV paratroopers deployed, as we discussed yesterday."

"Yes, sir, on it. But please, let Doc look at you."

"Get going."

Inside the command center, a dying signals technician had crawled to his comms console, one arm nearly blown from his body. He keyed the emergency HF transmitter and got out six words before he and the system went dark. "Constable Pynt...under coordinated...stealth...attack."

Chapter 51

RIDGELANDS

0511 Hours, 8 August

West of Constable Pynt Airport

Captain Lasse Holst saw the fourth blast before he heard it. The orange fireball on the horizon spread quickly just as a low, rolling concussion swept across the valley and bounced off the surrounding rock faces. Snow broke loose from the ledge above.

Holst led thirty-four operators from Denmark's elite Jaeger Corps. Every handpicked man had endured arctic survival training, long-range reconnaissance training, and silent kill drills. They had trained to fight deep behind enemy lines, often without support, and to fight with stealth, speed, and precision. In the frozen wasteland of Greenland, no force was better suited to lead a strike against a fortified Russian position.

As missiles continued to strike the Russians, Holst said over secure comms, "That's our window. Move out."

His team responded instantly, like predators closing in for the kill, precise, silent, and soon to be deadly. The squad of Jaeger operators and a dozen Home Guard reservists rose from the snow in staggered columns. Their ghillie suits, white on white over thermal-lined field gear, blended perfectly with the terrain. The effect was ghostlike, with figures seeming to appear from nowhere and moving as one.

Holst led the first fire team down a narrow draw carved by meltwater. The drop was steep, 15 meters down into a frozen creek bed. A twisted birch tree, blackened from past lightning, extended like a finger from the slope. He passed it without a glance.

Near him was his second-in-command, Lieutenant Emil Brandt. "Hold up, Captain," he said over secure comms. He scanned their approach route with high-powered binoculars. "Multiple secondaries. Heat signatures are still rising over the target. They hit more than just radar."

Holst ordered over comms, "Red One, break left and hold along the southern rise. Get eyes on the comms trailer. If it's still standing, torch it."

His reply was a double click.

As they approached their target area, Holst radioed, "We're in. Red One, status?"

There was nothing but static.

"Red Three?" he said.

No one replied.

0515 Hours, 8 August

Russian-occupied eastern Greenland

Inside the Russian defensive line, Barinov grabbed the binoculars from his spotter because he was taking too long. Barinov knew the enemy was coming. Standing in a sandbagged revetment north of the airfield, he pressed his binoculars tighter against his face, ignoring the pain from the gash on his forehead. He keyed his radio.

"This is Glacier. I've got movement, grid two-seven-five by eight-six-zero. Estimate squad-size element. No IFF signal. Could be enemy recon or an assault team. Hold fire until we get positive ID."

He wasn't going to kill anyone until he was sure they were hostile, but they were coming from right where he would have come.

"Activate tripwire Group Two," he said. "No gunfire until they are inside the kill zone."

Two dozen paratroopers lay waiting in the snow, rifles leveled and thermals active. They were dug into pre-sighted positions overlooking the southern trail. Behind them, two eight-wheeled BTR-82A armored personnel carriers sat dark but crewed, their engines idling under thermal blankets.

"Cut jamming," Barinov ordered. "Give them hope."

Within seconds of Holst's last transmission, the Jaeger's encrypted net flickered to life.

"Red One, do you copy?" he whispered again.

This time, he got an answer.

"Red One ambushed. We walked into—"

Gunfire, lots of it, interrupted the broadcast.

Holst didn't hesitate. "Contact. Red Two, fall back. Break north and regroup at Rally Point Bravo."

But it was too late. Muzzle flashes erupted ahead. Heavy-caliber machine gun tracers tore through the smoke. One Jaeger went down immediately, blasted across the chest. Another screamed as a grenade exploded just short of his position and peppered him with shrapnel.

"Cover fire," Holst shouted. "Move!"

Lieutenant Brandt turned to return fire, only to be dropped by a round to the side of his helmet.

Three more Jaegers sprinted toward a berm but were cut down by a burst from a machine gun.

One of the Home Guard reserves dropped to his knees and froze, hands over his ears, disoriented by the sudden noise. A round punched through his shoulder and sent him spinning backward. A second round struck him in the head.

Holst took cover behind the charred ruin of the birch tree. Blood dripping off his fingers, he didn't have time to check where it was coming from. He watched what was left of his team. Two Jaegers, one badly wounded, were bravely laying down fire and trying to hold the line. One of them yelled, "We're not getting out."

"No, we're not," Holst said to himself. He looked skyward where the F-35s had just been. "Ghost One," he whispered into his comms, "strike failed. No extract. Tell Copenhagen, mission compromised. We were never here."

He inserted his last magazine and fired at the Russians.

Chapter 52

THE WHITE HOUSE
8 August
Washington, DC

In the Situation Room, no one said a word as the assembled NSC viewed footage of the Danes' failure to retake their own land. Twisted wrecks littered red-stained snow, and bodies were scattered around the perimeter of Constable Pynt's airport. Flying in a stiff wind, a Russian flag reminded the world who controlled eastern Greenland.

President Mark Taylor, with bloodshot eyes from too many nighttime briefs, looked across the table at the people who would make the ultimate decision on Russia and, thereby, the entire world. "How many?" he asked quietly.

CJCS General Troy Kincaid answered, "Thirty-nine confirmed dead. Six captured and two MIAs. The air strike succeeded, but the ground element was overrun. We think the Russians laid in a secondary perimeter that the Danes didn't detect. They don't have the resources that we do."

"Elena," Taylor looked at DNI Ramirez, "any indication the Russians are packing up?"

"No, sir. We're seeing rapid reinforcements. IL-76s are landing at three-hour intervals. Our overheads show them unloading SA-21 components, electronic warfare vehicles, and construction equipment. They're expanding the runway and setting up camp as if there were no interruption."

The president nodded. "Are they entrenched?"

"They're in the process. If we don't act within a week, it will be tough to remove them. They're already moving construction equipment, attack helicopters, and heavier radar. Soon, they'll have a fully functional forward base within missile range of Pituffik and all northern shipping corridors. Additionally, their bastion defenses in the Barents Sea are mobilizing, and cruise-missile submarines are in motion. This is an Arctic line-of-control play. If they hold Constable Pynt, they cut the GIUK Gap from behind."

SecDef George Mitchell said, "Mr. President, we have two choices: let Russia lock down eastern Greenland and permanently fracture NATO credibility or act now bilaterally with Denmark."

"And what do you hear from NATO?" said the president.

SecState Brad Kelly said, "A lot of talking and nothing else."

"Any support?"

"No, Mr. President, not yet. Britain offered refuelers. And, according to them, they're watching closely. France and Germany want more time."

"Okay, so what options do we have?"

Mitchell pushed a button on his remote, and a three-columned slide filled the large screen. "We're calling it OPERATION FROST LANCE. We propose leading off with two B-21 Raiders. They'll deliver precision standoff strikes against hardened Russian C2 and air defense infrastructure. We have Marines staged in Iceland. The Ford carrier strike group is in the Greenland Sea and awaiting orders."

Taylor had heard that the operational testing of the B-21s was moving at an accelerated pace, but it had been kept under wraps. "First combat sortie for the Raider?"

"Yes, sir. Time to show what it's made of. To support the bombers, we deploy F-22 Raptors from Elmendorf to Iceland. They'll provide top cover and punch through any MiG-31 intercept attempts. We also have F-35s of the Ford. "

"And Denmark?"

"They'll lead the ground assault. They've got skin in this. They want the Russians out more than anyone, and they don't want this to turn into another Ukraine."

"So, no NATO?" asked Taylor.

"They're still arguing over Greenland's Article 5 applicability."

Taylor stood. "Then we move without them." He turned to SecDef. "Initiate OPERATION FROST LANCE. Coordinate with Copenhagen. I want troops in place within 24 hours."

"Yes, sir."

"And one more thing," said Taylor, "tell the Danes we're coming. This time, they won't be alone."

Chapter 53

CHRISTIANSBORG PALACE

9 August

Copenhagen, Denmark

General Lyhne looked over at his prime minister and thought how he looked twenty years older than he had a few days ago. Up on a large screen in the meeting room was one of the reasons.

<u>OPERATION ICE HAMMER</u>

KIA: 39

WIA/Captured: 6

MIA: 2

Target unsecured.

Russian forces remain in control.

Henrik Hansen had been prime minister for three years and had never seen or expected to see anything like this. He lowered his head into his hands for a moment, more out of respect than to shield others from seeing the tears streaming down his cheeks. His general stepped in.

"The Jaegers fought with distinction," Lyhne said, his voice low. "The F-35s hit the target clean. Radar, comms, and fire control were all destroyed. However, the Russians were prepared for ground contact. We believe they had layered defenses of overlapping arcs and presighted kill zones."

"Who tipped them?" asked the foreign minister, his voice tight. "We used every operational security protocol we have."

"No idea. SIGINT suggests they intercepted encrypted comms late in the staging cycle. Maybe a thermal drone caught the recon team. We may never know. The damage has been done, no matter what we find out."

Hansen still didn't respond. He looked at a list of names, his lips moving silently as he read.

"This will break us," the foreign minister muttered. "Public support was marginal before this. And now?"

The prime minister stood up. "No, this breaks them," Hansen said. "We bled for NATO's silence. Now they'll have to choose to either stand with us or be remembered as cowards."

NATO Headquarters
9 August
Brussels, Belgium

Inside the main meeting room, the screens displayed satellite images of Constable Pynt Airport. Around the table sat the ambassadors from all NATO countries. The question wasn't whether Denmark had acted but whether NATO would.

On one screen, for all to be reminded, was a blinking red dot next to the phrase: OPERATION ICE HAMMER – Mission Failure.

The ambassador from the UK was the first to speak. "This wasn't a rogue action. Denmark briefed us and asked for support. They were ignored. What did we expect them to do?"

The French ambassador said, "It's because the treaty obligation was unclear. Greenland isn't part of the European mainland. They—"

"The Russians aren't beaten by any means," interrupted the US ambassador. "They just wiped out a Danish special forces unit, and they're turning that airport into a forward operating base. If we fail to support Denmark again, we might as well hand the Arctic over to the Russians."

Silence took over the room.

With eyes on the satellite images, the Polish ambassador broke the silence. "The time for indecision is over. We must act now as one."

"We need to be clear," the German ambassador said while adjusting his earpiece. "Article 5 was not invoked. The Danish government acted unilaterally. The legal standing is ambiguous because of Greenland's territorial status. Also ambiguous is the escalation risk with Moscow."

Denmark's ambassador sat stiffly at the table, hands folded, face unreadable. He'd been offered condolences.

He'd received statements of sympathy. He hadn't received what Denmark wanted, and he wasn't hearing it now. "Ambiguous? Our special forces are dead. Killed and captured on NATO soil. You call that ambiguous, sir?"

"We sympathize," said the French ambassador, "but our posture must be deliberate. If we escalate without consensus—"

"Consensus? Denmark doesn't need consensus to defend our territory. But we need allies, and that's why this alliance exists, or so we have believed all these years."

The US ambassador slowly stood up, gaining the attention of those in the room. "Let me be blunt," he said. "Washington agrees that the current NATO posture is inadequate. While we debate, Russia is digging in, hardening defenses, reinforcing assets, and installing what damn well looks like a long-range ISR platform."

He paused for effect, then said, "The United States will not stand by while one of our closest allies is left out in the cold. We are deploying F-22s to Iceland to join elements of the 24th Marine Expeditionary Unit that are already there. The USS Ford, with its carrier strike group, is ready in the Greenland Sea, including some submarines. Denmark will no longer be alone." When he sat down, the only noise in the room was the creak of his chair.

Then a crescendo of mumbles filled the room.

The Italian ambassador spoke up, "Are these actions being taken under NATO command?"

"No," the US ambassador said flatly, "this is a bilateral operation between the United States and the Kingdom of Denmark. Countries in the NATO alliance are welcome to join us, and frankly, should. But we're not waiting any longer. Greenland is a strategic centerpiece to the Arctic, which is exactly why the Russians are there."

"And if Russia escalates?" the German ambassador said.

"They already did."

The US and Denmark ambassadors excused themselves and adjourned to a separate room. Both agreed it was time to reclaim Greenland—with or without NATO.

Chapter 54

THE WHITE HOUSE
10 August
Washington, DC

Framed by the American and Danish flags, President Taylor stood behind the podium before the Resolute Desk as the TV lights came up. He'd chosen this setting because he knew the American people had seen this office in the White House since they were old enough to watch TV. While the faces changed over time, Taylor felt that the office made the American people comfortable, as if they were a part of what he was about to say.

Good evening. Earlier this week, a company of Danish special operations soldiers conducted a limited strike against an illegal Russian military installation at Constable Pynt Airport on the sovereign territory of the Kingdom of Denmark in eastern Greenland. That operation resulted in the deaths of dozens of brave Danish servicemen and was met with silence by those who should have stood with them.

In the hours that followed, the United States of America was asked a simple question: Will we stand by our allies

*when they are attacked, or will we look the other way?
Tonight, I'm here to say that we will not look away. We
never have. And we will not start now.*

Taylor paused for a moment, allowing his words to
settle in a worldwide audience.

*Effective immediately and in coordination with the
Danish government, the United States is establishing a
maritime and air exclusion zone along Greenland's
eastern seaboard. The US Navy and allied forces will
enforce this zone by intercepting unauthorized aircraft
or vessels entering it.*

*Let me be clear. This is not an act of aggression. This is
a measured, defensive response to the illegal occupation
of allied territory. We do not seek war. We seek stability.
But if the Russian Federation continues to escalate and
threaten the security of the Arctic, our allies, and our
interests, we will respond swiftly and decisively with all
our military might.*

Taylor looked directly into the camera lens and thus into
the eyes of every single American watching.

To the soldiers on the ice, the sailors at sea, and the pilots in the sky, you carry our flag into the cold and darkness not out of conquest but out of duty. We stand by you. You will not fight alone.

And to our allies across the world, the United States is ready to lead. But leadership means more than aimless ramblings. It means action. Let history record this moment clearly. We did not yield to the cold, we did not blink in the dark, and we did not stand aside while others carved up what was not theirs to take. It is time for Russia to stop its expansionist advances. And that starts now.

Chapter 55

USS FORD
0550 Hours, 9 August
Greenland Sea

Jessie Hampton got his call sign, Swagger, because of his self-assured stride. He sort of slid across the ground as he strolled. In the cockpit of America's premier multirole stealth fighter, he was so calm under pressure, as if ice flowed through his veins, that he could have easily carried a different call sign.

As he taxied into position, he looked forward to the CAP mission he was about to fly. It was something that could easily turn into a shooting sortie. While he scanned the flight deck, the new ROEs echoed through his mind. US forces operating in and around eastern Greenland were authorized to conduct full-spectrum defensive operations against Russian military forces occupying Danish territory and to enforce exclusion zone protocols against unauthorized sea and air traffic. The mission briefer had said, "You will no longer defer or delay defensive actions when under threat. You will support the no-fly zone in the airspace near Constable Pynt to curb Russian air activity. You will respond to any surface threat, but whatever you do, don't be the one to start a war."

On the flight deck, the yellow-shirted shooter got Jessie's attention and gave the signal for a comms check. Jessie relaxed in his high-backed, armored seat, pulled the canopy down, and toggled his systems to life. The Distributed Aperture System lit up, piping external feeds directly into his helmet. The Arctic sky, horizon, and radar overlays made his aircraft an extension of his nervous system. Jessie was in his element.

He locked his helmet into place and flipped the last switches in the startup sequence. The canopy sealed. A secondary channel lit up in the upper right of his display, and speaking was Picket 11; there was no mistaking his wife's voice.

Lieutenant Commander Sarah Freeman was airborne, launched from Pituffik Space Base, where she was writing the manual for ground-based operations for the E-2 Hawkeye rather than flying off aircraft carriers. She was all business as usual.

"Raven 21, Pickett 11. Link is active, data clean. You're clear to push package Alpha toward objective grid. No threats airborne. Surface contact northeast has not escalated. You're eyes-on only unless instructed otherwise."

"Raven 21 copies, Danger. Arctic's quiet."

"For now, Raven 21," Sarah replied. "Push channel four if anything lights up, Swagger. We've got Growler support ten minutes off your nose."

Jessie watched as the orchestrated movement of focused specialists gathered around his fighter. The green-shirts swarmed underneath, double-checking tie-downs, cables, and access panels. But it was the red-shirts, the ordinance crew, who held his attention. One knelt at the starboard weapons bay, his gloved hand tapping on the panel just before it dropped open with a hiss of pressure bleed. Another stood back, clipboard in hand, calling out a sequence in a practiced rhythm. Jessie couldn't hear the words through the canopy, but he didn't need to. He knew the process by heart. "Left bay—two GBU-53Bs, serials confirmed, fused safe. Right bay—two AIM-260s, serials confirmed, fused safe."

The third red-shirt used a portable inspection wand to verify that the alignment and system integration part of the Built-In test was operational. Jessie wouldn't leave the boat if the aircraft couldn't see the weapons or if the fusing logic failed.

A green icon lit up next to each bay destination on his HUD. A message indicated ordnance was ready – configuration CLEAN.

Looking to his right, Jessie saw a final thumbs-up from the ordnance chief, who then signaled with a vertical arm motion, meaning "hot and verified."

Next, Jessie made eye contact with the yellow-shirt catapult officer as he directed Jessie into the final launch position. When he gave the run-up signal, Jessie went to full power and then focused on the shooter, who quickly scanned the deck to ensure it was clear. The shooter then performed one more visual assessment to confirm the flaps and slats were set and the launch bar was engaged. With all good, he crouched beside the cockpit and gave the final launch signal, a crisp gesture forward. Jessie responded with a salute, accomplishing an age-old tradition that indicated he was ready and that he respected the shooter's authority. The shooter returned the salute, dropped to one knee, and touched the deck, giving the signal to fire the catapult.

The catapult fired in a mix of controlled violence and precision. Jessie was pushed back into his seat with a force of over 3 G's. The F-35 shot forward, and he went from zero to nearly 170 knots in just over two seconds. He didn't even notice the cockpit rattling as the nose lifted when he cleared the bow. For a heartbeat, there was nothing but sky and sea.

God, how he loved this.

Chapter 56

THE KREMLIN

9 August

Moscow, Russia

While a white, blue, and red flag flew in the wind at Constable Pynt Airport, Russian leaders in Moscow sat around the large conference table in a windowless room lined with concrete and lead. President Andrei Petrov sat at the head of the table. He simply said, "Report."

Deputy Defense Minister Natalia Romanova began the discussion. "They're coming, and not just the Danes. Two American F-22 squadrons are now in Iceland. There's a carrier group north of Jan Mayen and submarine activity in the Fram Strait. And we suspect B-21s are at Pituffik, despite all intel that says they're not operational yet."

She glanced at the president. He remained motionless and expressionless, so she continued, "The Americans claim Denmark acted alone. Now they pretend this is a defensive move. But with their blockade and their bombers, this is war, just one without a declaration."

Romanova gestured to a map on a large screen. "Constable Pynt is secure. VDV elements have fortified the runway. The new S-400 battery is operational, though exposed. They took out the radar mast with standoff munitions, but we've replaced it. A second radar is being flown in via Arkhangelsk through civilian cargo channels."

"And the Danes?" the president said.

"Impulsive," Romanova replied. "They attacked without coordination with NATO, and we repelled them severely. With the US, they appear to be preparing for another assault with little or no help from the rest of NATO."

The admiral of the Northern Fleet added, "We underestimated their resolve. We thought they would stall. Instead, they're moving to retake the airfield and our foothold."

Petrov asked the question everyone was thinking. "Can we hold it?"

Romanova stood and pointed to the coastal ridgeline above Constable Pynt. "We've already reinforced. Two VDV companies, including an S-1 Pantsir SAM and triple-A air defense system, Tor mobile short-range air defense units, and S-350 Vityaz short-to-mid-range mobile SAM systems, were airlifted in through Arkhangelsk, along with communications jammers, artillery, and counter-mortar radars. We control the airstrip and the surrounding terrain. The key to holding it is fully committing with all our military might."

The room went silent as the assembled elite of Russia heard what they all knew must be done, Article 5 be damned.

The foreign minister pointed out, "If we escalate, the UN backlash will be immediate with sanctions, isolation, and more weapons to Denmark. Finland and Sweden will surely jump in."

Romanova replied coldly, "We're already sanctioned. We're already isolated. It's time we prove that doesn't matter and that the Arctic belongs to us."

All eyes fell on Petrov. He looked back at each person. "We hold Greenland at all costs. Do whatever it takes." With the knowledge that he would change that part of the world forever, he got up and left the room.

Chapter 57

NORTHERN FLEET HEADQUARTERS

9 August

Severomorsk, Russia

The briefing was conducted without distractions: no phones, no tablets. Printed copies of the top-secret Directive 35 operations order were distributed and were to be collected again before the room cleared.

Admiral Mikhailovich sat at the head of the table with senior commanders from the VDV, GRU, and the Strategic Rocket Forces joining him. He waited so each man could read Directive 35.

When all eyes were finally on him, he said, "Comrades, we're about to change the balance of power in the Arctic. Our VDV airborne forces are in place in Greenland. Air defenses are arriving, but the Americans have decided to do what most NATO countries didn't. They've initiated a no-fly zone while setting up a naval blockade around eastern Greenland, all to deny our access to our base at Constable Pynt."

He paused to note their expressions, and satisfied they reflected his seriousness, he said, "This is all about us holding Greenland. It's also about making it cost them everything to take it back. A public, painful loss for the

Americans will fracture NATO, discredit Denmark's leadership, and cement our control of the Arctic narrative. So we hold Greenland. Hold. Bleed. Delay. That is how we win, and win we will."

0420 Hours, 10 August

Greenland Sea

Captain Gromov stood in the dimly lit control room of the *Kazan*, the most advanced hunter-killer submarine in the Russian Navy. Events were escalating quickly, and his orders were specific. He was to position the *Kazan* off eastern Greenland, remain undetected, and disrupt any surface or undersea movement that would benefit the Americans as Russia rushed in reinforcements to Constable Pynt. If a foreign submarine was located, he was to engage at his discretion.

Tell that to a submariner, and that means everyone's a hostile.

Gromov had already loaded his torpedo tubes and was using his MGK-600 Irtysh-Amfora sonar to passively scan the sea, like the stalking predator he was. Fortunately, he had intel that his nemesis, the USS *Idaho*, was confirmed to be operating in the area. He'd found the Virginia class hunter before and felt confident he would succeed again.

Oftentimes, the captain of a warship, or in this case, a Virginia-class attack submarine, received orders that could raise one's eyebrows, yet if one knew the entire background, it all made sense. As with any soldier, "Theirs not to reason why, theirs but to do or die," as Alfred, Lord Tennyson put it in his poem "The Charge of the Light Brigade." And Captain Blake Stanton understood it all too well.

A few days prior, US Space Force SIGINT assets at Pituffik and an airborne P-8 Poseidon had detected encrypted Russian satellite relays consistent with Kalibr missile targeting data. The signals had originated from an area where only one Russian asset was unaccounted for: the *Kazan*.

At the same time, a civilian cargo ship, later identified as a disguised Russian naval support vessel, was caught laying underwater sonar relays used for fire-control signal transmissions. The conclusion was that the *Kazan* was preparing for a first-strike option either against the USS *Ford* or allied naval escorts running the blockade. As a result, *Idaho* had received flash traffic.

FROM: COMSUBLANT-USSTRATCOM FORWARD

TO: USS *IDAHO*

Priority: Flash // Eyes Only // OPERATION FROST LANCE

K-561 Kazan is confirmed operating within the threat envelope to the USN CSG and the Icelandic-Greenlandic corridor. SIGINT indicates launch prep activity for cruise missile employment.

You are authorized and directed to locate, track, and, if necessary, destroy Kazan.

The integrity of Operation Frost Lance and the survival of CVN-78 and its associated units depend on neutralizing this platform.

Proceed with maximum stealth. COMSUBLANT out.

After the past few days of hunting, Stanton was devising new tactics. He had directed the crew to take the *Idaho* under a thermocline at 900 feet and use the dense cold-water layer to mask their presence. Above them, the sea was a compressed pane of scattered ice, making them nearly radar-blind.

Stanton stood in the conn, his hands behind his back as if he were at parade rest, because he thought best in that position. His concentration was fixed on the sonar repeaters glowing across the combat control center. Every sound, every faint frequency fluctuation, was being evaluated by *Idaho*'s advanced sonar suite, which was one reason why the submarine was feared by other submarines.

"Deploy TB-29," he ordered. "Set narrowband mode."

Reyes worked the board. "Spooling now." The thin-line TB-29 paid out, two-and-a-half thousand feet of fiber-optic hydrophones trailing into the black, then the console lit as data flowed back, giving them a long-range passive look down the pipe.

Reyes analyzed the waterfall display as it scrolled slowly, each pass building a composite of the acoustic environment. Columns of data cascaded down the screen, marked by banded lines, a background wash, and occasional spikes that indicated biological interference. Sorting through it, she studied every gradient, looking for the elusive sound from a man-made Russian submarine. Hours passed, but Reyes never faltered.

As she was munching on her favorite snack of gummy bears, what had been a ghost began to take shape. It wasn't sudden or sharp, but something emerging with a reluctant inevitability. It started as a faint rhythmic modulation, like a whisper in a crowded room. She stopped chewing. Just a few decibels above the ambient noise, it was nearly lost in the reverberations of distant tectonic stress and the breaking up of Arctic ice to the north.

She pressed her headset hard against her ears. The signal wasn't constant. It wavered cyclically, then it was gone. But it came back. The timing was deliberate and methodical, not the irregular churn of natural noise, nor the disorganized slap of wave interaction. It was engineered motion, intentional.

Reyes's eyes tracked the pulse. Her mind filtered the data automatically, mentally subtracting biologics, seismic drift, and internal bleed-through from her boat's systems. What remained was a rotational frequency curve just where it shouldn't have been, too deep for a trawler, too steady for a whale, and too far offshore for civilian traffic.

Her heartbeat quickened. She could almost hear it: the low, deliberate beat of a five-blade skewback propulsor, slow-turning for stealth and optimized for acoustic masking. It was the exact configuration of a Russian Yasen-class sub.

She overlaid the signatures from her vast computer library, normalized for depth and thermal distortion, to confirm her suspicions. The overlay appeared as a red line against the fluctuating trace on the waterfall. It matched. Adrenaline rushed through her, alerting all her senses.

Keying her mic, she spoke deliberately, "Control, Sonar. Possible contact. New faint narrowband trace. Bearing two-seven-three. Intermittent screw noise, five-blade. Class match Yasen. Probable Kazan. Confidence moderate." As she talked, she had adjusted a filter on her screen. "Correction, high confidence. Contact is real. Contact is tracking."

Stanton immediately said, "Helm, all stop. Maintain depth. Bring rudder amidships. Hold position. Confirm bearing, Reyes."

"Two-seven-three, sir. Contact has consistent blade rate modulation. Contact faded but is reappearing at regular intervals. Bearing drift indicates slow movement, shallow angle."

"Sonar and Conn, log as Sierra 1. Helm, come left 5 degrees. Speed 1 knot ahead. We'll ride the layer and get a second bearing. Passive only. Let's draw them out and build a picture."

K-561 *Kazan*
0514 Hours, 10 August
Greenland Sea

On the *Kazan*, Gromov had directed the helmsman to go to 260 meters and operate under another thermocline. Rigged for ultra-quiet operations and equipped with passive sonar arrays to track faint broadband signatures, they waited for the *Idaho* to make a mistake and reveal its position. They had been submerged for four days, most of the time under strict emission control. No sound had escaped from the state-of-the-art submarine that wasn't filtered, suppressed, or absorbed. You didn't get second chances in the shooting war he was about to commence.

Looking over the chart plot projected on a hardened touch panel just aft of the command chair, Gromov noted that Constable Pynt sat 600 kilometers to the southwest. His boat approached the designated launch box, a preselected grid square cleared by GRU satellite recon and mapped for seafloor topology. It was one of several fire corridors prepared in advance for a potential missile strike using the sub's 3M-14 Kalibr land-attack cruise missiles or P-800 Oniks anti-ship cruise missiles, depending on the target priority. The time to prowl was over; it was time to strike.

He turned to his XO. "If we time this correctly, we'll be inside the launch envelope for Pituffik, the blockade line, and the forward carrier group, including the Danish frigate Huitfeldt."

He also knew the *Idaho* was lurking somewhere close, despite his efforts to search him out. Gromov had learned the habits of his adversary from their encounters over the past weeks. *Idaho* didn't follow directly but drifted and slid wide. It took time to reposition and hunted like a sniper, not a pursuer but a stalker. That told Gromov something important: the Idaho wouldn't chase but would flank and wait for errors. He'd seen it twice now, both times when he'd adjusted course through a thermal layer. The *Idaho* never took the bait and stayed below or above, letting him pass and collecting what it needed. That restraint meant its commander had confidence in his sensors and discipline in spades.

Gromov turned to his XO. "That American captain is patient. Too patient." He tapped a stylus on the combat chart. "He's not trying to track us. He's trying to get our bearing, range, and signature profiles. He's building his shot before we know we're targeted."

The XO nodded slowly. "So we bait him?"

"No, we force him to act on instinct. He plays the data, so we deny it to him. When we reposition next, do it off-cycle. Change bearing mid-transit. Vary shaft RPM. Break any consistent modulation. And just before we reach the firing box, we go loud."

The XO drew his eyebrows in. "Sir?"

Gromov smiled slightly, "If he's out there, he'll expect stealth. He won't expect a bold move. That's when we shoot."

USS *Idaho*
0754 Hours, 10 August
Greenland Sea

Back on *Idaho*, Reyes was frustrated and tried not to let it show in her communications. "Sierra 1 faded again. Last bearing one-five-eight. No course shift."

Stanton nodded. Let them think they lost us, he thought. For hours, they'd been shadowing the *Kazan*, never close and never fast. The Russian captain was good. He was conservative and disciplined, but perhaps too disciplined. Stanton didn't think he knew that the *Idaho* had him at range three times and never took the shot.

His XO was paying close attention. Stanton had told Harrington earlier, "He's watching us, studying and tracking how we behave. So I've been giving him a pattern."

Harrington then noted how the captain rotated the *Idaho* through quiet loops, deliberate turns, pauses, and bearing drifts. He knew the *Kazan*'s captain would build a profile of the American captain. Stanton let them believe that his sub hunted, staying quiet and hesitating.

Stanton had given another tip to his second-in-command. "We move when he does. We respond late. Not because we're slow but because we want him to think we are. The moment he commits to launch, he's got to think we're still processing."

Stanton stepped toward the fire-control console and pointed at the Target Motion Analysis screen. "XO, plot a probable intercept path into the launch box. We'll sit 3 miles outside it. If the Kazan fires, it will relinquish its position. And if it delays,"—he tapped the map, "we shoot first."

Harrington gave that some thought. "You think the captain will fall for it?"

Keeping his eyes on the map, Stanton said, "No, but I'm counting on him needing to believe he understands me. That's what makes him vulnerable."

K-561 *Kazan*
0812 Hours, 10 August
Greenland Sea

Yasen-class submarines carried thirty-two vertical launch system cells capable of firing the 3M-14K Kalibr land-attack cruise missile, the 3M-54T Kalibr anti-ship variant, and the P-800 Oniks supersonic anti-ship missile. All three types of missiles had been loaded just before going to sea. The submarine was also capable of launching the much-feared 3M22 Tsirkon, referred to by NATO as the SS-N-33 Zircon. No matter the name, the Tsirkon was a hypersonic cruise missile capable of reaching speeds up to Mach 9, flying at high altitudes before descending and executing violent terminal maneuvers, making it extremely difficult to intercept.

Since the *Kazan* was loaded and had so many targets in the vicinity of eastern Greenland, Gromov developed an in-depth firing plan.

Target	Missile Type	Quantity	Notes
USS *Ford*	3M22 Tsirkon	1	Highest priority

Target	Missile Type	Quantity	Notes
USS *Hudner*	3M-54T Kalibr AS	3	Dual vector attack
USS *Gravely*	3M-54T Kalibr AS	3	Spread shot
HDMS *Huitfeldt*	3M-54T Kalibr AS	1	Mid-range approach
Pituffik Space Base	3M-14K Kalibr LA	3	GPS-guided, land-attack

The remaining missiles would be held in reserve for defensive purposes and as a secondary launch option. Turning to his XO, he said, "The *Ford* is our primary target. However, we also want the escorts removed. Our goal isn't to kill them all but to overwhelm their intercept envelope. Punch through with just one, and we've succeeded. But first, we have to know where *Idaho* is hiding out."

Gromov examined the data in front of him, which was gleaned from the last six hours of collecting bearing drift and acoustic intercepts. He noted that the projected threat ring from what he presumed to be a Virginia-class submarine, likely the *Idaho*, had been shrinking, but no positive contact had been established. He looked over at his most experienced sonar operator, Senior Petty Officer Viktor

Sokolov. "Latest data. Any narrowband anomalies? Cavitation? Transients?"

Sokolov shook his head, never taking his eyes off his displays. "Negative, Captain. The last possible signature was six hours ago, bearing one-eight-seven. Faint and non-persistent. We've rotated all listening angles, but no modulation consistent with pump jet acoustics. If the *Idaho* is still nearby, it's either gone deep under the thermocline or drifted off-station."

His XO leaned in. "It might be further west, repositioning for a flank attack."

The captain gave this some thought but said, "No noise. No ping. No pattern. We've shown them nothing, and we're near the final vector. If they were planning to strike, it would have been while we were ascending."

It was time to act.

Gromov turned to his control station. "Navigation, bring us to launch corridor Bravo, depth 50 meters. Trim neutral. Ballast to firing configuration. Helm, course one-nine-five."

His orders were repeated for clarification.

He next turned to his weapons officer. "Begin missile system checks. Prepare Kalibrs in Tubes One through Seven for cold launch. Load Tsirkon to Tube Eight, final targeting packets *Ford, Hudner, Huitfeldt,* and Pituffik. Confirm with fire-control."

The weapons officer was more than ready for the order and quickly replied, "Confirmed, all packets preloaded."

Gromov said to no one in particular, "When we go to launch depth, we go quiet. No active sonar. If the American sub is out there and still blind, we don't tell them a thing until the sky lights up and their fleet is sinking."

Quickly, the order went out to the entire boat, "Combat status Level 1. All crew to action stations. Begin launch sequence when in position. This is not a drill."

Chapter 58

HDMS Iver Huitfeldt
1324 Hours, 10 August
Greenland Sea

Captain Steen Østergaard stood on the bridge wing, pulling his collar up against a cold summer wind and watching his breath drifting off against the red-tinged horizon—just another ordinary day in the Arctic. The sea was rough, the temperature hovering around -2 Celsius. His ship plowed through the icy chop at a steady 18 knots, and the *Iver Huitfeldt*'s SPY radar turned above him in a slow, unbroken rhythm.

His ship had been assigned to the northern arc of the USS *Ford*'s defensive perimeter, clearly in Danish waters. This was by far the most serious operation undertaken by Denmark in decades. The *Ford* and its escorts, the destroyers *Hudner*, *Gravely*, and *Ramage*, were operating south of his position, preparing to support a US-Danish thrust to retake Constable Pynt Airport from the Russians. No one wanted a repeat of Ukraine.

Just two months ago, Østergaard was assigned to command *Huitfeldt*, a multi-mission air defense frigate. It was a considerable promotion for the up-and-coming naval officer. While he felt confident in his position as commanding officer, he couldn't shake the feeling of responsibility for his crew of 101 sailors, who were mostly kids. One was the son of a close family friend.

He told himself to keep moving, stay busy, and let the crew see how confident he was. Such an attitude would rub off.

Heading into the CIC, he stopped to check the operations plot. Aegis-linked intercept grids floated on the screen in soft green lines. AWACS icons blinked offshore along with those of the aircraft flying the US CAP. The EA-18Gs and F-35s held a steady racetrack pattern off Greenland's coast.

He walked over to Sonar. "Any acoustics?"

"No, sir. Ambient is high from scattered ice movement, but negative on propulsion signatures. No transients."

"Perhaps they're gone." Or just waiting, he thought.

USS IDAHO

1425 Hours, 10 August

Greenland Sea

As the hours passed, Stanton stood behind his sonar operator, STSC Emily Reyes. It was nearing her relief time.

She said quickly, "Sierra 1 shaft RPMs just increased slightly. Bearing's drifting. Up-angle looks real. Kazan's ascending, Captain."

"Any pings?"

"Nothing active, sir. This does not appear to be an evasive run. Sierra 1 is climbing slowly, possibly going to launch depth."

The captain muttered, "I agree."

He stepped toward Fire-Control. "Update target motion analysis. Assume upward spiral. Plot probable launch corridor ahead of Sierra 1's current heading."

The fire-control technician responded instantly, "Calculating, sir. Target's still ascending and will be in Kalibr launch profile if it holds at fifty meters. All high-value assets fall within probable engagement range."

Stanton came back with a pressing question: "Time to weapons release?"

"Four minutes, Captain. Five tops."

Turning to his weapons officer, Stanton said, "Load Mark 48 ADCAP in Tube Four. Set passive homing. Enable at 1,200 meters. Do not flood."

"Aye, Captain," he said and then repeated the orders.

Stanton took a few steps back, looking at his combat display. The *Kazan* was still only an apparition, an echo beneath ice and silence, but it was moving with intent now. He felt it in his being.

He said out loud to himself, "They're not running. They're staging."

The crew around him heard him and understood the stakes had risen.

Fire Control said, "Still no solid range, sir. Do you want to shoot on bearing?"

"Not yet. Let's let them climb. If they open the hatches, we'll hear it."

Minutes passed. The crew was tense at their battle stations, waiting for their next order. Everyone was on top of their game, having never experienced anything like this, the real thing, not just training. One word from the captain and all their lives could change forever.

And then it happened.

"Control, Sonar," said Reyes, "new transient. Metal-on-metal. Multiple impulses. Read them as tube door actuation."

This was too important for misinterpretation. Stanton quickly replied, "Repeat."

Reyes came back in one second with additional information. "Confirmed missile hatch cycling. Launch prep noises, at least two separate impulses. Kazan is coming up and opening VLS."

The vertical launch system activity was all Stanton needed to hear. He had his orders.

"Weapons, flood Tube 4. Stand by on my mark."

The tube flooded with a low hiss, audible only inside the compartment. Cold seawater pressurized the launch chamber, equalizing with the surrounding ocean. The crew felt nothing, just the procedural cue through their headsets.

Stanton watched the digital timer tick. He held for two seconds, long enough for sonar to confirm any changes in bearing drift and range, and just sufficient enough for Fire Control to lock the final solution. There was no chatter, no countdown, just one more decision to be made by the captain of the USS *Idaho,* to make this a shooting war.

Chapter 59

KAZAN

1526 Hours, 10 August

Greenland Sea

The *Kazan* angled gently to port, responding to a trim correction. Deep inside its hull, water pumps cycled with short, muffled pulses to balance the sub for missile launch.

"Depth 55 meters and holding descent angle at 5 degrees," the diving officer reported.

"Level off at 50," Captain Ivan Gromov ordered. "Speed steady at 4 knots. Trim for missile launch profile."

Around them, the ice shelf's acoustic shadows would create just enough interference to mask minor course corrections. Gromov had ordered their approach along the western edge of Launch Grid Bravo, using a combination of pre-surveyed topography and the Global Navigation Satellite System. They glided into position.

"Kazan is stable," the diving officer said. "Depth 50 meters, trim neutral."

"Set Launch Sequence one," Gromov said.

The lighting inside the command sphere shifted to combat mode, bathing the compartment in red and amber hues. At the forward weapons console, the tube status indicators blinked to life as all eight vertical launch cells showed green. A soft chime behind the fire control officer confirmed that the missile launch sequencer was armed and the first salvo was ready. The *Kazan* was now committed.

Weapons reported, "Vertical Launch System: Tubes 1 through 6 loaded with 3M-14K Kalibr land-attack cruise missiles. Tube 7, 3M-54T anti-ship missile. Tube 8 Tsirkon on standby. Salvo interval 5 seconds. Fire-control is ready."

Gromov said instantly, "Tube 1, fire."

A soft mechanical thump vibrated through the deck as the first Kalibr missile was cold-launched from its vertical launch cell. On the overhead repeater, telemetry flashed green, booster ignition confirmed.

"Tube 2—fire."

USS Idaho
1531 Hours, 10 August
Greenland Sea

"Control, Sonar. Kazan fired a missile."

Stanton said, "Weapons, fire."

Tube 4 opened, and the Mk 48 ADCAP shot from the *Idaho,* targeting the *Kazan.*

The weapons officer immediately reported, "Weapon away. Wire guidance established. Depth separation holding. Torpedo in passive mode."

Fire-control said, "Shooter-One tracking. Target depth and course updated. Intercept in ninety seconds."

The crew began counting down the seconds.

In *Kazan*, missiles two through seven were fired at 5-second intervals. The console lit up, indicating that Tube 8 with the Tsirkon hypersonic missile aimed at the *Ford* was ready.

"Conn, Sonar. New transient. Bearing two-three-six. High-speed screw. Torpedo in the water. Confirmed Mark 48. Active homing initiated!"

Gromov didn't hesitate. "Fire Tube 8."

"Weapon away."

Tube 8's heavy ejection thud echoed faintly through the hull as the 3M22 Tsirkon was cold-launched from its vertical cell. Moments later, its solid-fuel booster ignited, propelling the missile into the upper atmosphere at speeds exceeding 11,000 kilometers per hour, streaking toward the *Ford* like a meteor on a programmed arc.

Gromov gripped the side rail of the command sphere. His ship had done her duty. The missiles were outbound, with targets marked and solid trajectories. As he was about to order evasive actions, sonar cried, "Torpedo active! Close range!"

Gromov knew they were out of time. No evasive measures could save them now, no dive angle, no emergency ballast dump nothing but to die with honor.

The sea around the submarine compressed and tore as the Mk 48 closed at over 55 knots, its active sonar hammering off the *Kazan*'s titanium hull. The guidance wire had long since been cut, so the weapon was hunting autonomously. And it had found its prey.

The torpedo struck below the sail, port aft and directly beneath missile compartments Six and Seven. The warhead's PBXN-103 explosive triggered its shaped charge at precisely the designed standoff distance. The resulting bubble pulse blasted into the hull, deforming steel and frame in an instant.

The pressure hull failed within milliseconds. Bulkheads buckled inward. Compartment Seven collapsed like a crushed oil drum. A bloom of fire, quick as a camera flash, ignited from missile residue and propellant remnants in the adjacent VLS modules.

The control sphere lifted and twisted, flinging crewmen from their stations. Dials spun. Consoles ruptured. The sound was not a roar but a tearing, followed by the groan of 3,000 tons of pressure reclaiming space. In a couple of seconds, before the captain and his crew of sixty-three sailors were shredded from the pressure and blast, Gromov's last thought was as a true Russian patriot. *We fired our missiles, and the Americans will now pay.*

On the *Idaho*'s sonar waterfall display, the contact line of Sierra 1 was fractured and broken into a series of echoes, reverberation tails, and low-frequency collapse harmonics, the sound of death in the sea.

Doing as she was taught, Reyes reported, "Control, Sonar, high-order detonation. Sierra 1 breaking up. Pressure hull failure confirmed. The Kazan is destroyed."

Stanton answered, "Mark the time. Retrieve the wire. Stand by for counter-detection."

The war had started, and Stanton wanted to ensure his boat would not be counted as a casualty. An eerie quiet descended as the crew didn't cheer, but instead quickly went about their work, concentrating on staying alive.

Chapter 60

USS FORD
1548 Hours, 10 August
Greenland Sea

The last act of aggression by the *Kazan* before being blown into a floating collection of wreckage was the launch of its 3M22 Tsirkon hypersonic missile, Russia's answer to US naval superiority. When the missile breached the surface in a bright flash, it left behind a boiling sea. As it cleared the surface, the missile's solid-fuel booster ignited, hurling it toward the upper atmosphere at an ever-increasing speed.

By the time the circling E-2 Hawkeye and the vessels of CSG-12 registered the vertical plume on radar, the missile was already at 80,000 feet and efficiently transitioning to a ballistic arc at nearly 7,000 mph.

Inside the CIC aboard the *Ford*, the Ship Self-Defense System, SSDS, immediately began aggregating onboard sensor data with that from the surrounding CEC-linked destroyers. As they fought their own battles against the Russian missiles aimed at them, Hudner and *Gravely* fed fire-control data back to the *Ford*. The SSDS tagged a new contact, a high-speed inbound.

"New contact," reported the radar operator, who was unable to control his emotions and spoke loudly. "Single track Mach 8. Rapid ascent. Bearing two-eight-zero. Likely SS-N-33 Zircon," he said, his voice rising an octave on the last three words. The young man swallowed hard, then reported, "Contact is executing a lofted trajectory." He adjusted the display to highlight the missile's behavior. "Boost phase complete, now entering glide. Altitude climbing through 130,000 feet."

USS THOMAS HUDNER
1532 Hours, 10 August
Greenland Sea

In the *Hudner*'s CIC, Jansen was more than prepared for what was coming. He'd been in two wars so far in his career, been fired on, and had his ship blown out from under him. But Jansen had learned from each experience, which gave him confidence as the XO aboard the *Hudner,* and when the ship's radar operator reported, "Multiple launches bearing two-seven-zero. Three low-flying tracks. Probable SS-N-27 Sizzlers."

In CIC, the ship's captain didn't flinch when he heard the NATO designation for Russian anti-ship 3M-54T Kalibr missiles. "Tactical, assign SM-6 to outer band intercept. Initiate full-spectrum surveillance. Confirm classification."

The TAO didn't need long to comply. "Confirmed SS-N-27 Sizzlers, sea-skimming. Launched from subsurface."

Jansen stepped forward, scanning the display. "Range estimate."

"Just over 120 nautical miles. Time to impact is ten to twelve minutes, depending on maneuvering."

Reynolds nodded. "Let's get ahead of this. VLS to ready. Assign two SM-6s per track. Keep ESSMs standing by for mid-to-low intercepts."

Jansen turned to the weapons console. "Set Condition One. Bring CIWS online. Reload chaff tubes and run a full decoy cycle. I want Nulka primed but not fired."

TAO called out, "Sizzlers now inside fifty miles. Two appear to be maneuvering. Probably terrain-following or decoy separation."

"Engage with SM-6, two birds per," Reynolds said. "Assign ESSMs for final pass."

"SM-6s away," came the reply. Everyone felt a thud beneath their feet as the Evolved SeaSparrow Missiles launched from four cells in staggered pairs.

Jansen watched the feed and heard the report, "First Sizzler down. Second missed. Adjusting lock."

The one missile entered its terminal sprint phase. Breaking from its programmed course, it weaved in tight S-patterns at supersonic speed and hugged the sea as it closed on the ship.

"CIWS, track and arm," Jansen said. "Manual override authorized."

"CIWS engaging."

The Phalanx filled the air with rounds, spewing tungsten. A wall of red tracers swept the horizon and met the missile 325 yards out. The Sizzler detonated in a flash, rocking the deck and showering the bow with debris. But no one was injured.

The TAO made it official. "Two Sizzlers destroyed. One leaker neutralized by CIWS. No direct hits."

Not everyone was so fortunate.

"New contact," the radar operator said. "High altitude. Mach 8.8 and bearing two-eight-zero. One track, climbing fast. No spiral. Single direct climb. This isn't a Sizzler."

The TAO's voice was hurried. "Probable Zircon. Repeat probable SS-N-33 Zircon."

Reynolds stepped to the screen. "They launched the Zircon last to let it leapfrog the slow movers while we're busy protecting our ships."

Jansen was already at the EW console. "Chaff Pattern 6, staggered release. Launch two Nulka decoys to emulate Ford's signature. Set pulse jamming on a rotating cycle — break the seeker's lock."

"Chaff away," said the lieutenant. "Decoys airborne. Jammers locked and transmitting."

Overhead, the destroyer's masts pulsed with high-powered bursts. The AN/SLQ-32 system sent tailored interference patterns, while the Nulka rounds drifted and emitted full-spectrum radar returns.

1549 Hours, 10 August
Greenland Sea

Even with Hudner's support, *Ford* was battling to survive against a hypersonic missile built to outrun and overwhelm any defense. At Mach 9, a Zircon could cross a nautical mile before its intended victims even took a breath. From detection to impact, the engagement window was measured in seconds, not minutes. The US had no proven defense against this new hypersonic threat.

But don't tell that to Lieutenant Pavati Talas, an electronic warfare officer. From the moment she heard of the airborne Zircon, she knew she had only seconds to act. She gave commands as fast as her fingers flew around her keyboard.

"Deploy Nulka port and starboard. Set them to drift high and emit false signatures. Chaff Pattern 5, wide dispersion, layer it thick. Activate full-spectrum jamming on targeting bands X, Ku, and Ka."

On the flight deck, the Nulka anti-ship self-defense system canisters fired with short hisses. Arcing away from the ship on rocket assist, the decoys deployed active lures to mimic the carrier's radar profile and to emit a convincing electromagnetic signature.

"Set Slick-32 to aggressive mode," Talas ordered.

Above the ship, the AN/SLQ-32's electronic warfare pods flooded the air with directed noise in an attempt to blind the missile's radar seeker. Every watt of the powerful emitters was pushed into creating chaos in the Zircon's terminal corridor.

The missile came screaming in, its skin ablaze from friction and its onboard seeker fighting through the carrier's wall of deception. The air was thick with a digital minefield of chaff, false returns, and pulsing jammers. The decoys mimicked the *Ford*'s massive radar signature, drifting in just the right geometry to lure it offline, or so everyone hoped.

Over the 1MC, the Air Defense Watch Officer said, "Twenty seconds to impact."

Ford had seen drone swarms and sub-launched cruise missiles, but nothing like this. The Zircon wasn't just another missile. It was a kinetic sledgehammer wrapped in plasma.

Everywhere on the ship carrying 3,000 souls, the 1MC announcement didn't change much. There just wasn't time. It was all up to the ship's systems.

The Zircon descended below twenty thousand feet. It had ignored the chaff, blown through the jamming, and bypassed two Nulka decoys. Its onboard guidance was built for terminal discrimination at hypersonic speeds and was aimed directly at the most significant radar return on the ocean: the *Ford*.

Aviation Electronics Technician Petty Officer 3rd Class Brian McCaffrey ran down the starboard side of the flight deck at a full sprint like he used to run two years ago at his high school in Fort Collins, Colorado. A call had gone out for a replacement communications cable for an F-35 that was hot on the launch pad. Clutching the coiled cable in one hand, he was twenty feet from the fighter when he saw a bright light flash out of the corner of his eye. His first and last thought was how unnatural that was.

All around what used to be Brian McCaffrey, the flight deck lifted beneath steel, shuddering like it had cracked open from the inside.

The Zircon struck with the force of a meteor on the starboard side near Aircraft Elevator 3, just aft of the island. At Mach 9, the kinetic energy alone was catastrophic, delivering the equivalent of a small precision-guided bomb before the high-explosive warhead even detonated. The explosion erupted upward and outward in milliseconds, tearing through bulkheads and blowing out compartments below the flight deck. Where Brian McCaffrey had stood, the steel deck tore apart like the lid of a can. A towering fireball erupted, climbing hundreds of feet and blotting out the morning sun.

The blast sheared the flight deck steel as if it were tearing through paper, opening a gash nearly forty feet wide across the hangar bay below. The F-35 that had been running up was utterly gone, and the shockwave hurled personnel off the flight deck.

Fire suppression systems were triggered but couldn't contain the initial inferno. Secondary explosions followed, aviation fuel lines ruptured, and a weapons locker ignited. The compartment just below the impact, crew berthing for the VFA squadron, was obliterated.

Sitting at her station in the CIC, Talas had just entered another EW command when she was hit in the head by flying debris. All around her, radar operators and critical CIC personnel were either wounded or killed outright. Cries of agony and desperation could be heard throughout the *Ford* as the massive carrier shuddered from the impact.

Emergency lighting kicked in on the bridge and throughout the massive carrier as the main circuit breakers tripped. Smoke rolled through the ventilation ducts, the acrid smell of burning aviation fuel and melting composites spreading quickly.

The captain crawled over to the bridge phone. Somehow pulling himself up, he grabbed the phone and said, "Medical to flight deck. Damage Control Teams One through Three converge on fire sector Bravo-Five and Delta-Two. Prep for flight deck triage. We've got mass casualties." He then blacked out and fell, cutting open a seven-inch gash on his forehead. His XO, who could still function, cradled the captain in his arms and yelled for a medic as the captain's blood soaked his uniform.

Chapter 61

USS FORD
1554 Hours, 10 August
Greenland Sea

The blast had been violent. In its short life, the *Ford* had been the victim of attacks by the Iranians, and now by the Russians. The Zircon hypersonic missile had slammed into the starboard aft section just below the flight deck, obliterating Elevator 3 and igniting a secondary fire in the hangar bay. The ship's lights flickered, then came back on. Quickly, the clatter of fire doors slamming shut echoed through the massive carrier. Above this adrenaline-producing noise were the ship's alarms that blared incessantly. However, through the bravery and training of the crew, the *Ford* held.

Chief Aviation Boatswain's Mate Warren Riley, known as Jet Bos'n Riley to everyone aboard, had been on the deck working. The moment the Zircon hit, he'd been thrown on his ass, and for a few moments he couldn't remember what he'd been doing or what had happened. But the forty-eight-year-old, barrel-chested brute of a man who'd been running flight decks since the Balkans, suddenly jumped to his feet, only to be met with flames burning around him.

He saw an F-35 sitting crooked near the blast perimeter, its rear landing gear wedged in a warped deck section and its tail scorched but intact. The bird was launch-ready, making it one hell of a large bomb.

Immediately, he put out a call on the emergency channel of his radio. "Tower, this is Jet Bos'n Riley. I need Crash 2, Chain Gangs 3, and Chain Gangs 5 to Spot 1. Bring two tow bars and prep a field dolly. Have DC Central send someone who can weld. That Bravo jet's ready to blow."

Riley heard a huge *whoosh* as a sudden gust of flame shot out from a vent seam nearby, likely fed by residual fuel vapor still burning below. The flight deck shook slightly beneath him. He debated his next move, which was getting close to un-assing the area.

Two sailors in silver flash gear turned toward the flight deck. The members of Crash and Salvage Team 2, who had been holding station aft while fighting the growing fire, saw flames heading toward a sailor bending over an F-35 landing gear. They sprinted with their hoses to help.

Each sailor dropped to a knee and swept a wide arc of white foam just forward of the F-35's tail. The flames that had been creeping toward the man receded. Riley gave them both a nod for saving his bacon. The two ran off to another hot spot.

Several green-shirts arrived with prepped steel pipe, clamps, and chain lengths. Working as a team, they built a makeshift dolly under the locked wheel strut.

Riley yelled, "Push!"

There was a loud shriek of metal as the fighter broke loose, then it rolled clear of the rupture. A spontaneous cheer erupted from everyone except Riley, who was already scanning the deck. He saw that the forward catapults were clear and signaled to the yellow-shirt standing near Catapult 1's blast deflector.

"Get her to the stroke," Riley barked, pointing down the deck. "Cat 1, now!"

The yellow-shirt nodded and immediately began spinning his arms overhead in rapid circles, signaling the tractor driver and brake rider. A green-shirt waved acknowledgment, and the tow team eased the jet toward Catapult 1, carefully avoiding the slick edge where foam still pooled from the crash team's last pass.

As the F-35 rolled into final position, Riley stood back, taking a moment to appreciate what he had just accomplished before sprinting down the deck toward the fire.

Sitting in the F-35 and getting ready to launch was Jessie Hampton, who was thanking the Almighty for saving his ass. He knew he needed to thank those on the deck, too, and would find out when he got back who the old-timer was who led the effort to get his F-35 away from the fire and onto the catapult. But right now, there was a war to fight, and he couldn't wait.

Chapter 62

HDMS Iver Huitfeldt
1534 Hours, 10 August
Northwest of the USS *Ford*

Captain Ostergaard stared at the tactical display aboard HDMS *Iver Huitfeldt*, his eyes scanning the data pouring through the NATO link. The ship's long-range SMART-L radar had just painted a fast low target, bearing one-nine-five. The captain had little experience with anyone shooting at him or his ship. Although he'd participated in several NATO war games, this was different.

He had to control the adrenaline rushing through his body. Slow down and think, he told himself.

His warfare officer was saying, "Profile matches the SS-N-27 Sizzler anti-ship missile. Sea-skimming. Speed around 403 kilometers per hour. No terminal stage yet."

"Set Condition One," Ostergaard snapped. "Bring CIWS and ESSMs online. Weapons free."

The Danish frigate's fire-control teams sprang into action in the Combat Direction Center. The SMART-L radar tracked the target as it skimmed in low, now under 40 kilometers out.

The Sizzler had been fired less than a minute earlier from the *Kazan,* and the *Huitfeldt* was at a distinct disadvantage. Due to the curvature of the Earth, even the flagship of the Danish Navy with its state-of-the-art shipborne radar systems couldn't detect sea-skimming targets until they were 40 to 47 kilometers away.

"Missile expected to enter terminal phase soon," the air warfare coordinator said. "It'll go supersonic to Mach 2.9 then."

"Time to impact?" Ostergaard asked.

"Forty-five seconds," came the reply.

"Fire ESSMs."

The forward Mk 41 VLS cells burst open in smoke and thunder, then immediately launched four ESSMs in rapid succession. The missiles arced up and banked hard, angling down toward the incoming threat.

"ESSMs away. Millennium Gun on standby."

In the Combat Direction Center, the track went red, hostile inbound.

"Sir, Sizzler has gone terminal. Pop-up maneuver confirmed. It's accelerating past Mach 3.3." The captain knew exactly what this meant. The cruise missile had shed its booster stage and deployed its supersonic terminal dart, a smaller aerodynamic warhead body designed for speed and penetration. When the dart executed a sudden pop-up maneuver, climbing sharply to gain altitude, it briefly disappeared from the ship's radar display, its signature masked by angle and velocity. Seconds later, it reappeared, angling downward in a high-velocity dive directly toward the *Huitfeldt*. They had thirty seconds to stop the missile.

"Captain, ESSMs are adjusting; two have lost lock. Millennium Gun firing."

The 35mm gun screamed, firing bursts of programmable advanced hit efficiency and destruction shells with air-bursting tungsten rounds designed to shred high-speed threats.

It was too little, too late.

Over 1MC, Ostergaard yelled, "Brace for impact."

A second later, the Sizzler dart slammed into the *Huitfeldt* just aft of the VLS, fire and steel shot into the air. The blast ruptured the starboard hull below the waterline and tore open several compartments amidships.

The ship pitched hard to port. Internal lights flickered. Fire alarms screamed throughout the ship. Ostergaard found himself lying on the deck. He looked around through the fog of his diminished eyesight and asked himself how long he'd been out. As he tried to get up, he saw bodies sprawled all around the bridge.

A faint voice said, "Situation report." The person kept repeating it. Still not hearing well or able to get up, Østergaard finally made out what was being said.

"This is Main Control. Fires are spreading through frames thirty to fifty. Forward seawater mains are severed. We're flooding fast."

"Abandon ship, abandon ship," Ostergaard yelled, but no words came out. Everything went black for the captain—for eternity.

Just under four minutes after being struck with the cruise missile, the HDMS *Iver Huitfeldt* rolled hard to starboard as it rolled over. A rush of seawater engulfed the hull. Within seconds, the ship slipped beneath the waves with only a handful of survivors struggling to stay alive in the freezing water. Of its crew of 165, fewer than twenty would be pulled out alive by rescue helicopters.

Chapter 63

1546 Hours, 10 August
Greenland

Before it sank, the *Kazan* had launched three 3M-14 Kalibr land-attack cruise missiles at Pituffik Space Base. Flying at subsonic speeds, the NATO-classified SS-N-30A missiles employed terrain-following profiles to reduce radar detection. Their navigation systems also received midcourse updates via satellite to refine their flight paths. Weaving through mountain passes and hugging the Greenlandic ice cap, each missile carried a thousand-pound warhead.

Pituffik's early warning radar did not detect the incoming missiles right away. Unfortunately, in the base's Operations Center, technicians first scanned their monitors looking for irregularities such as high-arc ballistic missiles, not terrain-skimming cruise missiles.

The newest team member, a nineteen-year-old just out of tech school, spotted it first. "Control, multiple returns bearing two-seven-one, low-altitude, and erratic. Might be clutter."

The controller had doubts about this excited newbie and decided to put her through her paces. "Confirm."

The newbie's screen flashed with updated information. She could now confirm. "Control, three inbound contacts. Range 35 miles. Speed subsonic. Profile is cruise missile."

The controller couldn't afford to keep doubting, so he hit a button. Alarms sounded throughout the base. Over the base-wide speaker system, he said as calmly as he could, "Missile attack. Missile attack. Take cover immediately." He had never thought he would ever have to say those words.

Although not originally built for heavy air defense, Pituffik had been partially reinforced over the past month as tensions in the Arctic escalated. A newly deployed National Advanced Surface-to-Air Missile System battery had been airlifted in and set up by US Air Force ground-based air defense crews. From that NASAMS, six AIM-120 AMRAAMs were launched in rapid succession out of static canister launchers as cued by the system's AN/MPQ-64 Sentinel radar. The AMRAAMs were then guided via midcourse uplinks from the base's integrated surveillance network through the Link 16 datalink system.

Inside the improvised command shelter next to the launcher site, a crew chief stared at his fire-control screen. "All targets confirmed. Three SS-N-30A tracks. Low-altitude. Speed 600 knots."

Smoke and flame blew sideways across the frozen ground as the AMRAAMs climbed sharply. Just as quickly, they tilted down to engage the targets.

"Missiles acquiring target," the crew chief said. "Time to intercept is ten seconds."

The newbie who first spotted the incoming missiles found herself mumbling, "Come on, come on."

Each AMRAAM was guided independently, using midcourse uplinks to adjust its path. At the final moment, their onboard radar seekers activated, locking onto separate approaching missiles with deadly precision.

The lead radar controller was the first to deliver some good news. "Intercept confirmed. One SS-N-30A neutralized. Splash at twelve miles."

Seconds later, another inbound missile disintegrated under a direct hit and ignited into a fireball that rained fragments onto the ice below. But one SS-N-30A had executed evasive turns, shifting vectors just enough to throw off the attackers. Two AMRAAMs passed wide, and the other two failed to reacquire before running out of energy.

The radar controller's voice changed to a pitch so high that one would have thought a different person was talking. "One leaker! Impact in ten seconds."

It turned out to be eight seconds when the Russian missile popped up from its cruise altitude, dove steeply, then struck a radar dome with surgical precision. The explosion obliterated the array and the room beneath it, sending concrete and steel fragments tearing through the operations center and killing six inside.

While all were fighting for their survival, they missed the Zircon hypersonic missile striking the *Ford*.

Chapter 64

THE WHITE HOUSE
10 August
Washington, DC

Sitting in the Situation Room with members of his NSC, President Mark Taylor was pissed off as he watched a video of the still smoldering wreckage of the *Ford*. Twisted metal ripped across the aft third of the flight deck. Smoke was still venting from near the carrier's island. Pieces of aircraft were strewn around like discarded toys.

"George, give it to me straight," Taylor said to the SecDef. "Don't sugarcoat anything. Got it?"

All eyes shifted to George Mitchell. Almost everyone in the room was hearing and seeing what happened for the first time, and everyone was as pissed off as their boss.

"Mr. President, at 0449 hours Zulu, the Russian submarine Kazan launched a coordinated missile strike. The first wave was a cluster of Sizzler anti-ship cruise missiles. They were not aimed at Ford but at the escorts on the outer protective screen. The Hudner intercepted two with an ESSM. The Danish frigate Iver Huitfeldt was hit directly amidships, starboard side, and sank in minutes. We expect heavy loss of life."

After a pause, he continued, "Then came the Zircon, a hypersonic missile that we're still playing catch-up with in defending." This raised several eyebrows, despite everyone in the room being aware of it. While funding for missile defense was gaining traction, development and deployment took time, and those in the Pentagon had hoped the Zircon wouldn't be used against the US for many years. Mitchell began to go into details about the ship's defensive measures, but the president interrupted him.

"Casualties, George."

"Sir, the current count, which keeps going up, is 126 dead and 212 injured. Medevac is underway. We've redirected our C-17s in Europe to Iceland for medical support. The carrier group is holding station but degraded."

The president fired off another request, "Confirm who did this and the outcome."

DNI Elena Ramirez cut in. "Mr. President, the Idaho was already tracking the Kazan in passive shadow. When the Zircon launched, the Idaho closed and fired one Mark 48 torpedo. We have confirmed imagery that the Kazan was destroyed. A debris field spread across six nautical miles, and there were no thermal signatures. No survivors."

Taylor leaned forward. "Does our intelligence believe this was a rogue submarine?"

Ramirez said, "No, sir. SIGINT shows command messages from Severomorsk to the Kazan, so this was most likely authorized through the Northern Fleet chain. We believe this was a planned escalation likely intended to test our threshold and intent."

Before anyone else could jump in, SecState Brad Kelly said, "Sir, this wasn't a probe. This was a decapitation strike. The Russians planned to knock the Ford out of action without technically triggering Article 5. Hitting the Danish vessel muddies the issue, but the missile that struck us leaves no ambiguity. This is an attack on the United States."

People in the room shuffled in their seats, but Kelly continued, "We're recommending immediate NATO Article 4 consultations. We're also drafting parallel messaging to London, Paris, Berlin, and Ottawa. We'll get unity, but Article 5 will depend on how we play this. The Danes are furious. The Norwegians are already on alert. But many in NATO will want verification and time before Article 5 is invoked."

"Okay, I've had enough," said Taylor. "Prepare for a speech to the nation tonight. We'll tell them what happened. And we'll tell them what's coming. In the meantime, begin surge planning. I want a second carrier strike group deployed. Activate all necessary units, no holds barred. If Russia is upping the ante, then we're going all-in." Taylor stood up. "Make it happen."

He walked out the door with his Secret Service protection surrounding him.

11 August

Moscow, Russia

Natalia Romanova, the Deputy Defense Minister, held that position due to her acumen in politics and, more importantly, her ability to control the narrative when the spotlight was on. In the anteroom to the Press Briefing Room, she peered at the security monitors. She saw representatives from *TASS, RT,* and *Izvestiya,* as well as journalists from a variety of foreign outlets, including the BBC, Reuters, and *Al Jazeera.* President Andrei Petrov had personally briefed her, so she was aware of what was expected of her.

After checking herself in the mirror, she walked into the Press Briefing Room and to the podium. Chatter stopped as she drew the room's attention.

She checked her three teleprompters, but her favorite was in the center because when she looked at that one, she landed right into people's living rooms. And once there, she knew she could win them over to Russia's take on things.

So, looking directly at the center teleprompter, she said, "Let me say right from the onset that Russia condemns, in the strongest possible terms, the reckless and aggressive behavior of the United States in the Arctic region."

Murmurs rippled through the room. Good, she thought, I have their attention.

"Yesterday, a Russian Federation naval asset operating in accordance with international law was destroyed in open waters in an unprovoked American attack. The Kazan, a submarine on routine patrol, was struck without warning by a US torpedo. We are currently reviewing sonar telemetry and diplomatic channels for confirmation, but initial data suggests no Russian weapons were fired before this hostile act."

As a professional, she knew to pause so translation feeds could catch up. She didn't want to leave anyone behind.

"In America's latest cover-up, US officials are spreading disinformation, claiming that the Russian Navy initiated hostilities. Let me be clear, no Russian missiles were launched at the Gerald R. Ford carrier or any NATO vessels. Their claims are a fabrication designed to justify further US militarization of the Arctic and deny Russia safe passage in international waters.

"The United States has long sought to dominate the Arctic through illegal military encroachment, sanctions warfare, and economic coercion. This incident is merely the latest provocation in a long pattern of destabilization."

A journalist from Germany's *Der Spiegel* stood up and interrupted her. Nothing new there, she thought.

"What about the Danish ship, the Huitfeldt?" the German reporter said. "It was sunk, and scores of sailors were killed. Is Russia denying involvement?"

The audience members seemed to move to the edges of their seats as they anticipated Natalia's response. Little did they know how much she had rehearsed just this answer.

Again using the center teleprompter, she said, "We mourn the loss of life, but we must ask, why was a Danish warship operating alongside an American carrier group in contested waters just miles from Russian sovereign territory? Had the West not surrounded Russian patrol zones with high-powered radar, stealth aircraft, and nuclear-capable platforms, this tragedy might never have occurred. We urge Copenhagen to consider whose fault this really is."

By getting that out, thanks to the impertinence of the German reporter, she had checked all her boxes, so she finished with, "That's all, thank you." She walked out of the room with reporters still yelling questions at her.

Chapter 65

NORTHROP GRUMMAN B-21 RAIDER HANGAR

12 August

Pituffik Space Base

Ever since the wing had received the OPORD for Operation Frost Lance, the two B-21s had been tucked away in their new reinforced hangars at Pituffik Space Base, where they sat like black phantoms.

It had been two days since the attacks on CSG-12 and Pituffik. The bombers were fully mission-capable, and having been so far removed from the battlespace, when the president wanted payback, something clean and deniable, the B-21s were just the tool.

Deniability would be simple. Over the past two years, the Pentagon had quietly leaked reports of B-21 program delays, such as production stalls due to integration issues. Whenever a rumor was planted, it quickly became a major story. The media created articles, newscasts, and even podcasts detailing all the production problems and slamming the Pentagon for ineptitude.

But in reality, the program had been ahead of schedule. The deception succeeded. The US intelligence community had confirmed that Russia's planners dismissed the Raiders as years away from being a real threat.

Presently, only a few on a need-to-know basis had any knowledge that the B-21s were ready for operational tasking. And one of those few sent the order.

In a Sensitive Compartmented Information Facility located in the office area at the back of the B-21 hangar, five men and two women were seated around a table. SCIF had all the latest bells and whistles.

The table projected a three-dimensional holographic overlay of eastern Greenland. Hovering above the surface of the table was pale blue topography indicating mountain ridgelines, fjords, and ice fields. The image occasionally flickered as the satellite feed refreshed. Bright red icons marked known Russian positions: an SA-21 Growler radar dish atop a ridgeline, a fuel depot near a glacier shelf, and a radar and navigational aids near Constable Pynt airport.

The B-21 wing commander, Colonel Ava Richmond, stood at the head of the table and used a stylus to point to the southern ridge above the airport. Across from her sat Major Logan Carter, the strike lead. Beside him was his co-pilot, 1st Lieutenant Megan Alvarez, who was calm and focused, holding a tablet. Besides the two other pilots in the room, the final seat was filled by Ed Munro, the NSA's Arctic Liaison, who monitored Russian comms and directed the fusion of intel streams feeding the holographic display.

"The mobile SA-21 battery here, Carter pointed to one of the red icons, "rotated in last week from Novaya Zemlya.

They're using terrain-masking line-of-sight coverage west, and it overlaps the SA-22 Greyhound radar net to the north. We've flagged their uplink activity as clean and disciplined. The operators aren't militia."

She moved the pointer to a glowing yellow icon several miles inland. "This is their POL site. Our principal targets will be two SA-21 Growler batteries north of the airfield, and the secondary target is the command center at confirmed grid four-seven-two and radar installations. There are also two MZKT 7930 trucks. The trucks are parked under camouflage netting near the ice wall. The thermal signatures are unmistakable. They're prepping for overland movement."

Carter leaned forward, arms resting on the table's edge and eyes locked on the rotating terrain model. "Any overhead confirmation on whether those SAMs are hot or if they're just decoys?"

Munro responded without looking up from his tablet, "We intercepted brief comms two hours ago. The coded uplink handshake is consistent with full readiness state. They're hot. We estimate three launchers, two search radars, and one command vehicle. All camouflaged. But the EM pattern is clean. They're running a tight beam sweep, not broadcast."

Alvarez was looking at the Petroleum, Oils, and Lubricants site. "Any thermal guards?"

Munro shook his head. "Thermals are minimal. They're relying on isolation."

"Looking at your armaments," Richmond said, "you'll be equipped with a full strike package. Each aircraft will carry four JASSM-XRs preprogrammed for the radar and POL targets. You'll cross the cap at altitude, drop to 25,000 feet just west of Scoresby Sound, and release from standoff range with no follow-through. You get in clean, and you get out the same way." Richmond paused, giving her aircrews time to apply the information to the hologram.

"The US has a large operation planned," she continued, "but no one can commit until we blind the Russians' net and cut their fuel. You take out their eyes, their reach, and their movement, and after that, they're stuck in the ice without radar or gas."

"Poor babies," Carter said, and smiled.

Chapter 66

NATO HEADQUARTERS
12 August
Brussels, Belgium

To most of the thirty-two NATO countries, Article 4 couldn't have been written any clearer.

"The Parties will consult together whenever, in the opinion of any of them, the territorial integrity, political independence or security of any of the Parties is threatened."

Yet here NATO was again, its hands tied by its bureaucracy and lack of unity. At the head of the room, standing beneath the NATO flag and facing the ring of somber faces, was Ambassador Henrik Hansen. He appeared haggard: his tie loosened, his suit wrinkled, and his hair out of place.

"Ladies and gentlemen, brothers and sisters in arms, Denmark has suffered a deliberate and fatal attack for a second time."

He tapped a remote. The chamber lights dimmed slightly as the central screen came to life. A satellite image filled the ten-foot display, showing smoke billowing from the waters east of Greenland, a heat bloom marking the spot like an exclamation point. "This is where Russian missiles brutally attacked the HDMS *Iver Huitfeldt.* There was no warning, no radio communication, just Russian missiles that killed 143 sailors and sent our flagship to the bottom of the sea. Make no mistake; this was an act of war."

The room was silent. Even the American ambassador and his aides sat still. They were watching everyone, trying to interpret facial expressions and body language to see what direction this was going.

"Has Russia confirmed or denied responsibility?" asked the French ambassador, as if no one had seen the broadcast from the Russian newscast.

"Sir," said Hansen, "you know the answer to that question. Why even ask it? Of course they denied it. They blamed it on the Americans, said that the submarine Kazan was sunk before any launch."

The American and British aides sneered out loud. Someone said, "Typical."

The US ambassador spoke next in a controlled voice. "We have full missile telemetry from Aegis radar and signature matches to Sizzler and Zircon cruise missile launches. They came from Kazan. Our submarine response to the start of hostilities by the Russians was measured and legal. Let's be clear here, the Russians fired the first shots."

The Polish ambassador, Anna Wilczek, jumped from her seat. "We must invoke Article 5."

This caused immediate consternation among several in the room, as if she had just declared World War III. Most nodded in agreement.

NATO Secretary General Marcus van Dijk stood and held up both hands. All eyes shifted to him. "Be reminded, we are here under Article 4 for consultation. A response is required, but it must be unified, measured, and above all else, strategic." He turned to Hansen. "What would Denmark request?"

Hansen replied, "We request immediate NATO reinforcement of the GIUK Gap, a no-fly zone over western Greenland, and maritime exclusion of all Russian naval assets west of the thirty-degree east meridian. Additionally, we request the formal preparation of Article 5 invocation, pending any further attack."

He let that sink in, then continued, "We are not here to grieve. We are here to prevent the next Huitfeldt and Ford from occurring."

The chamber went quiet again. The Italian ambassador whispered to his aides. Germany's representative shook her head, clearly weighing internal politics. It was so quiet that when someone clicked a mic, everyone stopped talking.

It was the Turkish ambassador. "If we escalate, Russia will strike again, and it may not be over empty ice."

Hansen fired back, "That's exactly why we act now and on our terms."

Van Dijk took back control of the session. "We will now enter a closed session. All advisors out." He remained standing as aides filed out and the doors were sealed. His eyes had stayed locked on the red-ringed satellite image of *Huitfeldt's* last location.

"We will vote on emergency force posture changes within the hour," he said.

Chapter 67

NORTHROP GRUMMAN B-21 RAIDER HANGAR
Early hours, 12 August
Pituffik Space Base

Carter had been involved with the B-21 program for nearly a year. However, as he prepared to leave the haven of his aircraft hangar, today would be different, the aircraft's first combat mission.

In the cockpit, all systems were green, his favorite color. "Engines stable. IR signature masked. Terrain following radar online," Alvarez reported.

The armored blast doors of the hangar eased open with a mechanical groan. Eagle 91, the B-21 Raider, rolled forward, its edges softened by the haze and the shimmer of heat from its auxiliary power unit. Under the golden wash of the airfield lights, its matte-black skin reflected almost nothing, making it appear less like an aircraft than a shadow sliding across the tarmac, a phantom built for war. In the cockpit, soft, filtered blue lighting illuminated the touchscreen interfaces, while amber outlines traced system health in real time. Known as pilot cognitive management, the display lighting and setup helped reduce pilot sensory overload. Instead of harsh buzzers, it employed subtle audio tones, directional cues, or haptic feedback.

In the right seat, Alvarez reviewed her checklist and checked on Eagle 92, since the other bomber's systems information was linked into her cockpit display.

"EO-DAS radar live," Alvarez said. "Terrain avoidance system online. Weapons systems safe. No windshear reported."

Carter scanned the flight parameters. "Copy. Taxi power to active."

Outside, the ground crew signaled readiness with hand gestures, not using radios or light wands. Eagle 91 and 92 began to move, rolling into the dusk, their engines barely audible over the steady wind flowing over the prairie. No tower cleared them. No call sign was logged. The launch wasn't in NATO's flight database. It didn't exist.

As their aircraft's wheels reached the runway threshold, Alvarez reported, "EMCON Alpha. Masking active. Polar ducting still holding. We are clean."

Carter eased the throttles forward. "Perfect. Then let's disappear."

The flight to the eastern shore of Greenland was all business with no idle chatter and just brief, necessary exchanges. Carter maintained a steady airspeed as the B-21 cruised through the upper troposphere at 45,000 feet. The plane's evolved stealth design rendered it virtually invisible to radar and difficult to track even by infrared satellites. He continually scanned the cockpit displays to verify weapon status and navigation tracks, while Alvarez monitored satellite imagery relayed through their secure datalink.

It was important. The closer they were to their target, the more everything mattered, since their lives were intertwined with how well they performed their duties. Carter constantly checked his instruments.

"Set Emission Control profile to Alpha-Plus," he said. "No active emissions. Passive sensors only."

As they neared their weapons release point, Alvarez double-checked all operating systems and said to Carter, "Hawk, verify primary objectives are two SA-21 Growler batteries north of the airfield, and secondary target is the command center at confirmed grid four-seven-two and radar installations."

Carter nodded, adjusting the flight path slightly. "Confirmed, Pixie. Ground units can't move until those radars are down. No warning, no counter-fire. We get one shot at each."

Alvarez enlarged the satellite feed, outlining the active radar signals. "Both SA-21 batteries are online. The command center's fortified, but it's above ground. One direct hit should do it."

Alvarez tapped on the TRN module and spoke again, "Terrain masking route holding. No LOS breach to Russian overwatch. Satellite occlusion window still open. Next Russian electronic intelligence in twelve minutes."

"Good," Carter replied. "No course adjustments. Hold this heading."

Alvarez checked the mission clock, then typed a single secure message directly to Eagle 92. "Four minutes to ripple launch. Stay in position. Fire on lead."

Less than a second later, the response arrived as just a green confirmation symbol on her lower display. There was no voice, no waveform, and no trail.

Carter adjusted the flight path slightly. "Weapons check."

"Four JASSMs armed and programmed. Targets assigned. Systems green."

"Master arm on," said Carter.

Alvarez worked the console. "Payload armed. Weapons ready."

"Weapons free on my mark."

"Bays confirmed open."

"Fire."

Carter felt a slight change in airframe balance as two missiles dropped cleanly and were followed a second later by two more. Faint flashes from below marked the ignition of the missile engines. They were gone almost as quickly as they had appeared. He watched the display as the weapon indicators cycled to empty. "I see clean release and no hung stores."

Carter adjusted the flight path, banking east. "Egress heading one-zero-zero. Maintain emissions control."

Alvarez verified their navigation and checked for the umpteenth time. "Course confirmed. No radar activity. Airspace remains uncontested."

Carter kept the Raider steady, climbing slightly to optimize fuel efficiency during egress. He radioed, "Weapons away. Eagle 91, returning to base."

Alvarez said something, but Carter didn't hear her. He was staring at the far-left panel, where a single pixel shift had flickered into existence for less than half a second, not a tone, not a lock, just a ripple, like light through water. Carter quickly reached forward, toggled the passive signal processor, and ran a loop-back diagnostic.

Nothing. The trace was gone.

Alvarez saw his motion. "What did you see?"

"Might've been an ionospheric bounce. It could've been the sun glancing off a Russian uplink dish and hitting us just wrong. Or"—he paused.

She turned toward him. Through her helmet's enhanced vis-light filter, Carter was right next to her. His face was half-lit in blue from the nav panel, his jaw clenched and eyes locked forward. Her augmented reality HUD marked his vitals in the lower corner, showing an elevated heart rate and mild stress spikes that would be barely perceptible in real life but were evident on her visor.

Carter was focused, his eyes continually scanning. A faint red ring hovered on his HUD, the last known location of the ghost trace and still marked with a question mark icon. The system hadn't dismissed it yet. It searched for more data.

"Could've been a lucky look," he said.

RUSSIAN AIR DEFENSE POST

0329 Hours, 12 August

Northwest of Constable Pynt Airport

Senior Sergeant Andrei Belov sat hunched over the scope inside a canvas-draped command shelter. One hand clutched a paper cup of strong tea that had gone cold.

He started to yawn, then stopped abruptly. A faint pulse crawled erratically across the display. It was in sector 160 at an altitude band between thirty and forty thousand. But it was neither a lock nor a return, just a shimmer.

He called out, "Comrade Lieutenant?"

"What is it, Sergeant?" said the officer in a tone that indicated he didn't want to be bothered.

"Sir, possible contact, bearing one-six-zero. Very faint, a single blip. Could be an EM shadow or just a reflection."

The lieutenant stepped in closer. "Show me."

Belov rescanned. Nothing appeared.

"Gone now, sir."

The lieutenant stared at the empty screen, then looked at Belov. "Could be atmospheric ducting. Sun angles are garbage at this latitude. I think you're chasing an apparition, Sergeant."

Belov was one of the best at what he did, which explained why he held this position in the first place. He also recognized that the lieutenant was unhappy with his new assignment and made excuses for many things. Thus, Belov hesitated. He felt the next logical step was to contact the S-400 unit and request an active sweep. Hell, even an AESA pulse from the Pantsir would suffice.

"You want me to mark it and report it to Command?" he asked.

The lieutenant shook his head. "Negative. If anyone's here, we'll know soon enough. Maintain passive scan. Don't wake up anyone for shadows."

B-21s
0334 Hours, 12 August
Over Constable Pynt

On the B-21, Alvarez monitored the launch firing. The 3D tactical display was refreshed with infrared imagery from a low-Earth orbiting ISR CubeSat, which showed heat signatures across the target zone in near real-time. Carter watched the feed on the center display. A sudden thermal bloom flared on the ridgeline, sharp, brilliant, and expanding fast.

Alvarez said, "Impact confirmed. Direct hit on radar site. Second impact in three—two—one—"

The sensors indicated four thermal clouds, all direct strikes.

"Good effects on targets," said Alvarez. "Battery's down. Fire-control offline. No secondary launch signatures. Eagle 92 reports good effects on all assigned targets."

Carter settled into his seat for the trip home.

Alvarez nodded, already verifying flight path masking. "Flight plan re-engaged. No emissions. We're clean."

Chapter 68

11TH AIRBORNE DIVISION – PATHFINDER DETACHMENT
1031 Hours, 12 August
Blosseville Coast near Constable Pynt, Greenland

The interior of the MC-130 Commando II with its AFSOC crew was a cavern of red lights and metal. Captain Robert "Frosty" Shepherd sat along the starboard wall of the aircraft, his M4 carbine across his lap, his gloved hands resting calmly over the receiver. Outwardly calm, that is. Internally, he was wound tight. He glanced at the altimeter display strapped to his forearm, just a few more minutes to jump.

Sitting directly across from him was his platoon leader, Lieutenant Elena Vasquez. She was studying her forearm-mounted tablet. On it was a 3D overlay of eastern Greenland. Like in the field, she sensed something, looked up, and locked eyes with her boss through her oxygen mask.

She thought this would be a good opportunity to give the captain the latest update. "Thermals picked up a shallow saddle just north of Hurry Fjord. It looks clear and flat enough for eight sticks to drop and assemble without scrambling over rock or ice. There are no heat signatures and no movement. Could be the best drop zone we get."

"That's our spot," Shepherd replied. "Get us on the ground quietly; mark it fast. Then we hold until the division comes in."

With a clenched fist, the loadmaster signaled the five-minute warning and pointed to the ramp. The cargo door began to lower, wind howling into the belly of the aircraft as if it were alive. The temperature dropped instantly as everyone pulled down their visors.

Shepherd stood up, as did the rest of the eight-person squad. He checked the tether on Vasquez's pack, then his own. She checked his. All the others were doing the same thing. No one spoke.

The MC-130 banked hard to the south, hugging the radar shadow line between two peaks. The airstrip at Constable Pynt was less than fifteen miles out, close enough for a Tor-M2 short-range missile system to engage them at low altitude. But above 30,000 feet, masked by Greenland's topography and flying in from the west, they should be good, or so they all hoped. That was up to the Air Force dudes.

"One minute to jump," the loadmaster called out.

Shepherd had always been a positive thinker, but somehow, a few negative thoughts crept in before he could dismiss them. This one was going to be tough. They were operating behind enemy lines in the Arctic, with no way out, and if they were spotted, things could get ugly fast.

He stepped to the front of the line, followed closely by Vasquez. They were the two most qualified to identify the landing zone in case of a scatter.

The red light clicked to green. Shepherd jumped.

He went headfirst, body tight, legs tucked, viewing the earth as a flat smear below. His altimeter blinked steadily, indicating the distance to the deployment point. All around him, the others drifted in formation. The butterflies had vanished; now it was just the hiss of his regulator and the rush of air past his ears. He was all business, focusing on where to land, how fast to orient, and checking on Vasquez.

At 5,000 feet, he deployed. The HALO chute jerked open with a brutal snap. He swung once, then steadied. The landing was hard; most were. Not unexpected. Wind at only 10 knots helped. Shepherd landed on his feet, unclipped fast, and drew his rifle. All around, dark figures landed and converged silently.

Vasquez landed 30 yards off his flank and hit the snow running. She was unhooking and scanning before she even yanked the chute free.

"Drone's up," Vasquez whispered. "Telemetry clean. The ridge is clear; the patrol grid at zero-four-seven appears to have two dismounts moving east.

"Mark the LZ," Shepherd ordered.

Vasquez knelt and activated the infrared beacon, which was coded for C-130 approach and unreadable to Russian NVGs. A second burst went to Pituffik: "Blizzard One: LZ secure. Commence drop. Window green."

USS *FORD* CAP
1035 Hours, 12 August
East Greenland

As Jessie prepared for the CAP launch, he reviewed the adjustments needed for Carrier Wing 8. In the immediate future, they could launch only from Catapults 1 and 2, as 3 and 4 were out of commission due to the missile strike. On the recovery side, only the middle arresting wire had tension. That meant you would only get one shot at catching that single wire, or you would become a bolter, hoping you had enough fuel for a go-around. Additionally, the carrier E-2s were grounded because they were too heavy for the current operational conditions. Thankfully, two E-2s were flying out of Pituffik, with one being Jessie's wife.

He was also thankful for the men who saved his ass when he was stuck on the deck with nearly 20,000 pounds of fuel and four internal missiles, with flames coming right for him. Being shot down was one thing, but getting blown up on the deck of a carrier wasn't how he wanted to check out.

For this CAP, they were going for a complete stealth profile. There would be no pylons, wingtip ordnance, or gun pods, just smooth angles and hidden firepower with four AIM-260 AMRAAMS tucked inside the aircraft.

Jessie was hooked up on Catapult 1 with his wingman, Lieutenant Jace "Cutter" Nolan, on Catapult 2. Two Growlers waiting their turn, one piloted by Razor. Their birds were loaded with electronic warfare ALQ-218 receivers and ALQ-99 jamming pods under each wing. For defense, they had AMRAAMs and Sidewinders.

Once airborne, they gathered up at 25,000 feet. As discussed in their brief, they would fly a four-ship box spread optimized for layered defense and radar coverage.

Jessie called it out. "Raven 22, Raven 21, move to the right side of the formation, five miles behind. Shadow 11, copy that, and take the left side. Keep the jamming perimeter tight. Shadow 12, shift into combat spread one mile off my right wing, same altitude."

"All units, this is Raven 21. Formation is set. Begin patrol. Stay in radio silence. Watch for enemy fighters. Keep the airspace clear."

Supporting the operation was the E-2 Hawkeye, piloted by Freeman. The experiment of flying E-2s from a land base was undergoing its first real combat test since *Ford's* E-2s couldn't launch. For Sarah's crew, the mission was straightforward yet critical. They needed to maintain airspace integrity east of the ice cap while the 11th Airborne prepared to drop into eastern Greenland in their attempt to drive the Russians from Constable Pynt Airfield.

The E-2's AN/APY-9 radar swept a 360-degree sphere out to 300 miles. Every return was analyzed, filtered, and transmitted via Link-16 to strike aircraft, CAP fighters, and AWACS controllers back at Pituffik. They were flying a classic racetrack pattern, 150 miles northwest of Constable Pynt at 20,000 feet.

"CICO, talk to me," asked Sarah, waiting for something to happen.

Her Combat Information Center Officer answered. "Tracking multiple IFF-positive friendlies: Ford Flight, out of home."

"Maintain wide scan. Prioritize low-probability threats east of Scoresby Sound."

As soon as the words were out of her mouth, it was her CICO, "New radar contact, bearing zero-eight-eight, range 210 nautical. Intermittent S-band. Sweep pattern consistent with Russian N011M Bars radar. Flanker-class emitter."

Chapter 69

AIRBORNE ASSAULT

1040 Hours, 12 August

Near Constable Pynt Airfield

Corporal Adam Dankworth stood second in line among sixty-five paratroopers from the 1st Battalion, 501st Parachute Infantry Regiment, ready to drop into eastern Greenland and face the Russians. He was far removed from the streets of New York City, where survival was a daily struggle and friendships held little meaning. Getting arrested had merely been another segment of his existence. When a judge offered him the choice of prison or the Army, he opted to enlist.

Dankworth proved himself during the war with Iran, earning recognition and a battlefield promotion. It was while in uniform that he found his true family, the US Army, and learned what loyalty meant. Now, others looked to him for leadership. He had switched his Military Occupational Specialty from infantry to airborne, and once again, he was heading into the thick of the fight.

The loadmaster's yell brought Dankworth back to the present. Just as the side doors opened, "Stand up" echoed through the cabin. Sixty-five paratroopers got up in one practiced move.

"Hook up."

The soldiers connected their static line to the anchor cable, the metallic clicks drowning out the sound of the engines for a brief moment.

"Check static line."

As the red light turned green, the order came: "Go."

Dankworth jumped out, feeling the familiar pull. He heard nothing but the wind whistling by and a sharp crack as his chute deployed. This was his life now. As the C-130 disappeared, he watched parachutes begin to bloom above the plateau like dandelions.

Then his world exploded.

He had a perfect aerial view as a mortar round struck 300 feet north of the drop zone. A brilliant flash erupted, and a puff of black smoke curled in the wind. Another landed closer, sending snow and a soldier flying through the air.

Dankworth pulled hard on his MC-6 risers, trying to avoid a crag near the drop's edge. His boots hit hard, skidding on the permafrost. He rolled as he yanked the chute in with numb fingers. His squad leader was already up, shouting, "Rally on me. North sector, use cover."

Another mortar round exploded near him as he ran in a combat crouch. He jumped into a shallow depression, landing next to a private who was face down in the mud, his chute still tangled around him. The next mortar landed closer, and shrapnel whizzed by his head. Overhead, he heard the thunder of a jet engine afterburner. Whose jet, he didn't know, but he kept moving towards his squad leader.

CAP

1112 Hours, 12 August

Near Constable Pynt Airfield

Jessie heard his wife's broadcast warning of incoming hostiles. "Three-bandit group, Mach 1.3, angels 35 and climbing. They're burning in fast."

"Flight, Raven 21, Confirming spike. Passive track only. Three contacts, echelon spread, high closure. ID as Su-35s. Classify bandits as hostile. Intercept and engage, weapons free. Shadow 11, 12, begin jamming tactics."

"Raven flight leader, Shadow 11, Burner's lit. Standoff jamming active denying Bars radar locks, deploying IR countermeasures for their IRST feeds."

Razor stayed calm. His Growler's sensors picked up radar signals from the incoming fighters while his electronics kicked into action. The jamming pod began flooding the area with interference aimed at the Russian jets to blind their radars. At the same time, he activated decoys that sent out false signals designed to trick the enemy into locking onto the wrong targets. The goal was simple: make it as difficult as possible for the Russians to get a clean shot.

Jessie thumbed the sensor mode, switching to active radar. He saw the triangle symbols go from "Hostile" to

"SU-35 Flanker-E." He told his wingman that he would target the first two 35s and assigned the third to him. The AESA radar locked on targets, and the fire-control solution stabilized in seconds.

"Raven 21, Fox Three."

Beneath his F-35, the weapon doors snapped open. Two AIM-260 AMRAAMs dropped clean from the internal racks, free-falling for a split second before their rocket motors ignited with a flash. He watched the twin contrails flare bright against the sky as the missiles accelerated past Mach 4, homing in on the radar signature of the Su-35s. He heard his wingman announce Fox Three. In his helmet, a line appeared, tracing the missile's flight path toward the Flankers. A small box lit up over the bandit distance, ticking down from 20 seconds.

Jessie knew better than to marvel at his missile release like a baseball player admiring his home run while standing at home plate. He skillfully threw his stick over, pulling into a steep climb, having learned that a straight vector after a launch was a good way to get killed.

He tapped the throttle forward, kicking into afterburner, and climbed through 35,000 feet, regaining the advantage of altitude and speed. As the Gs pressed him into the seat, he glanced toward his left display, watching the missile telemetry. Both 260s were holding track. Time-to-impact dropped into single digits.

The Su-35s reacted instantly. One went vertical, trying to drag the missiles high. The second broke left, releasing countermeasures. The third dove toward the terrain, going low to break the radar lock. Jessie saw the flash bloom in infrared as the seeker found its target. The box for the low flyer blinked off his display, replaced by a soft tone.

As Jessie maneuvered, his right thumb hovered over the HOTAS countermeasures switch. If the Russians had fired missiles, and they probably had, he was ready to deploy flares or chaff manually, even though the jet's electronic warfare suite could handle it automatically. The Barracuda system was already online, scanning for radar locks and preparing jamming pulses in case anything got through its stealth profile or evasive maneuvers.

On their way to leveling out at 28,000 feet, the flight saw the last parachutes disappear. Jessie's heart was getting back to normal. "Pickett 11, Raven flight leader, splash three. Holding Echo-Three. Fuel state green."

"Copy, Raven 21," said Sarah, holding back any sign of emotion or impropriety. "Maintain CAP, radar clean."

Jessie looked east, where the faint line of the sun was rising. "Raven flight, CAP parameters. Let's keep the sky clean and trigger fingers ready."

Chapter 70

2ND BRIGADE, 11TH AIRBORNE DIVISION
1125 Hours, 12 August
Near Constable Pynt Airport

Dankworth saw the last of the paratroopers landing around him, each quickly with their rifles at the ready, forming up, and moving out of the LZ into assigned sectors. Sergeant Duffy, his squad leader, yelled, "Perimeter, get eyes on the ridge." Everyone knew which ridge because mortars and small arms fire were pounding them from it.

Without warning came a *boom* as a mortar round landed nearby. The frozen ground vibrated, and shrapnel, ice chunks, and rocks flew in all directions. The Russians were marching their mortars closer into the LZ. Soldiers yelled, "I'm hit," and "help." Some just screamed in agony.

Someone hollered, "Mortars, north slope."

No shit, Dankworth thought.

Another explosion sounded, and the half-erected command tent vanished in a flash of fire. Dankworth heard Duffy yell to his radio operator, "Get us some air assets, now!"

The RTO crouched behind a boulder and immediately got on the line. "Any station, this is Echo 32. Troops in contact, grid November Tango zero-six-niner-three-five by one-two-four. We are taking effective mortar fire from the ridge line to our north, approximately 100 meters above LZ Echo. Request immediate close-air support. Danger close, say again, danger close. Marking with IR strobes and red smoke. How copy, over?"

1131 Hours, 12 August
Near Constable Pynt Airport

Inside the cockpit of his F-35, Jessie heard the clipped, urgent message on the secure VHF channel. Although he wasn't armed for ground targets, he knew how to help in another way. Checking his helmet display, he saw the coordinates and relayed them through his datalink. Instantly, his sensor fusion system mapped the overlaying terrain, friendly unit positions, and heat signatures. Six distinct thermal contacts pulsed along a rocky shelf above the LZ. Another flicker appeared, likely a vehicle attempting to reposition itself behind the ridge.

"Echo 32, Raven 21 in F-35 overhead. I copy you're in contact. I have visual on your red smoke and IR strobe. I confirm six enemy heat signatures on the north slope, plus one possible vehicle moving west. I am Winchester for ground strike, repeat, Winchester for CAS, but I can act as your FAC. Stand by for asset coordination." Jessie switched frequencies, reaching out to the two A-10C Thunderbolt IIs, better known as Warthogs, holding in the combat air patrol, ready to deliver their trademark firepower.

"Havoc 21, Raven 21. Say position and stand by for targeting info."

"Raven 21, Havoc 21. Two A-10s five minutes out. Say target data."

Acting as a forward air controller, Jessie loaded the target packet. His HUD crosshair blinked red over the mortar position. "Havoc 21, Raven 21. Target is six mortar positions dug into north-facing slope, elevation 900 feet. Red smoke is visible. IR confirmed. Secondary target is one vehicle west of the ridge, possibly a command element. Recommend ingress west to east. Danger close, friendlies 165 feet south of target."

"Copy all, Raven 21. I tally smoke and IR. Confirm you'll hold FAC through engagement."

"Raven 21, holding position as FAC. We'll handle battle damage assessment. You are cleared to engage." Major Lex "Hog-tie" Gaines locked eyes on the ridge line through his HUD. Red smoke billowed below like a flare from hell smeared sideways by Arctic wind. His targeting pod's feed showed six thermal contacts nestled in mortar pits, dug in hard and camouflaged for overhead ISR but useless against the A-10s sensors, linked to a battlefield network that sees everything."

The saying "the right man for the right job" fit Gaines perfectly. He'd flown almost every type of aircraft in his eighteen-year career in the Air Force, but for him, nothing matched the A-10. No other aircraft gave him the same feel in his hands: a low, mean connection to the ground fight. There was no stealth and no glamour, just titanium, thrust, and a cannon that could chew through armor as if it were wet plywood.

Gaines had flown the Hog over Fallujah, Kandahar, and the Kooringal. And now here he was, over the ice fields of Greenland, riding the old bird into its last days. The powers that be had tried to retire the A-10 more times than he could count, and they had finally succeeded in setting a non-negotiable schedule. He didn't blame them, because there were shinier, faster, sexier toys now. But none could look a grunt in the eye like the Warthog did. It wasn't built to fly pretty. It was built to keep people alive. And he was counting on that again.

He shoved the throttle forward and dipped the nose of the Hog toward the ground to pick up speed. In his helmet display, the aiming marker locked onto the enemy trench.

"Guns-guns-guns," he called out.

As the GAU-8 Avenger 30 mm cannon thundered, the A-10 shuddered, not violently, but with a rapid vibration, like tires skimming over wet pavement before gripping dry asphalt. Seven barrels spun in a blur beneath the nose, hurling armor-piercing depleted uranium rounds at nearly 70 per second. Each was longer than a beer bottle and capable of ripping through the toughest armor in the world.

The cannon's thunder rolled down the valley a split second after the rounds struck. The ridge line erupted. Snow vaporized, dirt exploded outward in gray-brown fans, and jagged rock splinters launched skyward. The mortar pits, vehicle, and the men inside were gone, erased in a spray of violence that left nothing moving but smoke. It was over in two seconds, just a sharp *brrrt* and then silence.

Jessie had to admit that the show the A-10 put on was impressive. He toggled the radio to provide the promised battle damage assessment. "Havoc 21, Raven 21. Confirm targets destroyed. All contacts cold. Good work."

"Roger that, Raven 21. RTB Keflavík. Let the brass know we brought the ugly one final time and cleaned it all up like the Hog has always done."

Chapter 71

THE KREMLIN
12 August
Moscow, Russia

As they had repeatedly done since making their move to Greenland, President Andrei Petrov and his council were examining a digital map of eastern Greenland. Red icons marked their assets near Constable Pynt Airport, while blue icons indicated the enemy, now comprising several countries. Recently, the US and its NATO allies, including Canada, the UK, Norway, and Finland, have utilized naval resources to block any Russian reinforcements. The seismic anomaly, attributed to a geological event but the Russians' calculated detonation of high explosives that had gotten them through the front door, was now so buried in news cycles that the door was slamming shut on them.

Deputy Defense Minister Natalia Romanova was holding her own in a room full of men because she said all the right things, thought Petrov. Sometimes, it takes a situation like this to reveal a person's true potential. He listened closely as she said, "If we do not draw a red line now, NATO will take the airfield. Once they hold the high ground and the runways, it's lost, and we will be thrown out on our collective asses. The time to escalate is now."

She slowly stood up as she pressed the remote. The screen changed from the digital map to show a mushroom cloud. This got everyone's attention, just as she'd planned. "Tactical nuclear weapons are a deterrent. Their value lies in what the enemy believes we might do, not what we actually do. If we detonate, we unify NATO. We give them justification for a strategic response, possibly even a full-scale one. But if we threaten detonation convincingly, we freeze them, allowing us freedom of movement."

General Andrei Smirnoff of the GRU chimed in, "Let them fear escalation. Let them argue among themselves. France and Germany won't sign off on a pre-emptive strike if the risk is nuclear fallout. We split NATO politically, delay their buildup, hold the airfield, and soon, all of Greenland."

President Petrov raised his right hand slightly. The room went instantly silent, and all heads turned to their leader. "Play the nuclear card. Make the message loud, but don't pull the trigger unless the West crosses a line we define. We must hold Greenland."

After another ten minutes of discussion, it was decided to communicate the nuclear threat to the US and, thus, the world. Within two hours, Russia released a statement via TASS. It was short and to the point.

The Russian Federation will consider the use of tactical nuclear weapons in defense of strategic territory if NATO continues aggressive operations in the Greenland theater. Our nation will not tolerate encroachment on legitimate Russian peaceful activities.

We demand that NATO withdraw naval and air assets from the Greenland theater. Cease all aerial incursions toward Constable Pynt. Any violation beyond these parameters may be met with non-conventional retaliation.

THE WHITE HOUSE

12 August

Washington, DC

As often as he was in the Situation Room, thought the president, he should furnish it with more comfortable chairs, even a sofa or two. Whatever happened to a quiet exit from his presidency?

Suddenly, SecDef slammed a printout on the table. It startled everyone, including one Secret Service agent who managed to catch himself before he drew his duty weapon.

"NSA intercepts confirm they've got nuclear-capable platforms on Alexandra Land," George Mitchell said. "Furthermore, the seismic event near eastern Greenland wasn't naturally occurring. It was a controlled blast to simulate seismic activity, which gave the Russians the excuse to occupy the country. And now they threaten the use of tactical nukes. We must call their bluff and strike them with overwhelmingly superior military force."

Instead of trying to take things down a notch, the president decided to let things go and see how it played out. Acquiescent comments were no longer being made; entrenched feelings were surfacing.

CIA Director Helen Morrow leaned forward, tapping the document. "This isn't just posturing. We've confirmed the presence of at least two nuclear-capable SS-26 units, what they call Iskander-Ms, on Alexandra Land. Satellite imagery shows active shielding bunkers and thermal activity consistent with warhead storage."

CJSC General Troy Kincaid said, "They're exploiting the gray zone between deterrence and escalation. It's a classic Russian doctrine to escalate and then de-escalate. They're daring us to test their resolve."

President Taylor scanned the room. "What are their red lines?"

"Any attempt to seize the airfield," Morrow said. "Or massed NATO troop movements in eastern Greenland. They're drawing a circle around that territory and daring us to cross it."

SecState Brad Kelly interjected, "If we call their bluff and they don't act, we win politically and militarily. But if we miscalculate..."

Kincaid nodded grimly. "We could lose a battalion of Americans in a flash. And then we're in an entirely different war."

The president turned to DNI Elena Ramirez. "Do the Europeans believe it?"

Ramirez said, "They're rattled. The Danes are calling for reinforcements, the Germans are seeking talks, and the Poles want to move forward regardless. NATO unity is fractured, and nothing seems to bring consensus."

The president sat up straighter in his chair. "So the Russians don't have to use the weapons, they just have to make us believe they might, and that's enough to splinter NATO."

"Sir," said Morrow, "if we yield now, we embolden not only Russia but North Korea, China, and even Iran. Our deterrent is only as strong as our willingness to stand firm. Petrov knows a nuclear strike will bring down the full weight of NATO's retaliation. He's gambling that we'll blink first, and I say we don't."

The president nodded once, looking again at the satellite imagery. "Then we let them hold their match over the powder keg and make sure they understand our match is lit as well."

Chapter 72

USS Thomas Hudner
1518 Hours, 12 August
Greenland Sea

As Russia attempted to hold the area around Constable Pynt Airport, the US and NATO allies were providing naval resources to block any Russian reinforcement. While Article 5 was still being considered, these countries acted through bilateral defense agreements. They supported a collective defense of sovereignty and stability in the Arctic, but it was nothing like a complete NATO response.

The USS *Hudner*, in collaboration with the *Gravely* and *Ramage* destroyers, was working in sectors between five and twenty nautical miles encompassing the *Ford*. Thirty miles out, the Virginia-class nuclear-powered fast attack submarine *Idaho* was also providing protection. No one wanted a repeat of what had happened to *Ford*.

Jansen was on the bridge, attempting to see something, anything, through the low gray clouds of Arctic summer. Holding steady at 12 knots, which was ideal for anti-submarine warfare, the *Hudner* patrolled the eastern picket line off Greenland. The warship towed a multifunction array system housing hydrophones and transducers to detect submarines at long range by listening passively for acoustic signatures. With American paratroopers having just landed near Russian-held territory, everyone was on top of their game and expecting the Russians to react.

Jansen walked over to the CIC. The air was cool inside, but it felt much warmer than outside. All through the room, young sailors slouched over glowing screens, interpreting every signal. The sonar officer was talking with Chief Mike "Gator" Gatlin, the senior sonar operator.

"What's up?" Jansen asked.

The sonar officer replied, "Gator's been following a weak return and getting modulation in the low band. Sub-harmonics are uneven, non-biological."

Keeping his eyes on his displays, Gatlin added, "Still faint, but yeah, it's not a whale. It might be prop cavitation, distant and slow, possibly Yasen-class, since they run quietly on low power."

Jansen considered this and made a decision. He keyed his handheld radio. "Captain, this is the XO. We've got a weak but persistent return. No classification yet, but I don't like the signature. It's anomalous and holding. Recommend we tighten our turn radius, keep the towed array on station, and prep to go active if needed."

The captain was on the bridge and responded immediately, "Understood. I'll be down shortly. Have fire-control ready and a holding track. We may be close."

Reynolds stepped into the CIC moments later and scanned the updated track. The ambient noise was low, the sonar clean, but the signal was still faint and deliberate. He studied the bearing line, holding it across the display, matching its rhythm against the patterns drilled into him over a career in undersea warfare. It was no fluke, no passing trawler or layer bounce. It was a submarine.

"You think he's sitting on the shelf?" Reynolds asked, eyes still on the plot.

Jansen considered what the sub's captain might be doing. "If he's smart, he is. That ridgeline gives him a shadow zone, especially with the thermocline where it is."

Reynolds thought for a moment, his expression unreadable. Jansen decided he was probably a great poker player.

"Very well," Reynolds said, "assume it's hostile and armed—weapons, prep ASROCs. Sonar, maintain passive track but stand by for active pulse. Tactical, notify the group we may have a submerged threat east of the LZ."

Suddenly, Gatlin half-jumped out of his chair. "Launch detected, bearing zero-four-three."

The sonar supervisor repeated the information into his mic, even though the captain and XO were standing beside him. "Launch detected. Initial signature consistent with submerged ejection."

The captain ordered general quarters, condition one.

Quickly, another three pulses rolled across the acoustic spectrum. Gatlin said, "Multiple events. Confirmed vertical launch and booster ignition. It's a cruise missile profile, bearing zero-four-three, range estimated under thirty klicks."

"TAO, alert the group of missile launch from submerged contact," Reynolds ordered, already turning to the weapons station. "Send flash priority warning to JTF Pike. Missiles are inbound, likely targeting our troops near the airfield."

"Captain," Jansen said quietly, "he fired on the rise. We can reach him before he clears the shelf."

Reynolds didn't hesitate. "Then we finish him."

Chapter 73

JOINT TASK FORCE PIKE
1520 Hours, 12 August
Eastern Greenland

Ground forces of JTF Pike were finalizing their pre-assault checks in the summer sun of the Arctic. Captain Shepherd moved between his company's platoons and reviewed positions on a laminated map while platoon leaders confirmed comms frequencies, ammo counts, and final coordination points. Nearby, a group of Army engineers secured a makeshift antenna mast for ground-to-air comms while two Marines fueled a portable generator humming beside the command tent. The mood was focused but calm, routine for a highly trained force about to roll into hostile terrain.

Back at the command tent, Shepherd heard over the radio, "Vampires inbound. Multiple missiles, low and fast."

Most had expected a missile attack, but now that it was a reality, it was truly unnerving. Heads immediately turned toward the radio while conversations stopped mid-sentence. Troops stopped what they were doing and were scanning the skies.

Shepherd brought those around him back to reality, yelling over comms, "Take cover!"

And just like that, everyone went from preparation to survival. Such is war.

USS THOMAS HUDNER

1520 Hours, 12 August

Greenland Sea

Even though the ship's captain wanted to hunt down the submarine that had launched missiles at US forces in Greenland, Reynolds knew what the priority was and didn't hesitate to give orders in the CIC. "Set Condition 1 Alpha. Prioritize inbound tracks. Initiate cooperative engagement capability using Link 16, all Aegis platforms."

All around the Greenland Sea, American destroyers and other NATO ships synchronized their ships' fire-control networks.

"Active CEC link established with Gravely and Ramage," the weapons officer called out. *Hudner's* Aegis Combat System had fused its sensor picture with that of the other destroyers guarding the *Ford*. Tracks updated in real time, forming a composite radar picture that spanned more than 100 nautical miles.

The Air Defense Officer said, "I recommend SM-6s using ripple fire, two interceptors per track."

Reynolds said, "Execute. Weapons free." As the Russian cruise missiles raced northward just meters above the ice and rock, the *Hudner's* VLS hatches flew open. Four

SM-6 interceptors roared skyward in quick succession, their booster stages trailing hard white flames before cleanly separating. The ship's Raytheon AN/SPY-6 air and missile defense radar maintained a firm track, feeding refined midcourse corrections through the fire-control loop. Two SM-6s banked hard to intercept the lead missile, their seekers locking on during the terminal phase.

Meanwhile, on the British destroyer HMS *Defender*, the operations team used the shared Link 16 data feed to lock onto the remaining missiles. In coordination with the American response, they launched two Aster 30 intercept missiles.

The British crew followed the tracks silently, watching the Asters close at over Mach 4 just as two of *Hudner*'s SM-6s slammed into their targets in brilliant flashes of fire and steel, reducing two Russian missiles to scattered fragments over the ice.

The combined NATO defense was having success until a short broadcast from the Brits changed everything. "Track 3 confirmed kill. Track 4 maneuvering, negative kill confirmation."

A collective *oh shit* sounded around ships and in the minds of all who were involved.

"Track 4 remains active. Missile evaded intercept. Terrain masking still inbound. Target is below radar horizon.

We have no shot. Recommend local ground units take immediate cover. Estimated impact fifteen seconds."

The *Hudner* put the call out to JTF Pike. "All stations, be advised, one vampire has penetrated the outer screen. Impact expected near friendly ground forces in ten seconds."

As a part of JTF Pike, Dankworth looked over the three other soldiers who made up his team. Like everyone else, he was preparing to step off for the move on Constable Pynt Airport. He moved from man to man to perform the last checks, ensuring magazines were secured in pouches, radios were powered up, and even that rucksacks were on. Dankworth had learned: don't assume shit.

"What the fuck, Adams?" he said. "You've got to secure that IR strobe." He tapped the blinking device clipped to the kid's shoulder. "You don't want fast movers lighting you up because they can't tell who's who, got it?"

"Roger that," said the kid, his hands trembling slightly as they worked on the strobe.

"Vampires inbound!"

Dankworth responded to the radio call by looking up. He saw three bright flashes and one dark dot.

Dankworth yelled, "Get down!"

He shoved Adams to the ground and waved for the others to take cover. Then he scanned the area. On a nearby low ridge, he saw two artillery spotters exposed, seemingly frozen as they stared up into the sky. Dankworth took off, sprinting up the hill and yelling for them to move. The men were slow to react.

When he reached them, he knocked one man to the ground and jumped onto the second. A split second after they were down, the cruise missile struck close by. The pressure wave hit them like a battering ram. Fire roared everywhere, shredding everything in its kill radius. Dirt, rocks, and shrapnel blackened the sky.

With his ears ringing, Dankworth didn't hear the initial cries for help as he forced himself up to his knees. Shaking his head in a feeble attempt to get his bearings, he got on comms.

"This is Charlie One-Niner, in sector two. We've taken a hit with casualties. Request medics. Initiating sweep, over."

Leaving the two spotters who had minor cuts, Dankworth found Adams bleeding from a deep leg wound. He went to work and tore a section of aluminum from a blown-out case to make a field splint. Adams was crying out in agony as Dankworth secured a dressing under the splint. He said, "You'll be fine, Adams. I'll be right back."

He began checking on the others who were around him. Fortunately, the medics started to arrive, so he went back to Adams. Just then, his captain arrived and instructed him to assemble his team, which was now reduced to three, and prepare to depart.

Chapter 74

RUSSIAN COMMAND POST
1634 Hours, 12 August
Constable Pynt Airport

A radio call came in. "American forces probing the western approaches. Request additional support."

As he bent over the operations map, Colonel Mikhail Barinov thought, Like I can pull forces out of thin air.

Before he could tell them to hold position with what they had, a new voice came over the radio, "Radar shows a new return, low-altitude, fast movers, bearing two-two-five. No IFF."

"I need more details," Barinov replied.

"Minimal radar cross-section. No uplink interference. No launch alerts. Possible cruise missiles."

Another voice cut in on the frequency, "Lost track at grid four-six-niner. Battery Two is down."

"Confirm loss," Barinov said to his staff in the command center. "Shift coverage to Battery One. Maintain perimeter integrity."

Around him, the operations staff moved fast, their trained reflexes overriding any reaction to the negative report. A junior officer rerouted surveillance feeds. Another technician attempted to link to secondary radar systems. But gaps were already appearing in their air picture, and Barinov knew what it meant.

Outside, the dimness was pierced by a flash to the southwest. The floor shuddered slightly under Barinov's boots. Alarms began to sound as a second impact shook the entire compound.

A report came over comms. "Multiple impacts near sector Delta. Secondary detonations in fuel storage."

Barinov grabbed the hardline radio and switched to the emergency channel. "Battery commanders, report status."

No answer came from the S-400 units.

The operations officer confirmed the worst-case scenario. "Both radar sites offline. No air picture. Main command uplink severed."

Barinov started to wonder where the hell all this had come from, but he quickly realized it didn't matter anyway because they were getting their asses handed to them. His defensive network was blind. It would only be a short time before he heard that the Americans were inside their perimeter.

He put out another order on the emergency channel, "Prepare fallback positions. Engage only if directly attacked."

The reply was nothing but static.

1640 Hours, 12 August

Northwest of Constable Pynt Airport

Dankworth moved with the weight of his full kit pressing down on his frame. His lightweight Crye Precision Jumpable Plate Carrier armor vest held six loaded 30-round magazines across the chest, a small first aid kit on his left side, and a tourniquet clipped high where he could grab it fast. His M7 rifle, outfitted with a stubby red-dot optic and infrared laser, rode tight on a two-point sling. The weapon was coated in a thin film of arctic lubricant to resist the elements.

It was cold, even in summer, but the light was good. Thin sun filtering through the high clouds was enough to see by without night-vision devices. The advance had started the moment word had come down that the Russian air defenses were offline. No radar coverage meant no coordinated artillery fire. The path was wide open, straight to the airport. Around him, the assault unfolded in layers.

To his left, two other squads from Charlie Company moved in staggered formation, each fire team moving forward in short rushes with one team advancing while the other laid down suppressive fire. From rocky outcrops, muzzle flashes winked in short, disciplined bursts, aiming at Russian positions dug around some shipping containers and burning fuel tanks.

Farther out, a squad pushed up the eastern side of the field, their movement carefully orchestrated as they used the broken terrain for cover. Smoke grenades blossomed along the fence line, thick white plumes drifting low in the cold Arctic air and masking the movement of breaching teams as they cut gaps through the perimeter wire.

Dankworth thought they were making good time with little resistance. He kneeled as he approached a large boulder, cautiously scanning ahead. Russian defenders were retreating in disarray and firing sporadically. There were no organized fields of fire, no armor, just isolated pockets of resistance being systematically broken apart. Close air support swept over the area.

He keyed his mic. "Charlie One-Niner at overwatch. Light resistance forward. Airport in sight."

The reply came almost instantly. "Advance and secure."

Dankworth stood up carefully and made a quick hand gesture, signaling the other two men on his team to move forward. Soon, they were on the perimeter road. As his boots hit the smooth surface, he was surprised by the firm footing.

His team gathered around a still-smoldering truck for cover while scanning the area, weapons at the ready. In the periphery, he caught sight of troop movement. Taking a better look, he counted five figures in Russian uniforms sprinting between two hangars 50 meters ahead.

Dankworth pointed. "Russians!"

He was the first to fire, letting loose with a tight volley at the two leading the group. A split-second later, his men fired in unison. One of the Russians tried to break from the path by sprinting for the shadow of a generator building. Dankworth dropped him with a 3-round burst, the man tumbling sideways across the pavement. Three more went down quickly.

"Grenade!" one of his men yelled.

It landed just to the side of their cover. Everyone dove to get away from the blast that was a second away. When it detonated, it sprayed jagged rocks and shrapnel. The nineteen-year-old who was closest to the explosion was killed instantly by a slash through his neck so deep it almost decapitated him.

Frozen in place, the team member who saw what had happened to his best friend began sobbing while throwing up. Rounds started ricocheting off their cover.

"Move—move!" yelled Dankworth.

The two men spread out, firing as they advanced toward the last Russian, then taking cover behind a building. Their combined firepower tore the small tin-metal structure into pieces along with the last Russian.

"We'll come back for our teammate," said Dankworth, "but right now, we gotta keep moving. Let's go."

Chapter 75

USS *HUDNER*

1641 Hours, 12 August

Greenland Sea

"Sonar, update," Captain Reynolds snapped, his eyes locked on the tactical plot. The CIC was tense after the Russian sub *Novosibirsk* fired several missiles in defense of its occupation of eastern Greenland.

Gator answered without hesitation. "Contact steady. Bearing zero-four-three. Depth fluctuating, he's moving deeper. Three hundred feet now. Small turns to starboard. Trying to get under the layer."

"He's trying to slip away," Jansen muttered.

"Negative," Reynolds said, already moving. "Helm, come to one-six-five. Weapons, prepare ASROC, target last reported depth plus five meters to account for descent drift. Fire on my mark."

The *Hudner* adjusted course, keeping tension on the towed sonar without overstraining it. The Multi-Function Towed Array gave steady, clean updates, signature modulation now matching a Yasen-class submarine.

"Target solution stable," reported Fire Control. "Firing window in ten seconds."

When Reynolds heard confirmation on his target, he ordered: "Fire."

The warship jolted slightly as the Mk 41 Vertical Launch System cell amidships launched the RUM-139 ASROC. A sharp mechanical thud followed, felt through the soles of every man standing near the CIC consoles, and accompanied by a brief, guttural *whump* as the cold gas generator pushed the weapon up and out. Half a second later, the solid-fuel booster motor ignited.

Above *Hudner's* flight deck, the ASROC climbed in a steep, low arc, the rocket motor burning hot against the pale sky. It accelerated quickly to nearly Mach 1, arcing downrange toward the predicted location of the Russian sub.

Inside the sealed canister, secured by a two-stage separation system, rode the real weapon: an Mk 54 lightweight torpedo configured explicitly for deep-water anti-submarine engagements.

At the pre-programmed point in flight, roughly 5 nautical miles downrange, the ASROC's rocket motor burned out. An explosive separation charge detonated, blowing apart the outer shell of the canister. Small drogue chutes were briefly deployed, stabilizing the Mk 54 and orienting it nose-down as it fell.

The torpedo splashed into the Greenland Sea in a tall, narrow plume, its minimal disturbance by design to reduce detection. It would have received a 10 if it were a diver in the Olympics. Immediately upon hitting the water, the Mk 54's onboard systems came alive. Its small propulsion unit engaged and its active/passive sonar head activated, searching for the faint noise signature of a submarine hull slicing through the thermocline.

Inside CIC, the weapons officer confirmed over internal comms, "Mark 54 splash acoustic acquisition sequence initiated." The torpedo's search cone opened on the tactical screen, sweeping wide as it dove deeper, hunting for its prey.

At the same time, sonar on the *Novosibirsk* reported: "New transient in the water, splash detected, bearing three-two-zero. Small displacement. Could be torpedo deployment." Captain Alekseev knew what was coming next, and it was confirmed five seconds later. "Contact active. Torpedo in search mode." A sharp metallic pulse echoed through the *Novosibirsk's* hull. Then another. Regular, crisp, growing louder. It was the sound of death.

"Decoys, deploy now," he barked.

The sonar chief knew that there would be few words left in his life but said them away, a sailor to the end. "Bearing closing, Comrade Captain. Fast."

"Stern right rudder, come to one-three-five, all ahead flank." Well, fuck it, he thought, he would give them something to think about. "Weapons, fire Tube Two. Target bearing one-seven-zero, shallow depth run, enable seeker on launch. Fire."

A single torpedo left the sub's forward tube in a hiss of compressed air, angling up toward the surface and hunting for its attacker.

There was an immediate reaction on *Hudner*. "Conn, Sonar, new contact torpedo in the water. Bearing zero-four-three, closing fast."

"Helm, emergency maneuver!" Reynolds barked. "All engines full. Hard to port. Deploy Nixie!" The *Hudner's* AN/SLQ-25 Nixie towed decoy streamed behind the ship, emitting acoustic signatures to fool the incoming torpedo's seeker.

"Weapons, engage the anti-torpedo system," came the second command from the captain. The *Hudner's* SSTD spun up automatically, launching a countermeasure torpedo to intercept the incoming threat.

Jansen leaned over the Combat Systems Officer. "Confirm countermeasure away. Helm, bring her hard to port; keep the decoy stream tight."

The ship heeled hard to port, the hull groaning under the strain as the helm threw the destroyer into a sharp, evasive turn. Astern, foam and shattered ice churned in the water. The *Hudner's* Nixie decoy streamed behind her, playing its false siren song for the enemy weapon racing in.

Confused by the abrupt course change and strong acoustic lure, the Russian torpedo drifted off *Hudner's* wake and homed in on the Nixie.

At that moment, the ship's Surface Ship Torpedo Defense countermeasure, already in the water and homing, intercepted the incoming torpedo with a rapid acoustic decoy burst, diverting its path just seconds before impact.

"Range five hundred."

"Impact in three—two—"

A muffled *boom* cracked through the water fifty yards astern. The blast sheared the torpedo and decoy apart, sending a heavy pressure wave that rolled across the ship's hull plates, making footing unsteady.

"Enemy torpedo neutralized!" Sonar Supervisor confirmed.

Jansen keyed the circuit. "Deploy second decoy. Set readiness for follow-on engagement."

Reynolds started to reply but was cut off as the sonar chief called out again, louder this time: "High-order detonation at depth! Bearing zero-four-one."

The plot lit up. A deeper explosion rolled up beneath the thermocline, far stronger than the first. "Confirming secondary explosion, contact breaking up," Sonar shouted over the net." Murmurs went through CIC and the ship. This was all new to everyone. They were in a shooting war with Russia.

"Debris rising, large air release, hull sounds of breaking up confirmed," came the call from Sonar.

Reynolds stood still, his face unreadable. Jansen, standing just off his shoulder, keyed the internal net. "Log contact kill. Initiate debris marking. Launch helo when ready for wreck site recon."

At the main tactical plot, Jansen stepped forward and checked the console. The red contact symbol, designating the hostile submarine, blinked once and then disappeared from the screen. Fitting, he thought, thinking how they could have been the symbol erased from the *Novosibirsk* console. Then he turned away, this hunt behind them, the next one already beginning.

Chapter 76

JOINT TASK FORCE PIKE
1647 Hours, 12 August
Constable Pynt Airport, Greenland

Shepherd moved along the wrecked service road, his rifle out front as he scanned the hangars to the east. His boots splashed through shallow puddles formed by the summer thaw. Mud made the cracked concrete slick. Around him, Bravo Company advanced in staggered columns with teams peeling off left and right to sweep through maintenance bays, barracks, and fueling points. He was happy with their progress but aware it wasn't over even as they cleared the final buildings at the sprawling airport.

Over the radio net, reports came in fast and furious. "Second Platoon contact front, small arms, Hangar 4. Engaging."

"Third Platoon clear on north apron. No resistance."

Shepherd keyed his mic. "Bravo Company, Bravo One. Push through. Clear every building. No holdouts."

Just then, Vasquez radioed, "First Platoon, multiple shooters in fortified positions, southwest corner. Engaging."

"Bravo Actual copies," Shepherd said. "Pin and flank, keep pushing."

Up ahead of him was some broken fencing with gaps that had been cut out. Smoke drifted across his view.

He and the troops in his team ducked behind a damaged loader. A group of Russian soldiers, maybe a dozen, had barricaded themselves behind a line of maintenance trucks and half-toppled cargo containers. Shepherd had a perfect view of Vasquez's team firing quick bursts.

"Bravo One-Zero, Bravo One. We will lay down cover fire so you can flank them."

Shepherd then yelled to his team, "Put fire on those bastards—now."

A wall of American rifles opened up, hammering the Russian position. Vasquez's team peeled off through the drifting smoke, moving fast and low, and slipped around the flank to get in position to cut the Russians down.

Dankworth saw what was happening and realized he was in a good position to lay down devastating fire as well. It didn't matter that he wasn't on comms with them because he was in a different company; you always helped a brother or sister out.

He said to the only person who remained from his team, "Keep 'em pinned! Short bursts, steady fire. Don't let 'em lift their heads."

They let loose with controlled three to five-round bursts and hammered the Russian cover positions from a new angle. The Russians had no choice but to keep down, and Vasquez's team slipped around their flank.

Vasquez used hand signals to tell her team to halt and line up along a low berm. The Russians were crouched behind their makeshift barricade, their weapons fixed forward, completely unaware of the new threat coming up behind them.

"Engage," she said.

Her team opened fire. The first Russian dropped instantly after rounds struck his center mass, a sign he wasn't wearing body armor. Another started to spin around, but Vasquez caught him with two quick shots to the chest.

One of her team lobbed a single 40mm round from his underslung launcher. The grenade arced low and detonated behind the Russian cover, shredding the last pockets of resistance. Within seconds, it was over.

Vasquez moved in, sweeping the wreckage with her rifle. Her team followed, clearing each body and confirming no survivors were ready to fight.

She keyed her mic. "Bravo One, Bravo One-Zero. area secure."

"Roger that, L-T," Shepherd said. "I had a great ringside seat. Nice job."

Now, with his full company able to move unimpeded, he and his team approached the main building, where the

Russians had set up a command post. Shepherd surged forward with Vasquez's team, leading them forward.

He crossed open ground in a fast-moving crouch, weapon ready, scanning for movement. A Russian soldier popped up from behind a rusted forklift, weapon raised. Shepherd didn't hesitate; he dropped the man with a tight double tap to the chest plate.

Pressing forward with more of his troops flooding the area, Shepherd could see Russian bodies strewn all about. Out of the corner of his eye, he saw movement in Charlie Company's area.

Dankworth and his troop had acquired a few more teammates thanks to the fog of war, and they approached a group of three Russians dug in behind a collapsed maintenance building. The Russians opened fire on the approaching Americans.

Dankworth took a knee behind a forklift and barked out, "Flank left. Smoke right. Crush 'em."

Seconds later, a wall of white smoke blossomed after Heckler & Koch M320 GLMs launched grenades. The Russian defenders' line of sight was cut. American troops pushed in from opposite sides, the sound of gunfire filling the air. One Russian tried to swing his rifle around, but Dankworth cut him down with two precise shots. Another fell a moment later, caught in a crossfire from Bravo Company's sector.

The last Russian dropped his weapon, raised his hands above his head, and yelled something. He was soon on the ground and cord-cuffed.

All-clear sector reports echoed across the net until the last one came. "South sector secure. Last enemy positions cleared. We hold the airfield."

American and Danish troops moved through the smoke, setting hasty perimeter defenses and sweeping remaining structures. Above the shattered airfield, the wind carried the last echoes of the firefight away into the endless Arctic light. Constable Pynt Airport was back in Allied hands.

Chapter 77

CONFERENCE ROOM 1, THE KREMLIN
13 August
Moscow, Russia

No one in the secured room needed to be told that President Andrei Petrov was upset; it was written all over his face. The invasion of Greenland hadn't gone according to plan. Lighting up the room were images that reinforced the point. Constable Pynt Airport was shattered with bombed-out aircraft littering the area and blackened craters punched through the tarmac. Denmark and US flags blew in the Arctic breeze.

The defeat stung. It was more than a battlefield loss. It was a blow to Russian prestige, a wound inflicted on the Arctic frontier that Moscow had claimed as its own.

"Turn it off, I've seen enough," Petrov growled.

The room went darker after the screen went blank. Petrov slowly got up from his position at the head of the large table and walked the room, taking time to stare at each of Russia's elites as they squirmed in their chairs. They all understood that the luxury they enjoyed could quickly be replaced with the horrors of Russia's notorious gulags.

Walking slowly, the leader of Russia said, "I ask each of you how you screwed up my brilliant plan for the takeover of Greenland, the strategic heart of the entire Arctic. How? This is not merely a battlefield loss; it's a strategic catastrophe. Now we have emboldened the West while weakening our own hand. I will not allow the Motherland to be shamed further. We will restore the fear that held them at bay. We will remind them that Russian power does not vanish because a few flags were planted in the ice."

He stopped at the front of the table. "This is my order: We will not retreat. We will move our tactical missile forces forward. We will place our nuclear readiness in plain view. And we will make Washington, Brussels, and everyone else wonder if they have pushed us too far. Strength will decide what comes next, not negotiations. Nor apologies." He nodded to GRU chief General Andrei Smirnoff.

"Mr. President, our next move must project strength without crossing the threshold that would justify a NATO pre-emptive strike. We still have our Kola bastion. Suppose we forward-deploy the 152nd and 536th Missile Brigades' modified Iskander-M units and stage them visibly near Polyarny, Severomorsk, and Alexandra Land. In that case, it will force NATO to reconsider any further advances."

Romanova interrupted the general when he paused to take a deep breath. "General Smirnoff, why move those missiles at all? We already have plenty of missiles with the range to hit Greenland and Iceland from their current silos.

Why expose our new missiles to NATO satellites and air strikes?"

The room went quiet. No one missed how she had just publicly questioned the most powerful general in Russia. Smirnoff turned to lock eyes with Romanova.

He unconsciously sat straighter before saying, "Because exposing the missiles is the point, Ms. Minister. We need them to see the new threat. We need NATO planners waking up at three in the morning and wondering if today is the day we fire our nukes." He jabbed a finger toward the satellite imagery on the screen. "They all know what the status quo is. What they don't know is that we have something else. Invisible weapons do not deter, just as words seldom do."

Smirnoff stepped closer to the screen and motioned for the slide to change. Maps appeared, showing circles of missile coverage extending from Polyarny, Severomorsk, and Alexandra Land.

"By moving the new Iskanders to within fifty kilometers of the Barents Sea and to an Arctic island, we cut launch warning times in half. We force NATO to spread its defenses thinner. We create uncertainty across every Arctic base and fleet anchorage they control."

He turned back to face the president, ignoring Romanova. "In simple terms, Mr. President, moving the missiles forward creates fear. That is our objective, and this will accomplish that result."

Petrov said nothing for a long moment, then gave a slow, deliberate nod. "Proceed, General."

Chapter 78

THE WHITE HOUSE

13 August

Washington, DC

President Mark Taylor had an hour off between meetings, which didn't take long for his free-spirited daughter, Jennie, to catch onto. It had taken her months to convince him to take yoga lessons, and she insisted he continue them, no matter what. As an accomplished instructor, she knew a quick session would help her father regain focus and maintain his mental and physical balance. Seeing him standing there in the White House's gym, wearing his worn Navy T-shirt and faded sweatpants, she couldn't help but grin at the leader of the free world.

"You sure this is going to help?" he asked.

Jennie let out a chuckle. "Dad, you're leading this nation on four hours of sleep and a gallon of coffee. Ten minutes of yoga is exactly what you need right now."

I give in, he thought. She always gets her way.

He gingerly dropped down beside her, and she took them through a gentle sun salutation flow. She kept her voice calm and steady, just like she did with her private clients.

"Inhale...hold...now exhale slowly. Feel the tension leave your body."

She took him through a series of other poses. Taylor followed along, clumsy but willing. The weight behind his eyes suddenly loosened somewhere between the breathing and the stretching. His hands stopped shaking. His thoughts cleared.

Jennie glanced at him as they held a low lunge.

"Better?" she asked.

He nodded, still focused. "Much better."

She gently smiled again and stood up. "Good. Now, please try and keep the world in one piece, Daddy-o." She began rolling up her yoga mat.

He chuckled, the first time he had done so all week. Watching his only child, he realized how much she meant to him.

The door opened, and a Secret Service agent announced, "Sir, you're needed in the Situation Room."

"Okay, but I'm going to change first." After giving Jennie a hug and a noisy kiss on her cheek, he left.

Not even ten minutes later, he entered the White House Situation Room. The men and women already seated jumped to their feet.

"Please, be seated," said Taylor. As he sat, he noticed all the screens in the room again showed real-time satellite feeds. One screen had a large map of the Arctic and Greenland.

"This is your meeting," Taylor said to his NSC. "What do we have this time?"

SecDef George Mitchell stood and clicked a remote. "Mr. President, the situation in the Arctic is evolving rapidly. We confirmed two hours ago that the Russian short-range ballistic missiles, the SS-26 Stone systems, have left the hardened depots near Severodvinsk. At least sixteen launchers are now moving toward temporary firing positions near Polyarny and the Severomorsk naval corridor. We also know some were loaded on a ship."

SecDef paused as he tapped another key. On-screen, high-resolution satellite images showed green mobile Transporter Erector Launchers moving through muddy roads under escort. "What is important to understand is that these TELs are mobile and can launch nuclear missiles. But the range of the missiles is about 50 kilometers. So this is a lot of effort for saber-rattling."

"Have they issued any statements?" Taylor said.

CIA Director Helen Morrow answered, "Russian media's quiet so far, but we're seeing indirect messaging on state channels. Phrases like strategic rebalancing and Arctic deterrence maneuvers. It's pure signaling, and it's not subtle."

SecState Brad Kelly asked the question on everyone's mind, "Is this a bluff, or are they prepping to escalate? Sir, I don't believe they intend to launch. This fits their escalate-to-de-escalate doctrine. They want us to pull back or stall our consolidation in Greenland."

The president asked, "And if we don't pull back?"

Morrow answered flatly, "Then they'll keep moving forces for naval drills, bomber sorties out of Olenya, maybe even have a sub pop a missile tube, all just to rattle us. They want the world to think we're on the edge of nuclear war, so countries will get involved in a debate loud enough to pressure us to stop what we're doing. They don't even have to fire a shot."

Taylor answered, "You all understand we didn't bleed in Greenland just to hand it back over on a bluff, right?" There were a few nods. Nobody said anything, so he did. "Options?"

CJCS General Troy Kincaid said, "I suggest we raise DEFCON for Arctic Command, deploy additional fighters to Iceland, get AWACS and tankers rotating 24/7, and quietly push another attack sub under the Barents Sea."

Mitchell said, "And we recommend beginning a low-visibility dispersal of our own tactical assets to Norway and our other bases in the Arctic. No press releases. Let them see it when they look."

Taylor retook the lead. "So to be clear, we don't blink, don't speak, and do not escalate publicly. We let our posture do the talking. But in case the Russians cross the line, if a single missile leaves the tube, I want targeting packages locked, submarines in position, and our CSG to respond without hesitation. Understood?"

"Yes, sir," everyone in the room said.

Taylor stood, ending the meeting. "If they want to walk the edge, let them. But if they think we won't answer when they step over it, they're wrong."

Chapter 79

Nagurskoye Military Base

14 August

Alexandra Land, Russia

Lieutenant General Alexei Morozov stepped onto the balcony above the airfield operations center, his greatcoat blown open by the Arctic wind. He didn't flinch at the cold. Summer on one of the Franz Josef Land islands was anything but sunshine and flowers. Instead, troops were treated to dirty melting snow, mud, and weak but ever-present solar rays.

The diminutive man was a leader with the ability to think through what was given to him and then devise a perfect plan. With early promotions and successful battles, he was one of Moscow's most trusted generals, and he'd been sent to Nagurskoye to get things done in the Arctic. From his point of view, this station was nothing but an opportunity that the Kremlin had provided for free.

With international and NATO pressure mounting against Russia after it lost its Greenland stronghold, the Kremlin had shifted gears, at least publicly. The politicians had begun airing statements calling for a diplomatic resolution to avoid irreversible escalation. President Petrov had issued a formal ceasefire proposal through backchannels to the UN Security Council, which had suggested a temporary freeze on Arctic hostilities to prevent a broader European conflict. The tone had been calm, almost conciliatory.

Morozov thought it was the perfect cover. Standing on the balcony, he watched as another IL-76 transport aircraft offloaded more men and crates under the direct supervision of his naval infantry officers. In the last seventy-two hours, the base had received two battalion-level tactical groups from the 61st Naval Infantry Brigade, who had flown in from Severomorsk. Some of the crates on their cargo pallets were marked Novator 9M729, missiles closely related to those used on the Iskander-M system but with extended range and nuclear capability.

Additionally, four Iskander-M TELs were now staged under arctic camouflage netting east of the airfield, each positioned with overlapping fields of fire toward the Greenland Sea. Their targeting packages could be changed in minutes from hardened American installations in Greenland to carrier strike groups off Iceland. A K-300P Bastion-P mobile coastal defense battery had also arrived, its P-800 Oniks anti-ship cruise missiles capable of striking either ships or shore-based targets up to 300 kilometers away. Though traditionally conventional, Russian doctrine permitted them to be modified for nuclear payloads in strategic scenarios.

Additionally, air defense S-400 Triumf launchers and supporting radar trucks were already concealed along the edge of the glacial ridge. Their 96L6 targeting radar was dark for now but could power up in seconds.

Morozov wasn't overseeing a defensive deployment, he thought. It was a battlefield taking shape.

He heard footsteps behind him. When he turned, he saw Colonel Nikolai Dmitry Orlov, a man with a reputation. His father had planted the underwater Russian flag at the North Pole years ago, and the son rode that heroic wave.

"Sir, all missile assets are in place and armed with conventional warheads as ordered by Moscow," Orlov said.

Morozov stared at his second-in-command for a few seconds before saying, "These weapons," he gestured to the nuclear weapons being offloaded on the ramp below, "have been used for training and exercises. Not one has ever been used in combat. I want half of all missiles to be armed with nuclear warheads. We are not bluffing. When we fire, it will be without a prelude. We will remove the Ford, its battlegroup, Pituffik, and bases in Iceland, Norway, Sweden, and Finland. Do you understand, Colonel?"

"Sir, if I may, Moscow made it clear in our orders that they want ambiguity. They want the Americans to second-guess our posture and what we might do."

"I don't care what Moscow wants. If Washington is watching, and they are, then they must see a force willing and capable of striking first and winning. So I will not say this again, Colonel Orlov. Make the change. No blanks, no dummies. In forty-eight hours, half the missiles will have nuclear warheads, and they will be fully combat-ready."

Turning back to look at the airfield ramp, Morozov added, "I will see Greenland burn before it stays in the hands of the enemy."

Orlov felt a cold chill run down his back and thought, What is this man thinking, the end of the world?

Chapter 80

NATIONAL RECONNAISSANCE OFFICE

14 August

Chantilly, VA

Deep inside the secure operations wing of the NRO, analysts were busy monitoring the orbital pass of one of America's most advanced spy satellites. The hush-hush KH-11 Block 5 electro-optical platform was beginning its high-latitude transit over the Arctic. At an altitude of roughly 160 miles, it drifted over the glaciated islands of Franz Josef Land. Its optical system was stabilized by precision gyros as its lens arrays extended like the iris of a mechanical eye.

As it arced downrange toward the Barents Sea, the satellite's onboard sensors snapped a high-resolution frame every few seconds, each image capturing thermal and visual data at a resolution sharp enough to read the markings on individual containers sprawled out on Alexandra Land's Nagurskoye tarmac and to capture open hatches on parked launchers.

A lead imagery analyst for Northern Command's Arctic Watch, Air Force Major Alana Bishop, reviewed the latest captures. An image rendered in false-color IR showed rows of SS-26 TELs at Nagurskoye Air Base. She compared the image to the ones from previous passes and noted that the

TELs had previously been positioned under concealment netting before. But what really worried the fifteen-year veteran was that the TEL was in an open firing posture. She casually mentioned this to the captain beside her and added, "This isn't an exercise posture."

Bishop further reviewed data from circling Lacrosse synthetic aperture radar satellites, which confirmed vehicle movement radiating out from the center of the base. It was a pattern consistent with pre-launch dispersal.

Something still didn't line up in her analytical brain, so she examined the images more closely. The KH-11's multispectral scan revealed crates being unloaded from a heavily guarded IL-76 aircraft, which was moved using distinct thermal handling protocols, including external coolant lines, mechanical vibration isolation, and radiation-shielding blankets. She called over a Department of Energy specialist, who looked at what she'd flagged.

The specialist thought for a moment before saying, "Those aren't standard warhead crates. That's thermal shielding. It looks like they're loading SSC-8 cruise missiles with selectable yield nuclear warheads."

Bishop asked, "Estimated type?"

The DOE rep said, "Likely RA-3 or RA-4 warheads with variable yields, estimated between 10–50 kilotons. They're compact enough for both the SS-26 short-range ballistic missile and the SSC-8 medium-range cruise missile variant."

Many in the know had long suspected that Russia's President Petrov might deploy nuclear assets in Franz Josef Land. Now they had direct visual and spectral confirmation of Alexandra Land. Showing that atomic warheads were on-site and possibly already mated to launch systems.

Bishop up-channeled the info, and the senior NRO liaison to the NSC took it all in. Immediately, he used the encrypted, direct line to the Pentagon, which he had previously only used for testing purposes. His palms were sweaty when SecDef answered. After identifying himself, the NRO liaison said, "We have imagery confirming short- and medium-range cruise missile systems plus nuclear warhead handling on Alexandra Land. Operational readiness drills are in progress. The Russians don't appear to be bluffing."

Chapter 81

THE WHITE HOUSE
15 August
Washington, DC

The Situation Room was at full capacity with the usual members of the NSC, some invited heads of other agencies, and everyone's aides, who stood in silence along the walls. Two Secret Service agents and two Marines stood at their posts outside the door. On the center screen were live satellite images of Nagurskoye Military Base. Everyone had already seen the confirmed nuclear-capable launchers. To each person, no matter their rank or position, it was clear that Russian forces were on the brink of making Greenland part of the Motherland, whether by conventional or nuclear means.

President Mark Taylor stood at the head of the table, and when he sat down, one of the Marines shut the room's door. With his tie loosened, Taylor's face was flushed even though the room was set at 68 degrees. The chief executive said, "Everyone here knows what we're facing since Russia has deployed nuclear weapons to the Arctic. They've also built a forward launch platform under our noses and attempted to conceal it behind diplomatic efforts. So now we have to decide whether we act before they do."

He paused and patiently looked around the room before saying, "We've modeled waiting and risking a launch against Greenland and our bases in the area and then retaliating. They escalate. We escalate. Cities burn, and thousands, if not millions, of people are disintegrated. So I bring up for discussion the option of striking now and neutralizing the threat before their first missile ever leaves its launcher. I mean by conventional means, of course."

DNI Elena Ramirez said, "Let's be clear, Mr. President. A first strike on Russian territory is a red line for everyone. If we hit them, even if we don't kill Russian civilians, they will call it an act of war."

"Some of you worry that this is how it starts," replied the president, "that this would be the spark to set off the next World War. I don't dismiss that. But I believe Moscow still respects one terrible truth: If they launch nukes, we all die per the mutual assured destruction concept. They know it, just like we do. And for all their saber rattling, they're not suicidal."

Ramirez had her doubts. "I suggest we wait for diplomatic backchannels to work. Let them make the first move."

SecDef George Mitchell cut in but directed his reply to the president, "If the Russians launch from Alexandra Land, sir, we won't have the time to intercept. Pituffik would go dark. Even worse, they'll no doubt go after the *Ford* CSG.

Everything we've collected points to imminent readiness. The missiles could be airborne within hours, leaving no launch signature. Once they're in flight, we have little time to stop them. So if we wait, we risk a surprise nuclear strike. If we act first, we control the timeline. But if we screw that up, we'll be reacting to a nuclear war."

Taylor shifted his weight as if he were holding the world on his shoulders. "We strike because it's the best option. A limited, conventional pre-emptive strike on Alexandra Land saves Greenland, protects our people, and keeps the Arctic from becoming the next Red Sea. Russia understands that there's no such thing as a limited nuclear exchange. The minute one of their warheads detonates, mutual assured destruction kicks in. We respond. They respond again. And within an hour, both nations cease to exist as functioning societies."

The president paused, then said, "They want leverage, not extinction. They want Greenland, not mushroom clouds over Saint Petersburg and Kansas City. Our strike will send one message: we won't be blackmailed by the threat of Armageddon. We're going to end their deception, not start a war. Launch the strike. Make it precise and surgical. We're risking everything to prevent something worse, and history will decide whether we did it too late or just in time."

Chapter 82

NAGURSKOYE MILITARY BASE
0836 Hours, 15 August
Alexandra Land, Russia

Lieutenant General Alexei Morozov was bent over the central operations table, studying his next move. He knew he had control of every missile, every man, and every decision. Highlighted on the map were Pituffik Space Base and the USS *Ford* Carrier Strike Group. Morozov was flanked by his second-in-command, Colonel Nikolai Dmitry Orlov, who hung around him like a pesky fly.

"What is it this time, Orlov?"

"Sir, with respect, you've ordered full nuclear readiness without confirmation from Moscow, coded release, or dual-key protocol. That's not posture, sir, that's provocation. And that's not our call."

The general didn't even look as he swatted at the fly with his verbal words. "No, Colonel, that's preparation. What Russia has lacked for far too long."

Orlov studied his superior. "Moscow was clear about creating ambiguity. They want Washington to guess, not react. This operational ramp-up was meant to pressure the US, not trigger a war."

Morozov replied as if he were explaining things to a little child, "Moscow no longer understands how to react from strength. They've been coasting on apathy since Ukraine. They think posturing works because we've never tested what happens when we stop bluffing." The general tapped his index finger on the map. "The US took Greenland. They disgraced us, and now they sit in Washington and dare us to act because they think we won't."

Orlov maneuvered so the general had to look at him eye to eye. "Sir, you're talking about independent nuclear deployment. Half of these crews haven't drilled under live conditions. There's no confirmation code from the General Staff. It crosses the line."

Morozov stared back for so long that Orlov felt like his life was about to end.

Eventually, the general said, "I'm not crossing the line, Colonel. I'm erasing it, for the Americans and for anyone in Moscow who thinks the future of Russia can be defended by indecision."

Feeling he had to be noticed to be heard, Orlov stepped closer to Morozov. "This could bring retaliation. The minute one of those missiles launches—"

"Then we go with everything," Orlov snapped. "We don't just hit Pituffik or the Ford. We strike every US ally within range so that the Americans lose their will before they find their response playbook."

Swat.

The general walked by the wounded fly, who was no longer a pest, and directed his orders to his communications captain. "Comms, initiate warhead mating for all TELs in Sectors A and C. Notify the 61st Naval Infantry Brigade to brace for follow-on strike conditions."

When listening to the conversation between the two men in charge of operations, the comms officer had agreed with Orlov. Now he asked himself if this action was worth it and decided it was. "Authorization, sir?"

The general walked over to the man and with steely eyes and a growling tone, he said, "Mine."

152ND MISSILE BRIGADE
0912 Hours, 15 August
Nagurskoye Military Base

It really bothered Senior Sergeant Nikita Karpov that his best friend had been whisked away by security forces a few hours ago. He had merely asked their captain why they were arming the missiles with nuclear warheads when they'd had little training about the safety aspects of the changeover from conventional warheads. He should have known better. Karpov had been around long enough to see that it was best to follow orders, never volunteer for anything, and do his job. He was good at that.

Still, nothing about this seemed routine. He double-checked the hydraulic arm status on the forward interface panel to ensure it had no pressure drop and was in solid alignment. He had watched earlier as the heavily armed security team in all black and wearing balaclavas had supervised the mating of the warhead with the missile.

He called out to his supervisor, a newly promoted lieutenant, "Sir, stabilization fins locked. External interface test complete. No thermal bleed. TEL-312 is fully aligned on bearing two-four-zero. Target uplink ready."

"You sound nervous, Karpov. You never handled a live one?"

"Negative, sir." In truth, he'd trained on simulators and dry runs, run warhead-separation diagnostics on inert test units, and even assisted once during a mock drill in Astrakhan. But he'd never stood in Arctic mud beneath a weapon that could level a NATO base and trigger the end of the world.

He said to himself, Shut up and do your job.

"You're doing fine," the lieutenant said. "Better than most."

Karpov kept working as he knelt beside the interface conduit and began logging the pre-launch telemetry file. He could feel the sweat running down his spine. He told himself repeatedly to keep his cool.

Out of the corner of his eye, he saw a second missile being loaded by another team. They were hanging around the azimuth gyro. He guessed it was probably set for a different target, but that was none of his business.

Karpov knew that if a launch order came down, he would be the one to unlock the fire-control safety and press the ready-state confirmation. Reality was much different than simulation. He had butterflies flying around that he could not tame. But like any soldier, he had a job to do, and he would do it.

After he completed the final item on his checklist, he said, "Lieutenant, warhead armed. Launch authority on hold."

"TEL-312 is in ready status," the Lieutenant said over comms. "Awaiting further."

Karpov wondered if, when the order came, he would be able to arm a nuclear bomb that would kill thousands. He pictured his wife and three-month-old baby girl and wondered if the Americans were arming one of their nukes to blast his hometown.

Just do your job, he repeated to himself.

Chapter 83

NORTHROP GRUMMAN B-21 RAIDER
1614 Hours, 15 August
Pituffik Space Base, Greenland

The mission's brief, which Major Logan Carter was now flying, echoed in his thoughts. "This operation is no longer deterrence. It's pre-emption. Strikes must be total; no fragments and no misses."

He looked over at his co-pilot and mission systems officer, 1st Lieutenant Megan Alvarez. She was busy reviewing the targeting information, checking it against the flight plan she had entered, and ensuring everything would proceed according to plan.

"Navigation locked in," she said. "INS alignment stable. Flight profile loaded as route Alpha to target zone. Stealth gate is green."

Carter reviewed the mission plan on his helmet display. "Launch in seventeen. Climb right after gear-up. Maintain altitude thereafter, stay low at 4,000 feet. Fly under NORLANT radar and maintain radio silence. Hit the hard TOT."

"Roger all, and time on target is confirmed," she said.

"Weapons check," he said.

"Four missiles locked in. Two bombs armed. All targets marked. We're ready, Hawk."

"This is it, Pixie," he said. "No mistakes."

USS IDAHO

1620 Hours, 15 August

Barents Sea

For the past two days, Stanton had kept his Virginia-class attack submarine in a holding position in its launch box. US analysts had tracked the repositioning of missile launchers under camouflage netting, the arrival of fuel trucks in staggered intervals, and a command trailer transmitting encrypted signals from a snow-covered ridge. The data was confirmed by infrared sweeps and intercepted radio bursts, then shared with his sub, which would deliver a package of Tomahawks to the Russians on Alexandra Land.

Stanton had to admit he was amazed that the Russians' usual bluff concerning the use of nuclear weapons seemed to be taking events to the next level. After all, bluffing had been their norm. He was also surprised that the US was making a pre-emptive strike on Russian territory. But he reminded himself that he was a naval officer and just did as ordered to the best of his ability. Besides, the type of attack he'd been instructed to execute fit his mentality perfectly.

"Sonar, report," he ordered.

Emily Reyes was on shift, as the captain had requested, and she replied instantly, "Control, Sonar. No surface traffic. No screw noise inside twenty nautical miles. We're clear."

"Helm, maintain current depth. Prepare for vertical launch. WEPS, status."

The weapons officer replied, "Tubes 1 through 4 loaded with Block V Tomahawks. Routes uploaded. Warheads live. Target packages verified." After a slight pause, WEPS continued, "Flight times calculated as 2 minutes and 42 seconds to first impact. All missiles are programmed for low-profile ingress. Terrain-masking active. Weather is clear above the ice cap."

"XO," Stanton said.

"All ready, Captain. Missile interface green. Torpedo room reports weapons checked and set."

Sailors stood ready beside the launch tubes. The Tomahawks sat cold and silent in their cells, the long, dark gray missiles sealed in canisters behind blast doors and ready to deliver their payload.

"This is the captain. Launch sequence is four birds staggered by 10 seconds. Target spread is west to east."

The weapons officer positioned his finger on the launch button, waiting for his orders.

1624 Hours, 15 August

Over Barents Sea

Back seater, Ronnie Harper flew 25,000 feet with a low electromagnetic signature and his radar off. His weapons officer, seated in the back, was hunched over his console, scanning frequencies.

"Talk to me, Gizmo," Harper said.

"I got S-band radar active, Razor. Long-range scan from the coast, so the Russians are reaching. Their SA-21s are online."

"Roger that." Flying at their five o'clock was his wingman, Shadow 12. Just ahead and above was his new bud, Swagger, flying flight lead in his F-35, and with his wingman, he was completing a diamond formation. They were nearly invisible to Russian radar.

"Shadow 11, Raven 21," Jessie said. "Five minutes from weapons release. Your show, Razor."

"Copy that," Harper replied. "Let's crack open the board." He flipped a switch.

The ALQ-99 pods that were slung beneath his wings came online. Electronic noise targeted the Russian search and tracking radars.

Harper's wingman followed suit, intensifying the jamming effort.

"Main radar is blind," Harper said. "They just started
painting ghosts."

Chapter 84

NAGURSKOYE MILITARY BASE
1630 Hours, 15 August
Alexandra Land, Russia

Lieutenant General Alexei Morozov stood alone in his private command office, the door closed, his uniform collar undone. Drops of his sweat bounced off the table in front of him. He'd opened the Russian version of the US "nuclear football" that was used to store launch authorization codes, targeting options, and programmed targets.

As he was making some last-minute, necessary adjustments on the launch terminal, a message appeared on the screen.

PACKAGE ECHO – TACTICAL STRIKE
PRIMARY TARGETS: PITUFFIK SPACE BASE, USS *GERALD R. FORD*, AND REYKJANES BASIN, ICELAND
STATUS: STAND BY – FINAL CONFIRMATION REQUIRED

He reached for the handset, his direct line to all the launch crews standing by for his orders to fire. As he picked it up, explosions rocked his building, momentarily throwing

Morozov to one knee. He got up quickly, mostly from the pure adrenaline burning through his system.

His office door opened. Colonel Orlov rushed in as more explosions seemed to be striking everywhere. Dust falling from the ceiling created a dark fog in the room.

Orlov immediately saw the general, the opened "football," plus the activated launch terminal, and he knew immediately what the general was doing. "Stand down!" he screamed above the clamor.

Morozov didn't even face his second-in-command. "I'm in command here. Don't you get it? We're under a coordinated attack. This is exactly the moment we've prepared for."

"You have no authorization to launch nuclear missiles. I repeat, STAND DOWN."

"If we don't retaliate, we lose the Arctic. We lose everything. No, not again."

Orlov moved in closer. "Let them take the ice. Don't sacrifice the world."

Morozov reached for the handset again.

Orlov drew his sidearm and pointed it at the head of his commanding officer. "If you touch that keyboard, I swear I will shoot you."

His hand hovering just above the handset, Morozov stood at attention.

Orlov applied more pressure to the trigger. "Don't do it, sir."

Morozov went for the handset just as the entire office went black from a massive bomb detonation. The two men were blown to smithereens; the sound of the gunshot was the last thing they ever heard.

THE KREMLIN
16 August
Moscow, Russia

Once emboldened by his Arctic gamble, President Andrei Petrov sat grim-faced at the end of the same table where he had first announced his ambitious plans. The same men and woman who had supported him surrounded him again, all exhausted from the outcome. The loss of Nagurskoye and Russia's entire Arctic offensive capability was a military defeat and a strategic collapse. Russia had poured personnel, materiel, and political capital into controlling the northern front and Greenland. Now, with satellite imagery showing the obliteration of their base, there was no impetus. Russia was back on its heels.

What had been a disjointed response by NATO was now a roar of condemnation. Russia had been beaten without NATO initiating Article 5.

While Petrov's hardliners demanded retaliation, the consensus was de-escalation. Russia's Northern Fleet was mauled, its airfield lost, and its long-range strike platforms either destroyed or secured well out of any threatening range. Sanctions would tighten. China had already distanced itself. NATO now stood unified.

Faced with rising dissent at home and the quiet mobilization of civil unrest, Petrov issued no further orders. A state broadcast portrayed the withdrawal from the Arctic as a strategic realignment, but the truth settled across Russia like an Arctic night: The war was lost, and with it, Petrov's grip on power.

THE WHITE HOUSE
16 August
Washington, DC

In the Situation Room, satellite imagery from a low-Earth orbit platform flickered across the screens. High-resolution visuals showed the aftermath of the attack on Alexandra Land and Nagurskoye Military Base. What had once been a fortified Arctic stronghold was now a wasteland of blackened craters and scorched snowfields. The skeletal remains of missile launchers, radar towers, and hardened aircraft shelters jutted from the ice like the broken bones of a dead empire.

Command bunkers had collapsed inward, their entrances buried under shattered concrete and twisted steel. The runways and taxiways were cracked open, fragmented by precision strikes. Fires still burned in isolated pockets, casting oily smoke into the polar sky.

The last Russian military foothold in the Arctic, the springboard for an assault on Greenland, had been annihilated. Across the main screen, in stark white against a field of red, a single message scrolled without pause:

TOTAL COMBAT EFFECTIVENESS ACHIEVED

A few months later, and on the day he was to leave office, President Mark Taylor stood alone in the Oval Office, the winter sun casting long shadows across the Resolute Desk. As he gazed out the window, he saw the grounds blanketed in fresh snow. His thoughts drifted to the Arctic conflict, the decisive strike on Alexandra Land, and the narrow escape from nuclear catastrophe. The weight of those decisions weighed heavily on him, but he found solace in knowing that, under his leadership, the nation had navigated through one of its most perilous chapters.

Before he went outside to meet the next person who would sit behind the famous desk, he had one final task to accomplish. He sat down, reached for his pen, and began to write a note to his successor.

"As I prepare to leave this office, I am reminded of the immense responsibility that comes with it. The choices we make reverberate through history, affecting not just our nation but the world. I urge you to lead with wisdom, courage, and a steadfast commitment to peace. May God bless you and the United States of America."

Present Day

Oak Harbor, Washington

The house was quiet, the kind of quiet a carrier fighter pilot seldom experienced. It had been two months since he'd come home from his Arctic cruise, and Jessie Hampton moved through the living room with a mug of coffee in one hand and the TV remote in the other. As he channel surfed, he couldn't believe how lost he was without Sarah. She was still deployed to Greenland but was due back next week. Damn, he didn't think he could wait that long. As much as he liked flying, he hoped they could spend some real time together, working but both coming home for dinner each night.

After going through six hundred channels and finding nothing worth watching, he turned the TV off and took a sip of his coffee.

There was a click at the front door. He froze.

"Hey, stupid, you left the porch light on."

The voice sounded tired, but it was unmistakable. He jumped off the couch, heading toward the door in one bound.

She stood in her flight jacket, her hair longer and pulled back. Her cheeks were flushed, and a go-bag was slung over her shoulder. She looked remarkable.

They just stared at each other for a moment.

"You weren't supposed to be back until next week," he said quietly.

"I wasn't supposed to miss you this much either," Sarah replied.

That was all it took. She threw the bag down. Jessie grabbed her and began to spin her around and around. They laughed and kissed, the whole while thankful to be together once again.

Jessie murmured against her cheek, "You're home."

"So are you."

And for the first time in months, they both finally exhaled.

Coming Soon: *Red Horizons*

Book 5 in the *Sea of Red* Series

North Korea strikes first.

A covert missile launch devastates a US ally, plunging the Pacific into crisis. As American forces mobilize, intelligence reveals an even darker threat: Pyongyang may be preparing a tactical nuclear strike against US forces.

Navy F-35 pilot Jessie "Swagger" Hampton deploys to hold the line, while his wife, Lieutenant Commander Sarah "Danger" Freeman, is in Japan, directing critical early-warning missions. Separated by war, both are thrust into a conflict where every decision could be their last.

From contested airspace and tactical submarine duels to covert ground operations and political brinksmanship, *Red Horizons* continues the high-stakes narrative of the *Sea of Red* series. War is coming, and the enemy is ready to go nuclear.

If you enjoyed *Arctic Red*, join the ranks of those who continue the fight. Pre-order *Red Horizons* on Amazon or visit me on my website at jamesbultema.com. I would love to hear from you.